HER SE

The prison governor stood looking down at Carla's naked body as she lay across the desk. She felt her cheeks glow with embarrassment as he ran his hands over the soft swell of her full breasts, then down to the curve of her hips. Her instincts commanded her to cover herself but her hands were firmly cuffed behind her back.

As his fingers reached her most secret place, shivers of excitement began to run through her and she bit her lip to prevent herself from crying out.

'You like the touch of a man, I see,' he said. 'Perhaps you will enjoy your time with us more than you think.'

Carla said nothing but her body was telling him everything he needed to know . . .

Also by Samantha Austen
in Headline Delta

Desires Unlimited
The Trial
Indecent Display
The Exhibitionists
Daring Young Maids
Maids in Heaven

Her Second Offence

Samantha Austen

Delta

First published in 1999
by HEADLINE BOOK PUBLISHING

A HEADLINE DELTA paperback

10 9 8 7 6 5 4 3 2

ISBN 0 7472 6144 X

Typeset by CBS, Martlesham Hearth, Ipswich, Suddolk

Printed and bound in France
by Brodard & Taupin.
Reproduced from a previously printed copy.

HEADLINE BOOK PUBLISHING
A division of Hodder Headline
338 Euston Road
London NW1 3BH

Her Second Offence

Chapter 1

Carla Wilde sat on the balcony of her hotel room gazing down at the busy streets below. To the young Englishwoman the traffic seemed impossibly thick, the cars jostling for position on the road, the sound of horns almost continuous. Between the cars rasped small motorcycles, dodging through the smallest gap in their determination to keep moving on.

She looked up at the sky. Its blue was stained with a brown smog through which the sun could produce no more than an orange glow. The heat, though, was oppressive, and she had very soon had enough, turning her back on the scene and returning to the relief of her air-conditioned hotel room.

Once inside, Carla flopped down on the king-sized bed, staring up at the ceiling. She always felt a little disoriented when visiting a foreign country for the first time, and this was no exception. She knew it would be a day or so before she was truly comfortable. She looked at her watch. There was no time to worry about acclimatising herself now. She was being picked up in less than an hour. It was time she was getting ready.

She rose from her bed and made her way across to the luxuriously appointed bathroom. She turned on the shower, then shed her dress and underwear and stepped into the cubicle. The water felt good on her bare skin, and she turned her face up into the jet as it cascaded down on her.

She washed herself thoroughly. The flight to this city had taken more than six hours and she was still very aware of the discomfort of having slept in her clothes. By the time she turned off the water, though, she was feeling much better. She towelled herself dry, then paused in front of the mirror, checking her naked body critically.

What she saw would have excited any man. Carla had a beautiful body. She was small in stature, about five foot three inches tall, but her body was perfectly proportioned. Her breasts were firm

1

and plump, the size and shape of ripe oranges, with pert brown nipples that stood high on her jutting orbs. Her belly was flat, her pubis covered with a mat of neatly trimmed dark hair. Below, the hair had been shaved from the thick, prominent lips of her sex, leaving them visible. Her legs were slender and shapely, her feet neat and small.

She pushed back her shoulder-length dark hair from her almond-shaped green eyes, revealing her classically beautiful face, with high cheekbones, a pretty nose and eminently kissable lips. Then she nodded her head in satisfaction. She was very proud of her body.

Carla went to the wardrobe and chose a short, black dress. She pulled it on over her head and zipped it up the back. She opened up a drawer and examined a pair of briefs, then decided against wearing any underwear. She always felt sexy when her vagina was bare under her skirt and her lovely breasts had no need of support.

She stepped into a pair of high-heeled shoes, then stopped before the mirror once more. She looked stunning, and she knew it, the low-cut neckline and short hem of the dress showing off her body beautifully.

Just for a second she paused, as a doubt about the outfit crossed her mind. It wasn't too sexy, was it? She screwed up her neat little nose. Just before leaving England she had been warned that women were somewhat oppressed in this country. Indeed a number of feminist organisations had been campaigning for years for women to boycott its misogynist regime.

Barovia was a country where women were expected to know their place and were decidedly second-class citizens compared to their male counterparts. Carla had seen scenes on television of the way the women were treated, and of the correction centres to which they were sent if they misbehaved. As far as she could understand it, it all stemmed from the country's ancient religion, a form of Orthodoxy, to which the locals belonged, and which preached male superiority in all things.

Carla was not exactly sure why she had come to this land in the first place. It was a job, certainly, but it wasn't as if she needed the money. And it wasn't a particularly lucrative commission anyhow. So what was it that had brought her here? She guessed it was simply her sense of adventure that had persuaded her to come.

Carla Wilde led an existence that was, to say the least, unconventional. When asked what she did for a living, she generally

2

described herself as a freelance assistant, though sometimes, she reflected, the title whore might not be too far from the truth.

Once she had been married to a successful lawyer and had lived a secure but bored existence in a large house in a salubrious suburb of London. Then, partly by chance, partly by the scheming of a mysterious woman called Phaedra, she found out that her husband, Eric, was having affairs with other women. When she had first discovered his infidelity, she had wanted to confront him and walk out on him, but things hadn't quite worked out that way. Instead, Carla had begun to seek her sexual pleasures elsewhere under the subtle guidance of Phaedra. The woman had led her down an increasingly slippery slope from casual screwing, to professional escort and from there to making pornographic movies. As this period in her life had progressed, Carla had discovered a sensuousness in her nature that she had never guessed existed. From single nights in hotel rooms with strangers she had gone on to whole weekends of sexual adventure and, before long, had abandoned herself to a life of pure wanton pleasure.

Then, one evening, all that had changed. To her utter horror and shame, she had found herself arraigned before a jury of her peers and her friends, naked and bound, on trial for her lasciviousness.

The ordeal had lasted all night, as she was forced to confess her wanton behaviour before an unsympathetic court, with Eric, her husband, as the main prosecutor. In the end, her guilt had been obvious to all, and she had been sentenced to spend time in a camp of correction.

It was only afterwards that she discovered that the whole event had been stage-managed by Phaedra in order to lure her into an undercover world of paid sex at the highest level. Phaedra had promised her highly lucrative affairs with the richest of men, and had offered to make the introductions she required. Since then, Carla had not looked back, going from one extravagantly paid job to another, giving her lovely body to whoever would pay the high price Phaedra demanded for her.

Her last assignment had ended a month before, since when she had taken a long holiday, then had spent some time with her lawyers, trying to finalise her divorce. Eric was being more difficult than was necessary over the split, and the whole thing was dragging out interminably.

Then had come the phone call, quite out of the blue.

3

It had been a man on the other end. He had introduced himself as a friend of Mitch, a photographer who had befriended her and had introduced her to the twilight world of porn movies in the days before her trial. The man had wanted a girl for a photo shoot in Barovia. Why he had chosen this country, Carla couldn't really understand, but he had explained something about the unique countryside and the quality of the light, and she had accepted that, as the photographer, the decision of where to shoot the pictures was his.

Normally Carla would not have been interested in such a small job. She knew too that she should have checked with Phaedra before taking on any commission, but the woman was out of the country, and all efforts to reach her had been in vain. Mitch, too, had failed to answer her calls, leaving Carla with the decision to make on her own. In the end it had been sheer boredom and frustration with the snail-like pace of the legal process that had led her to accept. After all, the prospect of a return first-class ticket and a stay in a luxury hotel in the sun seemed rather attractive to a girl trapped in rain-soaked London. So here she was, in Barovia, and about to meet the man who had extended the invitation.

Carla checked herself in the mirror for the final time, then picked up her room key and headed for the door. She went through and closed and locked it behind her, before crossing to the lift. When the doors opened there were two men inside, who looked askance at the young English girl, but said nothing. She rode the car down in silence, alighting at the lobby. There she stopped and looked about her.

'Mrs Wilde?'

She turned to find a man standing beside her. He was tall, at least six foot, with a dark complexion and jet-black hair. She guessed he was from an Eastern European country, and his accent when he spoke confirmed her suspicions.

'I am Moktar,' he said, bowing slightly.

'The photographer with an expensive taste in models?'

He smiled, and his eyes travelled up and down her petite form, taking in her curves.

'Well, I'm getting value for money, that's clear,' he said. 'I look forward to seeing you naked.'

'You intend to photograph me without my clothes on? That wasn't mentioned before.'

4

He smiled again. 'But you will strip for me?'

She looked into his eyes. Of course she would strip for him. She had known all along that that was what was required of her. She simply enjoyed these little conversational games, and besides, she didn't like to be taken for granted. She wondered if he would want to fuck her. Mitch had almost never screwed her during a photo session, preferring to get the job done first.

'My car is outside,' he said. 'Would you care to come with me?'

He held out his arm, and she linked hers through it. Then they headed for the door together. As they did so, all male eyes in the lobby turned enviously toward the tall man with the gorgeous dark-haired beauty on his arm.

Chapter 2

As the car left the confines of the city and began to climb up into the mountains, Carla felt herself relaxing once more. Moktar didn't say much, but she didn't mind. She enjoyed the silence and the magnificent scenery that was beginning to unfold about them. The countryside was certainly beautiful, and she was beginning to understand what it was about this place that made him want to photograph her here. All around were tall, snow-capped mountains, the road winding through steep-sided valleys that were reminiscent of Alpine scenes.

The further they drove from the city, the fewer people they saw until, when Moktar pulled the car off the road and began to follow a dirt track, it was as if they were the only people in the world. Carla stared dreamily from the window at the unspoilt countryside, her misgivings about the trip temporarily forgotten.

He drove on for about half a mile, then drew to a halt under a tree. They were in an open spot with, ahead of them, a huge expanse of bare rock that ended at a precipice. Carla climbed from the car and walked across. It was a drop of at least four hundred feet, and beyond it was a perfect panoramic view of the mountains that towered up on the far side of the valley. Far below Carla could discern cattle grazing and a few tiny farmhouses, but otherwise they were completely alone.

She turned and strolled back to the car. Moktar had the boot open and was pulling a photographer's bag out of it. He reached inside and took out a small leather pouch. This he tossed to his companion.

'Here,' he said. 'Put these on.'

Carla opened the pouch and peered inside. It contained a pair of black hold-up stockings.

'Where's the changing room?' she asked.

He laughed. 'Behind the tree,' he said.

'I don't think I'll bother.'

6

She sat down on the car seat with her legs dangling outside and began to pull on the stockings, sliding the sheer black nylon up the smooth skin of her legs. They came up to within about four inches of her crotch, so that, even with the skirt pulled down as far as it would go, the lacy tops of the stockings were visible. She slipped her feet back into her shoes, then stood up again. Moktar was fitting a lens onto his camera, but he paused to admire his lovely young companion as she strode across to him.

'That looks good,' he said, nodding approvingly. 'Go and stand by the car.'

Carla walked across to the vehicle, then turned to face him.

'Lean against the bonnet, hands behind you. Put your head back. That's right.'

Carla responded to his directions, and the shutter clicked. She looked at him coyly, one eyebrow raised.

'What next?'

He moved her about the vehicle, giving instructions as she went. Carla found herself responding enthusiastically to his commands. She loved to be admired and photographed. She loved too to show off her curvaceous body. When he asked her to lean forward over the car and raise her skirt she made no complaint, half baring the pert globes of her behind to the lens and glancing back seductively at him as he snapped away.

He had already used up two rolls of film before he gave the inevitable order.

'Now take off your dress.'

Carla turned to face him, her hands on her hips.

'Who's going to see these?' she asked.

'Does it matter? You're being paid, after all.'

She stared at him for a moment longer, then shrugged. There was really no point in being coy about it, though she did enjoy a little gentle teasing. She turned her back on him.

'Unzip me, please.'

She felt him take hold of the zip and slide it all the way down her back. Then his hand came back to her neck and he stroked it. Carla shivered slightly at his touch. Already the fact that she was about to bare all was bringing a warmth to her crotch, as a familiar feeling of pleasure flowed over her.

Carla had been seen naked by more men than she cared to count, but stripping in front of a new man was still one of the most exciting things she knew. Even now she could feel her cheeks colouring at the thought of taking everything off, especially here, in the open air, where anyone might chance along. She reached up and took hold of the straps of the dress, pulling them down off her shoulders and baring her exquisite breasts. She glanced down at them. The nipples were hard, as they always were when she took her clothes off in front of a man. She reached her hands up and cupped them momentarily, sighing lightly at the feel of her fingers on her bare skin. She hadn't been fucked for nearly a month, and she was suddenly reminded of her womanly needs as she caressed herself.

The sound of Moktar clicking his camera closed reminded her of what she was doing. Dropping her hands to her waist she took hold of the dress and pulled it down over her hips. She stepped out of it and, picking it up, dropped the garment through the window of the car. Then she turned slowly to face her companion, staring into his eyes, her arms by her side, her legs slightly parted.

Moktar stared at her, his gaze travelling up and down her naked body, taking in her succulent breasts, with their large, stiff nipples, and the pink cleft between her legs. Carla knew she looked good when she was naked and that the long, black stockings simply enhanced her nudity. Now, as the man looked her up and down, she felt a familiar thrill and the heat in her crotch began to increase.

'Over there,' said Moktar, indicating the bare rock at the edge of the precipice.

The naked woman nodded and made her way across, the cameraman close behind.

He began to photograph her again, posing her in every position imaginable. She lay on her back, her front and her side. She spread her legs and lifted her backside, thrusting her pretty cunt up at the camera lens as he snapped away at her. She climbed onto all fours, pressing her backside up and back and peering round at the lens. She stood, pretending to modestly cover her breasts and sex with her hands, though actually hiding nothing. For Carla the whole thing was an extraordinarily arousing experience, and she was soon very turned on indeed, so that it was all she could do to keep herself from masturbating as she flashed her luscious body at the lens.

At last Moktar lowered his camera. Carla was stretched out on her back on the rock, her thighs spread, her sex open. She could feel the wetness inside herself, and she knew that the man could see the glistening moisture that threatened to seep from within her most private place.

He smiled. 'That make you horny or something?' he asked.

Carla blushed, bringing her legs together.

'No, don't stop the show,' he said. 'It was just getting interesting.'

She rose slowly to her feet, brushing the dust from her bare backside. 'Is that all?' she asked.

'That's all the shots I want for the moment.'

'What does that mean?'

'Come over here, Carla.'

She walked across to where he was standing, her hands hanging at her side.

'Closer.'

She took another pace forward. He reached out a hand and stroked the smooth nylon of her stocking.

'Those look good on you,' he said.

'I know.'

He let his hand travel higher, and she shivered as his fingers touched the soft flesh of her inner thigh. He gazed deep into her eyes as his hand moved upwards.

'What do you think you're doing?' she asked.

'What you want me to do.'

Carla gave a little gasp as the man's fingers came into contact with her sex. She bit her lip, but said nothing. Emboldened by this he moved his fingers round, seeking out her love bud. He began to rub it in small circular motions, sending pulses of excitement through her small frame.

'You like that, don't you?' he said.

She nodded, not trusting herself to speak.

'Do you always give yourself to men who photograph you?'

'I haven't given myself to you yet.'

'Yes, but you're going to.' He slipped a finger into her vagina, and she knew that he could feel the wetness inside her. She moaned softly as he pressed his fingers deeper. She wondered at the ease with which she could be turned on. She had known from the start that, if he wanted her, she wouldn't be able to resist the temptation. Carla loved to screw and, standing here naked with this stranger, she was suddenly anxious to feel his cock inside her.

She stretched out her hand and ran it over the front of his trousers. They were already bulging, and she traced the shape of his cock with her fingers. She thought of his stiff rod straining against his pants, and suddenly she needed to taste him.

As he continued to finger her she pulled down his zip and

reached into his fly. He was wearing brief underpants and they were stretched taut by his rampant organ. She pulled them down, freeing his cock so that it stood proudly from his groin. It was long, the foreskin stretched back, allowing her to see the swollen glans. She ran her fingers up its length, feeling it jump as she squeezed his thick shaft.

'Suck me,' he said quietly.

The words sent a thrill through the young beauty. She dropped to her knees on the rocky surface, groaning softly as his fingers slipped from inside her. She grasped his shaft in her hand and, leaning forward, took him into her mouth, closing her lips about his stiff tool and beginning to suck.

There was something about having a thick erection in her mouth that Carla loved. It was something to do with the way the man reacted, his cock twitching uncontrollably as she fellated him. She took hold of his balls, stroking the puckered flesh as she moved her head back and forth, letting his organ slide in and out of her mouth. He gave a grunt of pleasure and she gazed up at him through lowered eyelids, her breasts shaking deliciously as she mouth-fucked him.

Carla would have been perfectly happy to bring him off between her lips and swallow his seed. She loved the taste of spunk, and the feel of a cock ejaculating in her mouth was one that never failed to excite her. But Moktar clearly had other ideas, and all at once he pulled her back from his rampant penis by the hair, making her gaze up into his eyes.

'Lie on your back and spread your legs, little English beauty,' he said. 'I want to take you properly.'

Carla obeyed at once, stretching out on the warm, hard rock and opening her thighs. She thrust her pubis up at him, suddenly anxious to have his cock inside her. He stood for a moment, staring down at her, clearly fascinated by the sight of her open cunt, which she knew was glistening with moisture.

'Come on, Moktar,' she gasped. 'I want you now. Stick your cock into me and fuck me hard.'

Moktar didn't need asking a second time. He dropped to his knees between her open thighs, then lowered himself down onto her prostrate form. She reached for his cock. It was still wet with her saliva and she guided it up between her legs, moaning softly as it came into contact with her slit.

When he entered her she cried aloud, loving the way he forced

10

himself inside her. He pushed himself home, penetrating ever deeper until the thick curls of his pubic hair were pressed against her own. Then he paused, watching her face as she groaned with arousal.

He started to fuck her, slowly at first, his hips moving back and forth with smooth movements as he slid in and out of her love hole. Carla's groans grew in volume as he did so. She pressed her hips up against his, urging him ever deeper inside her as her control began to slip from her.

As he took her, his heavy body bearing down on her own, Carla gazed up at the blue sky above. There was something about being screwed in the open air that she loved, and in an idyllic spot like this, with the sun beating down, it was almost perfect. She wanted the fuck to go on and on, to spend all day pinned naked to this hard rock whilst he rutted inside her like some primitive cave man with his young mate. But already she was beginning to sense the urgency in her partner, his thrusts becoming harder with every second.

He was screwing her with vigour now, his hips pounding down against hers, making her pert backside slap against the rocks in a way that was almost painful.

She felt his muscles stiffen suddenly, and his face contorted into an expression of extreme concentration. He drove into her again, then again, and then he was coming, his cock taking on a life of its own as spurt after spurt of hot spunk filled her vagina. Moments later Carla could hold out no longer and her own climax overtook her with a vengeance. She cried aloud as the intense pleasure of orgasm swept over her, bringing her the delicious release that she had been craving ever since she had stripped naked in this lonely spot. For Carla there was no sweeter sensation than that of a man shooting his load into her, and she savoured the moment as Moktar's rod continued to spit his seed deep within her.

He went on pumping his groin against hers until his energy was spent. Then he flopped onto his back, his stiff cock slipping from her. Carla lay beside him, saying nothing, her breath coming in gasps as she slowly recovered.

'Christ, that was good,' she murmured.

'For me too. You're a hell of a fuck, Carla.'

They lay side by side for about ten minutes. Then he buttoned his trousers and rose slowly to his feet, once again gazing down at the beauty whose pleasures he had just sampled. Carla felt his come seeping from her and trickling down her backside onto the rocks beneath her. She smiled at him.

'I needed that,' she said.

He picked up his camera.

'Stay there,' he said. 'I'm going to get more film.'

'You want to photograph me like this?' she gasped. 'But I'm such a mess.'

'I want to capture that just-fucked look,' he said. 'Don't move.'

She watched him as he walked across to the car, then let her head loll back onto the rock once more, loving the sensation of the sun's rays on her soft skin.

All at once a sound to her right made her turn. There seemed to be a disturbance in the bushes, as if some animal was coming through them. Then the bushes parted and she gave a gasp of dismay. There, approaching her at a run, were two men dressed in khaki uniforms, pistols clutched in their hands.

Chapter 3

For a second Carla froze, momentarily paralysed by the sight of the men approaching. Then, suddenly realising the danger, she rolled over and sprang to her feet. She looked wildly about her, and at once her heart sank. The car, wherein lay her clothes and safety, was all of a hundred yards away, but the men were barely twenty yards from her. In desperation, she started to run, the adrenaline spurring her on. But she never had a chance in her high heels. She had barely gone ten paces before a hand grabbed her arm and swung her round.

Carla found herself face-to-face with a tall, burly policeman with fierce eyes and a large black moustache. She struggled hard with him, twisting and turning to try to escape his grasp. But he was too strong for her, and the more she fought, the tighter he gripped her, until she feared that he might break her arm.

As she struggled with the first policeman, his companion ran past, shouting at Moktar. The young serviceman was running fast, but Moktar had had a good start and was already in the car, gunning the engine. With a screech of tyres he swung the vehicle round. He paused for a second, glancing back at Carla. Then he hit the throttle and in no time was disappearing down the track in a cloud of dust. The policeman chased him for a few more yards, then stopped, shouting and shaking his fist in vain at the departing car.

The man who had hold of Carla's arm began to shake her, yelling something at her that she was unable to understand. For her part, Carla was desperately trying to cover herself with her hands, suddenly very anxious at being the naked captive of these two powerful men.

The policeman who had gone after Moktar heard Carla's protests and turned. Seeing that his partner was in control, he strode across to where he was restraining the young beauty. By this time the man had pinned Carla's arms behind her, so that her attempts to preserve what was left of her modesty were completely

13

thwarted. The policeman stopped in front of her, and Carla saw his eyes travel down her body, taking in her jutting breasts and her bare sex, from which Moktar's semen was still dribbling. As he eyed her helpless form, the young woman wished to goodness that she hadn't left her clothes in the car. If only she had simply put the dress on the ground, she would at least have had something to wear. Somehow being dressed in only stockings and shoes made things even worse, the garments making her feel even more naked, being designed as they were to titillate rather than to cover.

The man facing her spoke, his voice harsh and guttural. She shook her head.

'I don't understand what you're saying,' she said.

'You English?' he said, with a heavy accent.

'Yes.'

'What you do here?'

She blushed. 'I was working.'

'What work?'

'I was posing. I'm a model.'

'You whore. You fuck with man.'

She said nothing, her face glowing.

'You break law. You come with us.'

'No. I didn't mean to do anything wrong. I was just posing.'

'You fuck with man.'

'All right, we were screwing. But we thought we were alone. We didn't expect anyone to come along.'

'Where your clothes?'

'They're in the car.'

'You come with us,' he repeated.

'Where to?'

'You come to police station.'

'Look, I'm sorry if I broke the law, but couldn't I have something to wear please?' she pleaded.

'You come.'

He said something to the man who was holding her, and he momentarily released her arms. She was free for no more than a split second, though, then she felt her hands grabbed again and the cold steel of handcuffs closing about her wrists. He checked that her arms were incapacitated, then pushed her away from him.

'You come with us,' he said again.

Carla stumbled off down the track between the two policemen, her hands cuffed behind her, her bare breasts thrust forward. As

14

they walked she reflected on her situation. She was in trouble, and she knew it. To have been discovered in such a compromising position at any time would have been bad news. Here, in this country where to be a woman was to be second class, her situation was even more serious. She eyed her two escorts. They were grim, uncompromising types, and she didn't expect much sympathy from them. She glanced down at herself. Her nudity compounded her problems a hundredfold. It gave her a vulnerability that she felt intensely, and she wished, more than anything, for something to cover herself.

They rounded a corner in the track and came upon the policeman's vehicle. It was an old, battered van, parked beneath a tree. The man who had spoken to her produced a key from his pocket and unlocked the back doors. He swung them open and indicated that Carla was to climb inside. It was awkward with her arms pinned behind her, but she managed to negotiate the steep step. Inside, the vehicle was stuffy and smelt of engine oil. A single chain hung from the roof, and the policeman dragged her over to it, wrapping it about her cuffs and locking it in place. Then he turned his back on her, jumping down to the ground and slamming the door shut. Moments later Carla heard the engine start and the van lurched forward, almost unbalancing her.

The journey was not a comfortable one for Carla. With her hands trapped behind her back there was no way she could hold on, and she simply had to try all she could to maintain her balance as the van swayed this way and that. The chain was almost useless as a support, occasionally tugging painfully at her wrists when she failed to anticipate a change of direction. The atmosphere in the back of the ancient vehicle was not exactly comfortable either. Carla was in complete darkness, and the smell of exhaust fumes wafted up through the floor, making her cough and splutter.

It was with some relief, therefore, that she felt the van reach smoother, metalled roads, though there was still some distance to go back to the city. By the time the vehicle finally came to a halt and she heard the engine die, Carla ached all over.

She listened as the doors at the front of the van slammed. Carla expected to be released at once, but in fact another fifteen minutes passed in the stifling heat before the doors were finally opened again, revealing the policeman with the moustache. He climbed in and undid the chain from Carla's cuffs, then indicated she was to get out.

'Isn't there something I could put on?' she asked, but he said nothing, simply indicating the door once more.

Carla jumped down to the ground and looked about her. The van was parked in a compound surrounded by high walls topped with barbed wire. The only comfort was that she couldn't be seen from the street, though there were a number of policemen lounging nearby and they watched with interest as the naked beauty was led past them.

Carla's face glowed as she ran the gauntlet of officers. Her body was covered in a sheen of sweat after her vigil in the van, and shining rivulets ran down between her breasts and on to her pubic hair. Her thighs were still streaked with Moktar's semen, which stained her stocking tops white, and she walked with her eyes cast down, aware that the comments the men were making were directed at her.

The policeman led her through a door and down a passageway with a stone floor and plain whitewashed walls. Carla's shoes made a loud ringing noise on the floor as she walked, and she wished she had been wearing something softer that would draw less attention to her. At the end was another door. He pushed it open and gestured for her to enter. As she walked in, she found herself in a reception room with a counter at one end. Behind stood a stern-faced sergeant, who eyed Carla with distaste. There were a number of other men in the room, and all eyes were turned in her direction as she entered. Her escort took her up to the counter and stopped her in front of it. He said a few words to the sergeant, then took a pace back. The man opened a drawer and produced a pad of forms, then picked up a pen.

'Name?'

'Look,' said Carla, 'would one of you people please get me something to put on? I'm not some sort of peep show, you know.'

'Name?' he said again.

Carla's shoulders slumped.

'Carla Wilde.'

'Address?'

'I'm staying at the Sheraton Hotel.'

'You rich lady?'

'That's none of your business.'

He glared at her. 'You not answer back. Women obey man here, not like in America.'

'I'm not American, I'm English.'

16

'English slut.'

'Listen,' she said, suddenly angry. 'I don't have to put up with that kind of talk. I'll report you to your superiors.'

'Age?'

'Twenty-five. Not that it's any of your business.'

The sergeant examined the document in front of him, then looked up at her.

'Carla Wilde,' he said slowly, 'you are charged with indecent behaviour in contravention of Barovian law. You will be held in custody until your trial can be arranged.'

Carla was flabbergasted. 'Trial?' she gasped. 'I was only posing for some pictures.'

'You broke the law.'

'Look, I'll pay a fine if you'll just get my stuff from the hotel.'

'Your belongings will be confiscated pending the outcome of your trial. Meanwhile you will be taken to prison.'

'No,' she cried. 'Look this is ridiculous. I've got to fly back to England in two days. I've already got a ticket.'

'That too will be confiscated.'

'You can't do this. I demand to see a lawyer.'

'There are no woman lawyers. And no man would defend a woman who has behaved as you have.'

'Then call the British Ambassador.'

The sergeant turned to Carla's escort and spoke a few words. Then she felt her arm grasped again.

'No!' she shouted.

Another policeman moved in and took hold of her other arm. Carla tried to struggle but the petite English girl was no match for the two hefty officers, who frogmarched her out of the room and back down the corridor as she protested loudly.

They emerged into the yard, but instead of taking her to the van in which she had been delivered, they dragged her toward a truck parked on the other side. The back of the truck was barred, like a large cage, and inside it she could see figures. Standing beside the vehicle were two men carrying rifles. As Carla approached they unlocked a door at the back of the cage. Her escorts hustled her up two steps and through the door. There were four other occupants, all men, and all dressed in scruffy clothes. They eyed the naked beauty with some amusement as she was led in with them. All had their arms trapped behind them as she did, their cuffs attached to a rail that ran about the inside of the cage so that

17

they were facing out through the bars. The policemen took Carla to the bar and attached hers in a similar way. Then they turned away.

'Wait!' she shouted. 'You've got to give me some clothes. I can't go like this!'

But the guards were already locking the door again as the officers strolled back into the station.

Carla couldn't believe what was happening to her. She realised now that she should have listened to those who had warned her not to visit this awful place. It was too late for that, though, she mused. She was here, and she'd just have to make the best of the situation. After all, she had been in tight spots before. Even so, she wished she had some clothes. It was difficult to be dignified when wearing only a pair of black semen-stained stockings, and she felt her cheeks glow red as the other prisoners stared at her beautiful young body.

It was nearly half an hour before anything happened. Half an hour during which three more prisoners were brought into the cage, and half an hour of enduring the constant comings and goings of the policemen who came to gaze at the naked young Englishwoman so temptingly displayed in the yard.

At last, though, one of the guards made his way round to the cab of the truck, and was joined by a driver. They climbed in and, moments later, the engine roared into life. Then Carla was on the move again, the vehicle lurching over the rough terrain of the yard and through the main gates of the police station.

As they pulled out onto the open road, Carla became more aware than ever of the vulnerability of her situation. She was perfectly visible to passers-by through the bars of the cage, and many an amazed eye turned in her direction as the truck raced through the busy streets.

They stopped at a set of traffic lights, and a group of youths gathered round the side of the vehicle, laughing at the young beauty. As she listened to their jeers, the hapless woman couldn't help but reflect on the irony of the situation she found herself in. They had arrested her for indecency, yet at the time of her arrest nobody had seen her but the policemen. Now here they were displaying her to all and sundry. She stuck her tongue out at one of the men who was making a particularly lewd gesture in her direction, bringing a peal of laughter from those looking on.

The truck moved off again, much to her relief, and they sped on through the city. As they progressed, the areas they passed through became less and less salubrious. Modern shops and houses gave way to scruffy shacks, with dogs roaming the streets and shabbily dressed people lounging aimlessly about. At last the vehicle came to a halt before a massive pair of iron gates, guarded on each side by armed men.

Papers were passed out through the window of the truck and examined by the guard. One of them wandered round to the back, stopping in amazement at the sight of Carla. The girl said nothing, trying not to meet his gaze as she stood there, her charms on open display.

Eventually the massive gates were swung open and they were waved through. The vehicle rumbled into a large compound, surrounded by tall, thick walls topped with barbed wire. In the distance Carla could see a group of people marching back and forth in grey uniforms and all around were gun-toting guards.

The prisoners were unloaded into the yard. As before, there was no shortage of interest in the naked girl amongst the group of ne'er-do-wells who were her companions. The prisoners were forced into a line by the shouting guards, then turned and marched through a thick oaken door into a tall grey building. Inside the décor was even more drab than that of the police station, and Carla found herself once again embarrassed by the way the clack of her heels on the floor drew attention to her as she followed the man in front.

They came to a desk, not unlike the one at the police station, behind which sat a bored-looking guard, who perked up somewhat at the sight of Carla. The prisoners were made to line up in front of the desk, then called forward one at a time. The man questioned them in turn, filling in a piece of paper in front of him as he did so. Then each man was made to stand with a board bearing his name hung about his neck and was photographed, before being led away.

When it came to Carla's turn, she dutifully answered the questions put to her in broken English. The man took down her name on the paper in front of her and scribbled it onto the board. Before handing it to her, the photographer lengthened the strap on the board so that her breasts were left uncovered. There was much laughter as he took the shot. Carla said nothing as, for the second time that day, she was asked to stare into the cold eye of the camera, though she couldn't help contrasting this occasion with the previous one, when she had been more than happy to display her body.

Once the photograph was taken, she was taken by the arm and led through another barred door. On either side were cells, and there was a good deal of whistling and shouting by the inmates as she passed, her hands still trapped, her breasts thrust forward.

The guard led her to a door at the end of the passage. He opened it and pushed her in. Carla found herself in an office. It was starkly decorated, the walls being painted gloss white, the floor without a carpet. At one end was an old, rather tatty desk behind which lounged a man in a similar uniform to those of her guards, but with gold braid on his shoulders. He was writing something as she entered, and it was a good thirty seconds before he looked up. Carla studied him as he wrote. He was about forty-five years old, with a receding hairline and rather overweight. At last he put his pen down and sat back.

'Mrs Wilde, I presume,' he said in almost perfect English.

'That's right.'

'Good. Now, Mrs Wilde, you seem to be in something of a predicament.'

'You could say that,' she replied, trying to maintain an air of calmness, despite the turmoil that raged inside her.

'Well, this can be a pretty uncomfortable place. I just hope you're sensible enough to appreciate how you can make your stay a little less unpleasant than it might be.'

'How do you mean?'

He let his eyes travel down her body to her crotch.

'I think you understand what I have in mind,' he said.

Chapter 4

Carla looked the man in the eye, trying not to let him see the shock that his last statement had given her.

'Just who are you?' she asked.

'My name is Colonel Pakat. I am in charge of the remand wing of this prison. Here we hold prisoners awaiting trial. All prisoners must call me sir. As a prisoner yourself, I suggest you remember the courtesy.'

'What did you mean just then . . . sir?' She pronounced the title in a slightly mocking way on purpose, and she saw his eyes narrow as she did so.

'I advise you to take me seriously, young lady,' he said. 'I'm about to tell you about this place, and you may not like what you hear.'

'Do all your customers get this kind of service?'

'Not all my customers arrive naked, and with such a delectable body.'

'That's probably a good thing.'

'You're forgetting that courtesy already.'

'I'm sorry, sir.'

'Good. Now, I must tell you that remand prisoners in this jail have very few rights indeed, and female prisoners even fewer.'

'I see.'

'I'm not sure that you do. For a start there are no prison clothes for remand prisoners. Prisoners are expected to wear what they arrive in.'

'But I . . .'

'But you arrived without clothes, I know. Rather unfortunate for you, but good news for the other inmates.'

'Can't you get me some clothes, sir?'

'It may be possible, but in your case I'm not inclined to make it a priority.'

Carla stared at him, then down at her bare body. It seemed

things were even worse than she had thought. 'In addition,' he went on. 'Remand prisoners have no right to food or other requirements.'

'What, nothing at all?'

'It is normal for the families of the accused to provide what is needed for them. The state has no obligation for such things.'

'But what am I supposed to live on?'

'It appears you will have to earn your keep.'

'What on earth can I do?'

The man smiled. 'A young, beautiful and naked woman in a prison full of men? Use your imagination.'

Carla's eyes widened. 'What do you mean?'

'I should have thought that was obvious.'

'You . . . You mean you want me to sell myself?'

'Not at all. I shall handle the sale. All you need to do is to perform. There are a number of quite wealthy men languishing in this place for one reason or another. They will pay well for the kind of diversion you can provide.'

'But I'm not some cheap whore.'

'Most certainly not. I shall see that you are quite an expensive whore.'

'I won't do it,' she said angrily.

'Then I'll just have to put you in one of the common cells. There's one that's got four suspected rapists in it, that should do.'

'You wouldn't dare!'

'I assure you that one touch on this button and the guard will be back in here. Then you'll see whether I dare.'

She glared at him.

'Look, young lady,' he went on. 'All you need to do is what you obviously enjoy doing. After all, the man whose semen is running down your thigh, how well did you know him?'

'We . . . we met this afternoon, sir.'

'Yet you let him fuck you?'

'That was different. He was paying . . .'

Carla's voice trailed away as she realised what she had said.

'He was paying you? So you are no stranger to getting paid for sex?'

'He was paying for the photo shoot.'

'And you just got horny?'

'Something like that.'

'Then I can persuade you to get horny with some of the inmates of this place?'

Carla said nothing. There didn't seem anything to say. What he was suggesting made perfect sense, she had to admit. Her greatest asset in this place was her beautiful young body, and it was a very saleable commodity. She supposed that letting this man pimp for her was no worse than some of the other things she had done in her time. After all, she was no angel when all was said and done. Besides, there would be little else to do in this place, so why not do what she enjoyed doing most?'

'If I do this, sir, you'll see that I come to no harm?' she asked quietly.

He smiled, seeing at once that he had won the argument.

'Apart from having your backside thrashed occasionally, you will come to no physical harm,' he said.

'All right, then. I'll do whatever you ask of me, sir.'

'Sensible girl. I knew you'd see my point of view eventually. Now, I think I'd like to sample the goods myself.'

'You?'

'Naturally I must ensure my customers are getting value for money.'

'You can see what they're getting.'

'Please, no more arguments, young lady. Just sit down on that desk, then lie back and spread your legs.'

'What, just like that?'

'Just like that.'

Carla opened her mouth to protest, then closed it again. There seemed little point in prolonging this interview. This was obviously a man who was used to getting what he wanted and, in this particular situation, he held all the cards. Silently she crossed to the desk and, turning her back on it, felt for the edge with her hands. Raising them up behind her back she sat gingerly down. Then she prostrated herself across it and slowly spread her legs.

Colonel Pakat rose to his feet and stood, looking down at her. Carla felt her cheeks glowing as he ran his hands over the soft swell of her breasts, then let them travel down to the open cleft of her sex, the lips still wet with Moktar's spunk. Her instincts told her to cover herself with her hands, but the cuffs that still immobilised her wrists prevented her from doing so. Instead she simply lay still as he reached out a hand and stroked her clitoris. As his hands lingered in her most private place, they sent tingles

23

of excitement racing through her, and she bit her lip to prevent herself from crying out. He rubbed a little harder, and she felt the muscles in her sex contract, forcing a dribble of semen to escape from her.

'You like the touch of a man down there, I see,' he said. 'That's good. A man enjoys a fuck much more when he knows he is giving satisfaction to the woman. You like to have your nipples sucked too?'

Carla said nothing, but when he leant forward and placed his lips over her teat, a sigh escaped from her. At the same time her nipples puckered to hardness in silent answer to his question.

Despite herself, Carla was becoming more aroused by the second. The sensation of his gentle sucking, his tongue flicking back and forth over the hard brown knob whilst his fingers continued to explore her vagina, was delicious and she groaned once more as he slipped two fingers into her pulsating love hole.

His hand left her crotch, and she heard the sound of a zip being pulled down. Then she felt something hard press against her leg. His cock felt hot, and she glanced down at it. It was long and rigid, with a thick blue vein running up it. He was holding his shaft between his fingers and, as she watched, he ran them up and down its length. It seemed to take on a life of its own under his hands as he began to work the foreskin back and forth.

He lifted his face from her breast. 'You want it inside you, don't you?' he murmured.

Carla said nothing but her body was telling him all he wanted to know.

He moved round so that he was standing between her thighs, and she raised her head, gazing down at him through the valley of her breasts. She shifted her position slightly. The cuffs were digging into her wrists under the weight of her body, causing her some discomfort, though the bondage was actually increasing her pleasure as she lay there waiting to be taken.

He placed his hand on her thighs, pulling her forward so that her backside was clear of the table and her open sex was exactly where he wanted it. Then she felt his cock pressing against her, and she gasped as he forced himself into her.

Carla couldn't suppress a moan as he penetrated her, pressing himself deeper and deeper. The exquisite sensation of her cunt being filled with a rampant penis brought new and more violent convulsions from the muscles of her sex as they closed about his organ. Despite the way he was taking her, with utter disregard for her own desires, Carla was more turned on than ever now, and she thrust her hips up at him, urging him still deeper inside her.

He started to fuck her with long, even strokes, his cock sliding back and forth inside her, bringing yet more moans of desire as she abandoned herself to him. As so often happened, Carla's inhibitions were soon forgotten once her carnal desires took control. Now, as he took his pleasure in her, she found herself overcome by the lust that was never far beneath the surface of her psyche.

Carla gazed up at the man who was taking her. He had the confident air of one who knew how to pleasure a woman, his hips moving easily back and forth as he looked down on the wanton young beauty who was giving herself to him. He reached out and took hold of her breast, massaging it and bringing a sigh from the girl as he did so. A smile crossed his face, and he took her nipple between his fingers, eliciting new sparks of pleasure deep inside Carla.

His pace began to increase, his thrusts rocking her body back and forth, making her breasts shake with every stroke. Carla was consumed by desire now, her young body positively on fire as she pressed her hips up at him, his strokes making her pert bottom slap down noisily on the surface of the desk.

He came suddenly, filling her vagina with yet more spunk and bringing her to her own climax, the sensation of his seed pumping into her making her scream out loud. He went on screwing her with unabated vigour as she writhed beneath him, her orgasm totally engulfing her.

When, at last, he began to slow, Carla moaned with disappointment. She loved the sensation of a man coming inside her, and wanted to savour the moment for as long as possible. But she too was beginning to come down, the violence of her movements slowly decreasing until she lay flat on the desk, her pretty breasts rising and falling with her panting.

He withdrew slowly, bringing more sighs from the sated woman as she watched his shining cock emerge from inside her.

He wiped his penis on her thighs, smearing the juices across her pale skin, before tucking it back in his pants.

'You'd better get yourself cleaned up,' he said. 'You'll be servicing your first customer soon.'

Chapter 5

Carla's heart was hammering against her chest as she followed the guard along the prison corridors between the rows of cells. The cell occupants all had their faces pressed to the bars as she passed, and the whistles and shouts, though in a foreign language, told the young beauty that they appreciated the sight of her naked body being paraded before them in this way. Their cries attracted the attention of other convicts ahead, and already more men were rushing to their doors for a glimpse of the girl as she was taken past them.

Pakat had allowed Carla a night's sleep before calling on her services for the first time. She had bathed in a common ablution area amongst the other female prisoners and had been instructed to wash her stockings. Then she had been led to a small, bare cell with a low bed covered with just a thin mattress. There she had been allowed to sleep, though the light had been left on, and she had been disturbed a number of times by prison guards coming to stare at her.

In the morning she had been taken back to the shared bathroom, after which she had been given a small meal. Then she had been locked in her cell once more.

She had sat, gazing up at the sky through the small window far above her bunk, reflecting on her fate. Of all the things she had ever done, this was much the most bizarre and, in a way, the most alarming. Still, she knew she had to keep her wits about her and, if to survive meant to whore for Pakat, then she was more than capable of doing that.

Despite her sanguine reasoning, though, she had felt a tight knot at the pit of her stomach when the guard had opened her cell door and ordered her to don her shoes and stockings. She had done so quickly whilst he had stood and watched her, then he had handcuffed her and they had set off together.

The guard took her up a number of flights of stairs to the very top of the prison. They arrived outside a door marked 'Special Wing' and he spoke into an intercom. Moments later came the sound of a key turning, and the door opened. Carla's guard took her through to another corridor. This one was very different from anywhere she had visited in the building before, though. There was a carpet on the floor, and the walls were freshly painted. The doors to the cells were distinct too, being of solid oak rather than the bars that fronted all the other cells. The guard stopped outside one of the doors and, to Carla's surprise, he knocked. Clearly these were not ordinary prisoners.

The door was opened by a burly man in prisoner's uniform. He was about thirty years old, and the scars on his face spoke of a violent past. He eyed Carla up and down, then nodded to the guard, who took a key from his pocket and undid the girl's handcuffs. Then he pushed her forward and the man stood aside to let her into the cell.

Once again, Carla had to suppress her natural instinct to cover herself with her hands as she stepped into the room. Her experience had showed her that this was no time for modesty. If a man invited her to his room clad only in stockings and shoes, it was because he wanted to see her naked body. She came to a halt and looked about her. There were two other men in the room apart from the one who had admitted her. One of them wore the grey shapeless suits that the other prisoners wore. Like the man at the door, he gave the impression of being a bit of a tough and, from his appearance, she guessed he had been in a few fights. The third man was much older, about fifty she estimated. He was about five foot nine inches tall, heavily built and dressed in a dark business suit. He was lounging in an armchair whilst the other two remained on their feet. They were, she guessed, almost certainly his bodyguards.

The one who had opened the door took hold of Carla's arm and pulled her to the centre of the room.

'You stand,' he ordered, in a heavily accented voice.

Carla stayed where she was, her arms hanging at her side, her legs apart, the way she knew men liked to see her. If she was going to do this, she reflected, she might as well do her best to please her client.

The man in the armchair looked her up and down coolly.

'Pakat was not exaggerating when he said you were sexy,' he said. 'And the redness in your cheeks does you credit. I like to see

27

a girl who retains a little modesty even when she's parading about stark-naked before strangers.'

Carla remained silent, acutely aware of the three pairs of eyes that were inspecting her breasts, buttocks and crotch. She wondered when they had last had a woman. Already she could see the bulges in the younger men's pants as they took in her beautiful form, and the first stirrings of her own arousal began as she contemplated what was to happen.

'What is your name?' asked the man in the suit.

'Carla, sir.'

'And when did you last fuck, Carla?'

'Yesterday, sir,'

'With whom?'

'With Colonel Pakat, sir.'

'And with a photographer before that, I understand.'

Carla's colour deepened. 'Yes, sir.'

He nodded. 'Your frankness is becoming. You know, I take it, that you will be fucked this afternoon?'

'I assumed I wasn't invited for tea.'

He smiled. 'My name is Daran,' he said. 'These are my servants, Olak and Javin. I am here because I was careless about who I bribed when arranging my tax affairs. I'll be released in about two months for good behaviour. Meantime, I have my men here to look after me and, for this afternoon at least, I have you to amuse me.'

Carla listened in silence. This was clearly a very wealthy and powerful man. She was used to dealing with such men, as her chosen career, by its very nature, brought her into close contact with them. She wondered, though, at the influence required to secure a suite like this in a prison.

'Which of my men would you like to bring off in that pretty little mouth of yours?'

'Sir?' The question had taken Carla by surprise.

'I'm offering you the choice of which of my men to suck off.'

'I . . .'

'Take your time. I'm interested to know which one's spunk you think would taste better.'

Carla looked from one face to another. The men were grinning broadly. She was determined not to appear intimidated, though.

She pointed to the man who had opened the door.

'That one,' she said decisively.

'Olak? A good choice. I'm sure Olak thinks so. Go on, then, take a look at what you've chosen.'

Carla looked at him in silence for a moment, then turned to the bodyguard, who was standing, his hands on his hips, watching her. The young woman stepped forward, then dropped to her knees in front of him and reached for his fly. The prison trousers were held closed by buttons, and her fingers trembled as she fumbled with them, only too aware of the two men watching her.

The buttons came undone at last and she slipped her hand inside. He wore no underpants and her fingers closed about his shaft. It was already rock hard and she eased it gently into the open. She stared at it. It was thick, with a circumcised end. She ran her fingers up and down the shaft, noting his sharp intake of breath as she did so. She suspected that it was some time since he had last had a woman, and she could sense the tension inside him as she caressed his meaty manhood.

She leant forward slowly and, protruding her tongue, licked tentatively at his glans, feeling the muscles in his groin twitch as she did so. Then she opened her mouth and took him inside.

As she began to suck he emitted a grunt, and for a second she feared that might be about to come already. But he stayed in control, and she began to move her head back and forth as she sucked at him.

No matter how often Carla performed for a man, she could never quite believe her own promiscuousness. Less than two years earlier she had been a faithful young housewife, whose desires were hidden, even from herself. Yet here she was, on her knees before this rough prison inmate, sucking his cock with enthusiasm whilst his companions looked on.

All at once she felt a pair of hands grasp her at the waist. Then they slid around her body, reaching upwards toward her breasts. As they closed over her soft orbs, she felt the roughness of a prison uniform press against her bare back, and she knew it was the other bodyguard, whom Daran had referred to as Javin. He squeezed her breasts in his rough hands, kneading the pliant flesh and making the nipples harden at once. Carla loved to have her breasts caressed, and she gave a muffled sigh as he mauled her, her mouth still closed over his companion's erect tool.

He removed one of his hands, and she sensed him fiddling with his fly. Then she felt the unmistakable sensation of another rampant cock pressing into her back.

29

Carla knew what was coming. She had taken on two men before, though never in a prison cell. Now, as Javin took hold of her thighs and began pulling them apart, she recognised at once what was required of her.

Whatever inhibitions Carla had brought with her to Daran's cell had long been abandoned. She was here to perform, and perform she would. After all she had nothing to gain by resistance to this powerful man. Pressing her breasts downwards, she thrust her pert bottom back at him, presenting him with the access he required to her already wet cunt.

He guided his weapon to the entrance to her honeypot and began to push. Carla responded by thrusting her backside back still further, and in a moment he was inside her, pressing himself all the way in and sending waves of pure pleasure through her young body as he filled her.

He fucked her hard. Thrusting himself against her so that her small body was shaken back and forth and she had to cling to Olak's thighs as she continued to fellate him. She glanced across at Daran, who was sitting back in his chair, watching her ravishment. She wondered what she must look like, naked apart from her stockings, her lips closed about one stiff member whilst another invaded her vagina from behind.

All at once her attention was brought back to Olak as his cock began spitting great gobs of semen into her mouth. She almost choked as it splashed against the back of her throat, and at once she began swallowing greedily. So copious was his ejaculate that it began leaking from the sides of her mouth, dribbling down her chin and onto her breasts. Still she sucked at him, draining every drop from his balls until the flow ceased and he withdrew.

No sooner had Olak shot his load than she felt Javin withdraw his cock from inside her. Carla had been on the brink of orgasm, and she moaned with frustration as he spun her round and threw her onto her back. Then he was astride her breasts, forcing his throbbing erection between her lips, and she was rewarded with the taste of her own juices as she found herself obliged to start sucking again.

This was as violent a face-fucking as she had ever experienced. Javin rammed his penis into her mouth with gusto, his heavy balls slapping against her chin with every stroke. She grasped hold of his shaft and began to wank him as she sucked, pulling his foreskin back and forth, her senses overwhelmed by the taste and smell of

30

male and female arousal that came from his tool.

His movements became even more frenzied with this new stimulation, and she felt his ball sac tighten and his body suddenly stiffen. Moments later she received a second mouthful of hot, creamy spunk in her mouth. She swallowed it down as fast as she was able as he continued to thrust his thighs against her face, grunting aloud with every spurt that escaped from his throbbing cock. Once again Carla felt sperm dribble from her lips and down her neck, despite her efforts to keep it all inside her.

She went on wanking and sucking at him until he too was done, and he pulled away from her. Still he wasn't finished, though, and a final jet of semen splashed down onto her upturned face as he rose to his feet, a satisfied expression on his face. Carla lay where he had thrown her, her legs spread, a trickle of spunk running down her bright red cheek as she slowly regained her breath.

Moments later she heard a door close. Surprised, she looked up to discover her two violators had gone, leaving her alone with Daran. He was sitting where he had been throughout her ordeal, staring down at her from his chair, a smile on his lips.

'You wanted that spunk in your cunt, didn't you, little one?' he asked.

Carla did not answer, but she knew that the wetness in her vagina and the stiffness of her nipples told him all he wanted to know.

'It is unusual to see a girl so aroused by such treatment,' he said. 'You must have been well trained.'

The words struck Carla as odd. Certainly she had been trained, but how could he possibly know that? His next words, though, gave her much more of a jolt.

'I'm afraid you'll have to wait a little longer for the orgasm that I know you crave.'

'Sir?'

'You see, I intend to take you in that tight rear hole of yours.'

Carla looked at him with wide eyes. She hadn't expected that. She had been buggered before, of course, but only on one or two occasions. Now she felt a sinking feeling at the pit of her stomach as she wondered whether she would be able to accommodate him in the tightness of her anus.

'Over here,' he ordered. 'Bend over the couch.'

Carla rose slowly to her feet and moved across to where he was indicating. Her legs trembling, she dropped down to her knees and bent forward against the rough material of the couch. As she did so, Daran rose to his feet and walked across to stand behind her.

'Spread your cheeks for me.'

Carla moved her hands back and, taking hold of her buttocks, pulled them apart, revealing the tight star of her anus to his gaze. She felt him run his fingers down the crack of her backside and shivered slightly as he touched her there. He rubbed his finger about the hole, testing it, and she felt her muscles contract as he pressed the end of his finger into her.

He gave a grunt and crossed the room to a cabinet. She saw him take something out and move back to where she knelt. Then she felt something cold and soft against her flesh, and she realised that he had produced a jar of ointment of some sort and was rubbing it into her there. She gritted her teeth as his finger slipped into her rear hole again and twisted round.

'Hmm, very nice,' he murmured.

He placed the jar down on the floor beside her, then she heard his zip come down. She glanced behind to see that he had eased his stiff cock from his trousers and was working the foreskin slowly back and forth. She studied his member. It curved up proudly from his groin. It wasn't the biggest she had ever seen, but it was quite thick, with a large blue vein running down its length. As she watched him masturbate it seemed to grow even thicker, and she wondered anxiously if she would be able to accommodate it in her rear.

She was soon to find out, as he pulled back his foreskin and began pressing his glans insistently against her backside. Carla bit her lip. Her instinct was to tighten her sphincter and to refuse him entry, but she knew she had to fight that instinct. Closing her eyes she forced herself to accept him, willing herself to relax as he pressed still harder.

As he penetrated her she gave a cry, screwing her eyes tight at the inevitable pain. Still he pressed, easing his member deeper and deeper into her rectum until she felt his stomach pressed against her backside. Then he began to move, his stiff rod sliding back and forth inside her rear hole as he took his pleasure inside her.

Despite the discomfort of the anal penetration, Carla couldn't help being struck by the eroticism of her position, bent naked over the couch whilst this man rammed his cock into her rear hole. Giving herself this way seemed to her the final surrender to the cult of eroticism to which she had been a servant for so long. Her body was a vessel for the use of men and, whatever they chose to do with it, it was her pleasure to comply. Now, as she was buggered hard by this man, she felt the contentment of one who did what she did with perfection.

He began fucking her harder, grunting with pleasure as his body slapped against Carla's behind. She held on to the material of the couch, pressing back at him, urging him on now that the edge of the pain had receded. That seemed to spur him on all the more, and he gripped her thighs, thrusting her small body hard against the sofa and pressing the wind from her body.

He came suddenly, his rock-hard cock spurting his hot semen deep into her rectum. Carla gasped as she felt her rear filled with his seed. It was like no other sensation she knew and, despite the fact that she wished desperately that it was her cunt that was being so filled, she too found herself able to enjoy the exquisite pleasure she sensed in him as his orgasm overtook him.

He kept his cock buried in her behind until all his spunk was drained. Only then did he withdraw, leaving the young beauty slumped over the sofa, blinking back the tears from her eyes. He ran his hand over her smooth flesh, then leaned forward and kissed her in the middle of her back.

'Yes,' he murmured. 'You really were well trained.'

Chapter 6

For the next three days, Carla settled into her role as prison whore. Her services were much in demand, and, despite Pakat's assurances, she found herself being summoned five or six times a day. She worked out that he must be charging for her by the amount of time she spent in the cell. Some of the more affluent prisoners, like Daran, would keep her for long periods, making her perform for them with others before taking her themselves. Others would simply throw her down on their beds and fuck her hard, coming quickly inside her before shouting for the guard to take her away. In either case, she seldom managed to suppress her own desires, and was almost always rewarded by an orgasm in the hands of her customers.

Meantime Pakat was true to his word, and Carla ate and drank well, the food being brought to her in her cell. The only clothing she was permitted, though, was stockings and shoes, a new pair of stockings being delivered to her every day.

Carla found herself being taken to every corner of the institution. Soon there wasn't a man in the prison who hadn't feasted his eyes on her lovely body, and a fair number had enjoyed the pleasure of fucking her or coming between her lips.

It was on the fifth day that something quite unexpected happened. The guard arrived at her cell, and Carla rose with a sigh, pulling on her stockings as she was always required to do. Then he clicked on her cuffs and led her out. This time, though, he took her not into the depths of the prison, but back along the corridor she had come down on first arriving there. She was led out across the reception area, where she had to endure the jeers of some newly arrived inmates, and into a low building that she had not seen before.

She found herself in a room, divided in half by a glass partition that ran all the way across. Set high in the glass were a series of manacles on short chains. Carla's escort took off her cuffs and, pulling her hands above her head, attached her wrists to two of these, leaving her arms stretched apart and her pert breasts almost pressed against the glass. Then he left her, alone and puzzled, in the large room.

For about five minutes nothing happened. Carla's mind raced as she stared about her. Was she to be beaten? Was she in the hands of some bondage freak? But why the glass? It just didn't seem to make sense.

All at once a door opened in the other part of the room and someone stepped in. It was one of the guards and, as he came through, he held the door open for another, slighter figure. A figure very familiar to the young captive. For a second Carla couldn't believe her eyes, but then the woman smiled, and there was no mistaking who it was.

It was Phaedra.

Carla's mouth fell open as Phaedra walked in. This was the last person she had expected to see, yet it was certainly her.

'Phaedra!'

'Hello, Carla.'

The woman was still smiling, but Carla could see the concern in her eyes as she surveyed her young protégée.

In a sense, it was because of Phaedra that Carla found herself in the situation she was in. It was Phaedra who had first propelled Carla toward the life of debauchery that she had so embraced in the past two years. Ever since they had met, she had encouraged Carla to share her body with others, and had introduced her to the dating agency from which she had begun to sell her body. Phaedra too had been a prime mover in the extraordinary trial that the young woman had had to face in order to explain her misdeeds, and which had culminated in her leaving her unfaithful husband and taking on full-time the life for which she was so well suited. Now, to see her here, was scarcely believable.

'What on earth . . .'

'I heard you were in trouble, so I thought I'd better come and find you.'

'But how?'

'Why, Daran of course.'

'Daran?'

'Yes. Surely you'd have guessed that a man of his standing would be one of our customers. I've supplied him with at least three girls in my time, and he soon sussed you as one of ours. He got on the

35

phone to me straight away, and I flew out here on the first plane.'

Carla shook her head. Of course, that explained Daran's comments about her training, but it hadn't occurred to her for a moment that he might know Phaedra. Clearly the woman's influence spread further than even Carla could have guessed.

'But what can you do to help?' asked Carla.

'Quite a lot I hope, although there's something very fishy about this whole affair.'

'How do you mean?'

'That guy, Moktar.'

'The photographer?'

'He's no photographer. I checked with Mitch. He reckons he's just a small-time crook.'

'But he said he knew Mitch.'

'Oh he knew Mitch all right. He owes Mitch a lot of money for a shoot he did a couple of years ago. They're not exactly pals.'

'So I was brought out to this place under false pretences.'

'That's the way it looks. The point is, why? And more particularly, why to this bloody awful country, where women are treated as third-class citizens?'

Carla was stunned. Until now she simply thought she had been unlucky to end up in this predicament, but as she listened to Phaedra the whole thing began to seem more sinister.

'What do you think's going to happen to me, Phaedra?'

Phaedra ran her eyes up and down Carla's naked, chained body. 'It looks like it's already started to happen,' she remarked. 'How are they treating you?'

Carla glanced down at herself, so cruelly stretched by the chains that held her.

'This place is not exactly a conventional prison,' she said. 'I've got no clothes, and the prison boss sells me to the inmates all the time.'

'So I've heard. Daran told me all about your friend, Colonel Pakat. He sounds a bit of an opportunist. Daran reckons you're reasonably safe with him, though, as long as you behave yourself. Or misbehave,' she mused.

Carla blushed. 'I'll do as I'm told,' she said. 'But how long am I going to be stuck here?'

'That word is that the trial is early next week.'

Carla sighed. 'That long? Why can't they just put me in front of a magistrate and have done with it?'

'I'm not sure. Listen, I'm convinced that all is not as it seems. I'm going to do some investigation. Meanwhile, you'll need a lawyer, so I'll see what I can do.'

'Thanks, Phaedra. God, it's good to see you.'

'It's good to see you too, honey,' said Phaedra with genuine affection. 'I'll get you out of this as quickly as I can. In the meantime I guess you'll just have to go on doing what you're good at.'

'I guess so,' sighed Carla.

'Well, you know what they say. Lie back and think of England!'

Chapter 7

During the next few days, Carla's life continued in the same bizarre fashion. At any time of the day she would receive a visit from one of the guards, who would take her off to a cell in another part of the prison where a man or men would be waiting for her. Carla knew that no ordinary woman would have tolerated the treatment she received at the hands of the other prison inmates. But Carla was no ordinary woman, and her lascivious nature carried her through the ordeal. In fact she soon lost count of the orgasms she had had and the amount of spunk she had swallowed during those hectic days.

All the time she was whoring for Pakat, Carla had been expecting word from Phaedra. Each time her cell door banged open she looked up hopefully, only to see the grinning guard gesturing her to don her stockings. When the mail was distributed in the mornings she looked hopefully for an envelope addressed to her, but none came. Before long she was beginning to wonder what had become of her friend and mentor.

Then, one morning, the pattern was broken, and for the second time she found herself being led, not up to the cells, but to the reception area. This time, though, she was taken past the visiting room and outside into the yard.

Carla had mixed feelings as she was led across the gravel. On the one hand, it was good to feel the sun on her again after the days of incarceration in the bleak, damp jail. On the other, though, there was the humiliation of being led naked in the open air, where anyone who wanted could see her. She tried to ignore the shouts and whistles from the men around her as she walked along, her firm young breasts bouncing with every step. As usual her hands were cuffed behind her, so there was no opportunity to cover herself. All she could do was stare straight ahead and make no sign that she heard or saw her tormentors.

They rounded a corner, and ahead she spotted a lorry similar to the one in which she had been brought to the prison. Her heart leapt as she realised that she was being taken toward it. She knew it could only mean one thing. They were taking her away from the prison. But where?

There was only one place she could think of: the courthouse. That meant that her trial must surely begin today. The thought filled her with trepidation. What would happen to her? There was little doubt in her mind, after what she had witnessed so far of their justice, that she would be found guilty. The charge was indecency, and there was no denying that she had been naked when they had arrested her. In fact, the evidence was still plain for all to see, since she had never regained her clothes. She had hoped that they would at least clothe her for her trial, but it seemed that that was to prove a forlorn hope. Even for the formality of the court, she would be allowed no modesty whatsoever.

As they marched her along, Carla's thoughts went back to the last time she had been made to stand trial. Then it had been in an English country house, surrounded by her peers. She had been naked then too. Now, though, it all seemed a lot worse. She was in a foreign country, amongst total strangers. She shivered at the thought of standing up before so many people with all her charms on show.

They reached the truck and the guard indicated that she was to board. Once again, with her arms trapped behind her, Carla found it difficult, but achieved the feat with as much dignity as she could muster. Then she stood quietly whilst she was cuffed to the bar beside the other prisoners who were to travel to court with her.

Ten minutes later the vehicle bumped out of the compound and headed off toward the city. Once again Carla had to endure the stares of the people on the street, all anxious to get a look at the beautiful young woman, clad only in black stockings, as the lorry rumbled by.

The drive to the courtroom took about half an hour. Half an hour of humiliation, as the wolf whistles and shouts reached Carla's ears. She stood, staring straight ahead of her, refusing to look at the people or to acknowledge them as they rumbled through the busy streets. At last they reached their destination, and it was with relief tinged with anticipation that Carla saw the gates to the building close behind them.

Once they had pulled up, the door to the cage was opened, and the prisoners were let out one by one. The girl watched as they were led through into the building. She was the last to be released, and the court guard eyed her up appreciatively as he undid her cuffs. He allowed his hands to stray to her bottom as he did so, squeezing her soft young flesh in his rough hands before refastening her wrists behind her.

Once freed, Carla jumped down from the cage and went to follow the route taken by her fellow prisoners. However, it seemed that the guard had other ideas for her. He took her arm and led her away from the main courtroom toward a long, low building to its left. He knocked on the door and Carla heard the sound of bolts being pulled back. Then she was inside and being taken down a long corridor to yet another guarded door whilst the one behind her was locked shut once again.

After more twists and turns, Carla found herself in a large room, clearly set out as a courtroom, though a lot of the furniture seemed rather makeshift and she had the distinct impression that the whole set-up was somewhat temporary. This surprised her. It was almost as if the whole thing had been set out for her benefit. She thought back to what Phaedra had said to her, and the fears she had voiced about this whole case, and once again she began to wonder whether this was to be an ordinary trial.

The guard took her forward to a dais about three feet high in the centre of the court and led her up the steps at its side. Once she was on the top she saw that there were shackles, chained to rings, set in the floor. The guard began to attach them to her ankles, forcing her to stand with her legs apart as he secured them. Once these were in place, he stood in front of her and reached for her breasts, taking them in his hands and squeezing the soft, pliant flesh. Carla said nothing, standing still and helpless as he felt her up, embarrassed by the way her nipples hardened under his fingers. He ran his other hand down her belly, stroking the wiry triangle of her pubic hair before seeking out her clitoris, bringing a muffled gasp from the girl as he rubbed it with his fingertips. Carla closed her eyes, trying to deny the excitement within her as this stranger took advantage of her bondage. He slipped a finger into her vagina, and she felt the wetness flow within her as her body responded to his advances. She was panting slightly now, her nipples standing proudly from her breasts as he continued to tease them.

Carla looked at the man. His eyes were fixed on her lovely body as he began to frig her. There was an expression of amusement

40

on his face, and she knew that he could sense her control slipping away. She glanced round at the empty room. She was certain that what he was doing was illicit, but she guessed that any complaint from her would fall on deaf ears.

He began moving his hand faster, and, despite her reluctance, she gave a little moan of arousal as the excitement inside her increased. She was pressing her pubis forward now, her legs slightly bent as her body responded to his probing.

She came suddenly and unexpectedly, gasping with sheer lust, her body shaking as she let herself go. The guard watched her expression as she climaxed, continuing to keep her impaled on his fingers as she rocked back and forth, moaning aloud.

All at once the door behind Carla opened. The guard snatched his hand away. Carla was standing with her back to the door, and she guessed that whoever had come in could have seen nothing of what was happening. She tried hard to bring herself back under control, but her orgasm continued, even though he was no longer stimulating her. Still gasping, she turned to see a woman standing there.

It was Phaedra.

'Hello, Carla.'

'H-hi,' she puffed.

'You look a bit flushed.'

'It's nothing.'

Phaedra moved round in front of her, and Carla knew she could see the wetness of her sex, the muscles still twitching with the last vestiges of her climax. The woman eyed the guard, then looked back at Carla, but she did not comment.

'I-I guess today's the day, then,' said Carla, trying to make her voice sound normal.

'Yes, but I'm still convinced that something fishy's going on.'

'What do you mean, fishy?'

'This isn't the proper courthouse. And you're still naked. Normally they'd give you prison clothes. This is obviously not going to be an ordinary trial.'

'What do you think's going on?' asked Carla nervously.

'I just don't know. But I don't like it. Nobody will tell me anything. Anyhow, you'll be pleased to know that I'm going to be your defence lawyer.'

'You?'

'Don't worry, I know what I'm doing.'

41

'I'm not worried. I'm sure I couldn't get a better defence.'

At that moment the large double doors at the end of the room swung open and Carla turned to see a crowd of people entering. As they came in, each one stopped short in astonishment, staring at the naked young beauty for a moment before the person following shoved them forward, only to stop themselves as the vision of beauty met their eyes. Carla's face glowed as they took in her bare charms with frank interest.

They began to take their seats. The ones that filed down to the desks at the front of the court were dressed in sober suits. Behind them more casually dressed people were filling the public area.

Then Carla spotted a face that was all too familiar to her and she gasped in recognition.

'Oh my God!'

'What it is, Carla?' asked Phaedra.

'It's my husband,' she whispered.

Carla could scarcely believe her eyes as she watched the man stroll into the courtroom. She hadn't seen him since the end of her previous trial, after which she had entered a new life. Her only contact with the man since then had been via lawyers as her divorce made its slow and tortured way through the legal system. Now here he was, suddenly turning up in this dreadful country. Worse, here she was in an even more uncomfortable situation than she had been in then. He gave her a sidelong glance as he took his seat at the front of the court beside a tall, dark-suited man with whom he began to talk in a low voice.

Phaedra moved close to the base of the dais on which Carla was chained.

'I was afraid of this,' she said quietly.

'I don't understand. What's he doing here?'

'I think this whole thing was engineered by him.'

'What?'

'I reckon he set up that photo shoot with Moktar and arranged for you to get caught in the act.'

'Would he really go that far?'

'Of course he would. That bastard has had it in for you ever since you walked out on him. What better way to get back at you than this?'

'But it's just an indecency charge, for God's sake.'

Phaedra shook her head. 'I think it's more than that. This country has some very strange laws, particularly where women

42

are concerned. I think he may have some kind of surprise up his sleeve.'

'What kind of surprise?'

But before Phaedra could answer, somebody banged a gavel down hard on a table and Carla turned to see a large figure enter the court. He was dressed in a black gown and wore a chain of office about his neck. As he strode in the officials and observers rose to their feet.

This was clearly the judge.

Carla studied him as he took his place in a high-backed seat at the front of the court behind a raised bench. He was in his early fifties, stern-faced and with an undeniable air of authority about him. A cold feeling gripped her stomach as he glanced across at her.

When he sat, the rest of the court sat too, so that Carla was the only one left standing.

Another man, whom Carla supposed was the usher, arose from the bench just in front of where the judge was sitting.

'Court is in session,' he called. 'Mr Wajir prosecuting.'

'Go ahead, Mr Wajir,' said the judge.

There was silence for a moment, then the man who had been sitting next to Carla's husband rose to his feet.

'If it please the court,' he began, 'we would like proceedings of this case to be held in English to facilitate the accused and accuser.'

The judge inclined his head. 'Your request is granted, Mr Wajir,' he said. 'Usher, read the charges.'

The Usher turned to Carla.

'Carla Wilde,' he said, 'you are before this court on a charge of gross indecency in that you did expose your naked body in a public place.'

All at once the man called Wajir rose again.

'Your Honour,' he said, 'we wish to extend the charge against the accused.'

'Yes, Mr Wajir?'

'We intend to show that the accused deliberately insulted the superior sex, and particularly the gentleman sitting beside me, her rightful husband in law.'

'Wait a minute,' said Phaedra, rising to her feet. 'You can't bring in a new charge after the trial has begun.'

The judge banged his gavel. 'Silence!' he shouted. 'Mr Wajir, can you substantiate these charges?'

'Yes, Your Honour. We will show that this woman deliberately used her charms to mislead and to rob men in the most insulting manner, contrary to the laws of gender that exist in this country.'

'In that case, add the charge to the sheet.'

'But that's unfair,' called Phaedra. 'I've prepared my case on the charge of indecency, not this new charge.'

Bang! Down came the gavel again.

'Silence,' barked the judge. 'Another outburst like that and you'll be in contempt! The defendant will answer to the charges.'

The courtroom official turned to Carla.

'Carla Wilde, you have heard the charges against you. How do you plead?'

Carla glanced at Phaedra, then turned to face the man, a defiant expression on her face.

'Not guilty,' she said.

Chapter 8

Carla stared out at the crowd of faces that gazed up at her from the court. She tried to look composed, but it wasn't easy, standing there totally naked before all these men. She was still trying to understand the charge that Wajir had thrown at her. Insulting men? Surely that was something she had never done in her life? Apart from the ridiculous nature of the charge, it was something of which she was certain she was innocent. Yet Wajir seemed confident of his case.

The group of well-dressed characters at the front of the court, it transpired, was the jury, and a clerk began swearing them in. Carla studied their faces. All were men, and all seemed hostile to her as they stood up and took the oath. She was glad of the presence of Phaedra, the only other woman in the court. She certainly felt isolated, standing there chained and on display, like some kind of exotic specimen.

During the next half hour the court busied itself with procedure. Once the men had all taken the oath, Phaedra was introduced as the defence lawyer and the charges were formally set down. Then Wajir rose to his feet once more.

'If it please the court, the prosecution would like to call the first witness.'

The judge inclined his head.'

'The prosecution call Joseph Stone.'

Carla and Phaedra both looked up sharply as the name was called out. It was one that was only too familiar to both of them.

'That bastard,' whispered Phaedra from her seat just in front of where Carla was standing. 'I might have known that he was mixed up in this.'

The door at the back of the court opened and a man walked in. He was strongly built, with a craggy, unshaven face. He wore an ill-fitting lightweight suit, his tie askew. He strode confidently to the front of the court, running his eyes over the soft curves of Carla's body as he did so.

The clerk swore Stone in, then Wajir was on his feet again.

'Your name is Joseph Stone?'

'That's right.'

'Mr Stone, do you recognise the accused?'

Stone feasted his eyes on Carla's nude form.

'Oh yes,' he said. 'That's Carla Wilde.'

'Mr Stone, were you previously employed by the Hartfurt Institute?'

'I was. For about two years.'

'And did you encounter the accused there?'

'Yes, sir.'

'In what capacity?'

'She was an inmate. A trainee.'

'And what exactly was taught at this institute?'

'They taught women how to exploit men.'

'To exploit men, you say? In what way?'

'They taught them to use their bodies to tempt them, then they gave themselves to them in exchange for money.'

'So it was a school that taught them feminine wiles?'

'That's correct. The whole intention was to find rich men, then get as much from them as possible.'

'And Mrs Wilde was a good pupil?'

'She took to it like a professional. She positively revelled in it, and she took every opportunity to learn new ways to trick men into parting with their cash.'

Stone went on to describe an institution where the women were shown precisely how to use the men they targeted, and how to use their charms to seduce them. The jury listened to him in silence, occasionally turning dark accusing stares towards Carla. The girl wished that she hadn't been forced to display herself so blatantly. She knew that the immodesty of her situation wasn't helping her case at all.

Wajir questioned Stone for about half an hour, before finally turning to Phaedra.

'Thank you, Mr Stone. Your witness.'

Phaedra rose to her feet. She had been making notes whilst Stone had been giving his testimony, and she studied them momentarily before speaking.

'Tell me, Mr Stone, why did you leave the Institute?'

'It didn't suit me.'

'Isn't it true to say you were sacked?'

Stone looked uncomfortable. 'I was planning to leave anyway.'

'But, in fact, you were sacked. Why was that?'

'It doesn't matter, does it?'

'Wasn't it for stealing money from the petty cash?'

Wajir sprang to his feet.

'Objection, Your Honour. Is this line of questioning relevant?'

The judge turned to Phaedra.

'Well?'

'I think the witness's character is a material factor, Your Honour,' she said.

The judge nodded. 'Continue.'

'Well, Mr Stone? Did you steal from the petty cash?'

'That's what they said.'

'So, in fact, if anyone was extorting money from men, it was you?'

'It was the women, I tell you.'

Phaedra turned to the judge.

'With your permission, Your Honour, I'd like my client to explain precisely what went on at the Hartfurt Institute.'

'I object,' said Wajir. 'The defence will have plenty of time after the prosecution has finished presenting its case.'

'Listen,' said Phaedra. 'We all know this is no ordinary case, and it's not being tried in the ordinary way. You only have to look at my client to see that. I want her to be given the opportunity to answer her accusers directly. Only then will we hear the truth.'

The judge nodded. 'As you say, everything about this trial is unusual. Unlike the West, we have no rigid rules about how these things are done. Let the accused answer.'

Phaedra moved across to where Carla was chained.

'Carla, you recognise Mr Stone?'

'Yes, I do.'

'And you remember the Institute?'

'Of course I do.'

'Is it a place where they train women to exploit men?'

'No. It's precisely the opposite in fact. It's a place where women learn how to bring pleasure to men.'

'Perhaps you'd like to tell us about your time there?'

'What, all of it? I'm not sure. . .'

'Now, Carla,' interrupted Phaedra, 'this is no time to be coy.

47

You've done this sort of thing before. This time it's really important.'

Carla looked about at the sea of expectant faces once more. Then she took a deep breath.

'All right then.'

'So how did it all start?'

'Well, I arrived at the Institute shortly after my trial . . .'

Chapter 9

When the long, black car pulled up outside the Institute that warm May morning, Carla was already disoriented, having spent much of the journey blindfold. Now, as the driver applied the handbrake, she didn't know what to expect. She was glad of the fact that Phaedra was sitting beside her in the car, but she suspected that she would soon have to face things alone. She turned to the older woman questioningly, and Phaedra reached out and squeezed Carla's hand.

'This is the place,' she said. 'Out you get.'

'Aren't you coming with me?'

Phaedra shook her head. 'No, you're on your own from here.'

The driver opened the door and Carla looked out. They had stopped outside a tall, imposing edifice surrounded by a high wall. Carla wasn't even sure what country they were in. The flight from London had taken about two hours, and the temperature told her that they were some way south of Britain.

She stepped from the car and the door was closed behind her. Then the driver climbed back inside and the car swept round the drive and out between the heavy iron gates. The moment it was through, the gates swung closed with a clang. Then she was alone.

Carla felt very isolated. She had no luggage with her. She had been instructed to bring none. All she had, in fact, was the tight black low-cut dress that Phaedra had given her before they had left England. Now here she was, alone in this strange place. She turned to the house. There were wide steps leading up to a heavy oaken door. Her stomach knotted at the thought of what awaited her inside, but there was nowhere else to go.

She mounted the steps warily. Beside the door was a large brass bell push and she pressed it. A minute passed, then she heard footsteps and the sound of a key being turned.

The door creaked slowly open, to reveal a figure framed in the doorway.

'Yes?'

Carla gaped at the young woman in front of her. She was blonde, about twenty years old, Carla guessed, with long flowing hair. But what had made Carla gasp was her state of undress. She was totally nude, apart from a pair of red high-heeled shoes. Carla stood for a moment, taking in her magnificent breasts which stood out proudly from her chest, the pink, bud-like nipples surrounded by large, circular areolae. She let her eyes drop to the girl's trim waist, then lower to her fair pubic bush and the slit of her sex beneath.

'Yes?' said the girl again.

'I . . . I'm sorry,' stammered Carla, returning her gaze to the girl's face.

'You must be the new girl.'

'Yes. I'm Carla.'

'Hi, Carla. I'm Bennie.'

The girl stretched out a hand and Carla took it.

'You'd better come in.'

She stood aside, and Carla entered. The hallway was cool after the heat of the sun, and the light streamed in from high windows. Bennie locked the door again, then turned to Carla.

'Follow me,' she said, and set off.

Carla watched her as she walked ahead. She had a perfectly shaped bottom, and it wiggled seductively as she walked. To Carla the sight of the nude girl, apparently quite unconcerned about her lack of clothes, was a strange one, and one she found very erotic. She wondered what it would be like to caress the girl's breasts, and a small shiver of arousal flowed through her.

They continued through the house. It was a large building, sparsely furnished with rustic furniture. Everywhere the ceilings were high and the carpetless floors cool. Most of the walls were painted plain white, here and there hung with mats or baskets.

They arrived at a door and Bennie knocked lightly.

'Come!'

She pushed open the door and ushered Carla in.

'This is Carla, Master. She's the new arrival.'

The burly man glanced up from his desk. Carla's first impression of him was of a muscular man, about thirty-five years old, with thin lips and cold eyes. Later, she was to come to know him as Joe Stone. He pushed back the chair.

'Carla, eh?'

He ran his eyes up and down her body, his gaze making the girl

50

feel as naked as her companion. Eventually he spoke again.

'You know why you're here, Carla?'

'To learn how to please men.'

Bennie nudged Carla, and the young girl looked at her quizzically.

'Master,' she whispered.

'Pardon?'

'Call him master.'

'I'm sorry. To learn how to please men, Master.'

Stone eyed Bennie coldly.

'You're not doing your job, Bennie,' he said. 'You should have instructed her on the correct form of address before you brought her in here.'

'I'm sorry, Master.'

'Such forgetfulness must be corrected, mustn't it, Bennie?'

'I said I'm sorry, Master.'

'You'll be sorrier soon. Go and fetch a cane from the rack.'

'Yes, Master.'

If the order had come as a shock to the young blonde, she didn't show it. Carla watched in amazement as she walked calmly across to a rack on the wall on which were hung a variety of whips and canes. The blonde beauty selected a long, thin cane from it. Then she crossed the room again and handed it to Stone.

'Over the desk.'

The girl turned to his desk, pressing her body against it. Then she leant forward over it, sticking her lovely backside up and back and spreading her legs. As she prostrated herself, Carla saw for the first time that her hair about her sex lips had been shaved so that her long, pink quim was perfectly visible.

'Six strokes,' said Stone.

'Thank you, Master.'

Carla watched as he positioned himself beside the girl and tapped the cane against her soft flesh. Then she bit her lip as he drew his arm back.

Swish! Whack!

The cane descended with terrible force, cutting into Bennie's rear and leaving a white stripe that immediately began darkening to an angry red.

Swish! Whack!

He brought it down again, the force shaking the girl's body, yet still she made no sound.

51

Swish! Whack!

As Carla watched the punishment she found herself unaccountably aroused by the sight of this beautiful girl who was accepting such an awful beating. Carla knew that the pain must be dreadful, yet the girl submitted without protest. She remembered when she herself had been caned by Lindy, the jealous daughter of one of her customers, during her trial. She had known then that men became aroused at the sight of a naked girl being caned, and now she began to understand why.

Swish! Whack!

She was snatched back from her reverie as down came the cane again, laying yet another stripe across Bennie's pale behind. She looked at the girl's clenched fists and the expression of agony on her face, yet still there was no sound from her.

Swish! Whack!
Swish! Whack!

The final two blows were delivered with undiminished force, both shaking Bennie's body as more fierce weals were cut into her buttocks. Then Stone lowered the cane.

'Stand up!'

Bennie rose slowly. As she turned, Carla saw the tears that ran down her cheeks. Still she said nothing as Stone handed her the cane, but her walk was stiff as she returned it to the rack.

Stone turned to Carla.

'Let that be your first lesson. The first of many I hope.'

'Yes . . . Master.'

'Strip her.'

'I beg your pardon, Master?'

The order had come so suddenly that Carla barely understood what he was saying. Bennie knew, though, and she immediately moved across to where Carla was standing. She stood in front of the petite, dark-haired beauty, staring down into her eyes for a moment. Then she raised her hands and reached behind her. She unhooked Carla's dress with a flick of her fingers, and began pulling down the zip. She stood close to Carla and, being taller, her luscious breasts jutted right in front of Carla's face. Carla could smell the thin sheen of sweat that had broken out on Bennie's body during the beating, and there was something intensely erotic about being so close to this naked beauty.

Bennie slipped the dress from Carla's body, leaving her in her brief black underwear. Carla looked into her eyes, wondering if

Bennie felt the arousal that she did at being so close to a beautiful girl. If so, Bennie gave no sign as she reached behind Carla once more and unhooked the catch on her bra. The garment fell away from her firm breasts and Carla felt the heat rise in her cheeks as she realised that her nipples were stiff.

Bennie dropped to her knees in front of Carla and dragged off her panties, pulling them down her legs and over her feet. Then she stood back to admire the pale young girl who stood red-faced and naked in the middle of the room.

'Sit on the desk and spread your legs,' ordered Stone. 'I want to see your cunt.'

Once again the order was issued with a cold authority that sent a shiver of excitement through the young beauty. There was something about a dominant male that Carla found very arousing, particularly when he was clothed and she was naked. Obediently she moved across to the desk and sat as ordered. Then she slowly opened her thighs, revealing the pink flower of her sex to the watching man. He stood between her legs, examining it critically.

'Get it shaved,' he ordered curtly. 'Just leave a patch on your pubis, like Bennie's.'

'Yes, Master.'

'Well, Bennie. What do you think of Carla's cunt?'

'It's a lovely cunt, Master.'

'Wouldn't you like to lick it?'

'Yes, Master.'

'Then do so.'

Once again Carla was astonished at his audacity in issuing the order and at the coolness with which Bennie accepted it. It was as if he had asked the girl to perform the most ordinary of tasks, yet the intimacy of the act he demanded was extreme. Bennie was unruffled, though. The girl simply stepped forward and dropped to her knees between Carla's open thighs. Then she leant forward and protruded her tongue.

'Oh!'

Carla was unable to suppress the exclamation as the girl's wet tongue came into contact with the hard nut of her clitoris and began to lick at it. She could scarcely credit what was happening to her. Just minutes ago, both these people had been complete strangers to her. Now here she was, perched naked on a desk, being fellated by a gorgeous blonde whilst a man looked on.

'Ah!'

She squirmed as Bennie probed inside her vagina with her tongue, alternately licking and sucking and sending the most delicious sensations through her body. The blonde was clearly an expert at performing oral sex on a woman, seeking out the hot spots in Carla's gaping cunt and teasing them with her tongue, then sucking her clitoris into her mouth and running her teeth gently back and forth over it. Carla had never experienced anyone with such ability to arouse her. She began to moan aloud, her pubis pressed up into Bennie's face, urging her on. The fact that she was naked and being watched by a complete stranger was forgotten in her passion.

She came suddenly, her moans turning to screams as the release of orgasm swept through her body. Bennie kept her mouth locked onto her sex, riding the writhing newcomer, holding her at her peak for as long as she was able, then slowly bringing her down once again.

By the time Bennie had finished, Carla was gasping for breath, her body stretched out on the desk, the other girl's saliva coating the creamy flesh of her inner thighs. She stared into the face of the blonde, who was wiping her lips on the back of her hand, then she glanced across at Stone.

'Get up,' he ordered.

She rose slowly to her feet, her legs still slightly unsteady. Bennie too got to her feet again, standing to one side of Stone, her face without expression.

Stone nodded. 'Not bad,' he said. 'I shall take great interest in your training, Carla. Take her to her room now, Bennie, then come back here. I fancy coming between those gorgeous tits of yours.'

'Yes, Master,' said Bennie. 'Come on, Carla.'

She opened the door. Carla glanced down at her clothes, which lay on the floor where Bennie had dropped them. Then she saw the blonde give a little shake of the head and she knew at once that she was to leave them where they were.

As Bennie closed the door, Carla reached out and took hold of her hand.

'Sorry about what happened in there.'

'What, licking your cunt? I enjoyed it. I love making a woman come.'

'No, I mean the caning.'

'Oh, that's Joe Stone for you. He's a complete shit.'

'Yet you obeyed him so willingly.'

54

'That's what we're here for, Carla. To please men. Joe likes total obedience, so that's what he gets. Other men want loving care or total sluttishness. The trick is knowing what they want and giving it to them. You'll learn.'

Carla looked at the stripes that crisscrossed Bennie's behind and shook her head doubtfully.

'He laid it on pretty hard.'

'I can take it. I knew that if I complained he'd just have doubled the punishment.'

'Did he mean that about coming between your breasts?'

'Yeah. Joe's got a thing about tit-fucking me. With you I suspect he'll prefer your mouth. Come on now, Carla. If I don't get back to him quickly I'll get some more strokes from that cane.'

Chapter 10

In fact, as it transpired, Carla didn't encounter Stone again for some days. She was allotted a small room at the top of the house, where Bennie left her, instructing her to appear for lunch at one o'clock and giving her directions to the dining hall. In the bathroom she found a razor with some shaving cream. After showering, she settled herself on a stool in front of a mirror and, spreading her legs, set about the delicate process of denuding her sex lips of hair. By the time she had finished, her cunt was quite smooth, and she shivered slightly as she ran her fingers over the sensitive flesh. She wanted to masturbate as she stared at herself in the mirror, but she feared someone might be watching, so instead she prepared herself for the impending meal.

When the time came, she entered the dining room with some trepidation, feeling extremely uncomfortable without clothes. There, seated at the table, was Bennie, along with two other girls. One was nude like herself. The other wore a black maid's outfit that was far too small for her. The skirt was extremely short, so that her bare crotch was on view, and the white apron at the front was cut so low that the tops of her nipples were visible over the top.

Bennie introduced Carla to the other two. The nude girl was called Petra. She had long flaming red hair and a loud laugh, and she greeted Carla warmly. The other girl, Rita, was much quieter, and Carla sensed her embarrassment at the sexy outfit she was wearing.

Over lunch Carla learned that Petra was in her last week at the Institute, whilst both Bennie and Rita had more than a month to serve before their training was complete. The new arrival felt very young and inexperienced compared to these three, but they treated her as an equal, and soon she was enjoying their company very much.

She learned from them that the Institute was run on strict lines, though Bennie's thrashing that morning was not a very common

56

occurrence. They gave her a timetable, showing where she should be and when. Carla surveyed the curriculum with some anticipation. The subjects included obedience, deportment, make-up and sexual techniques. That afternoon she was scheduled for a session intriguingly entitled orgasm. She asked the others what it involved, but they simply giggled and changed the subject.

It was with some trepidation, therefore, that Carla found herself knocking at the door of a room at the top of the house half an hour later.

She pushed the door open to find herself in a room with bare floorboards and white-painted walls. There were no curtains at the window, and the place had an air of starkness about it. It reminded Carla of a gymnasium, and the variety of pieces of equipment placed about the floor strengthened the impression. She stared at the objects, but could find no clue as to their function.

There was nobody in the room, and Carla paused uncertainly just inside the door, wondering what to do. The door swung shut behind her with a bang, then there was silence.

The naked girl began to walk about the room, inspecting the equipment. There were pieces that resembled vaulting horses. Others were low benches, the tops upholstered in leather. There were large wooden frames and low pedestals. Each had shining chains attached, with cuffs and shackles on the ends. All around were large full-length mirrors clearly designed to allow anyone using the devices to see herself and what was being done to her. Carla shivered slightly as she imagined to what use these strange objects could be put, running her hands over the rough leather and feeling the cold steel of the chains.

The sound of the opening door took her by surprise, and she swung round to see that a figure had entered the room. It was a woman, about thirty years old, tall and slim with dark hair cut short. She had high cheekbones and deep blue eyes, and she wore a simple skirt and blouse, her full breasts pressing the material out in front. Carla stood, feeling awkward and embarrassed, her hands hanging at her side as the woman walked across to her.

'You must be Carla.'

'Yes . . . Mistress.'

The woman gave a little nod, so that Carla knew she had assessed the woman's status correctly.

'I see you've been observing the equipment, Carla,' she said.

'Yes, Mistress.'

'I'm sure you'll soon become familiar with it. My name is Laura, and I'm an instructress here. Now lets see if we can get off to a good start together.'

'I hope so, Mistress.'

'Good. I want you to stand with your legs apart and your hands behind your head whilst I inspect you.'

'Yes, Mistress.'

Carla did as she was told, and the woman walked round her, running her eyes critically over the younger girl's lovely young body.

'I see you've shaved your cunt.'

'Yes, Mistress. Mr Stone ordered me to.'

Carla had almost forgotten her depillation but, on being reminded, she became aware once more how her bare sex lips felt strangely cool as she stood with her legs spread.

'Ah, yes,' said the woman. 'Phaedra told us you were beautiful, and she wasn't exaggerating. Your breasts are exquisite.'

'Thank you, Mistress.'

'Do you masturbate, Carla?'

The question caught the young woman off guard.

'Er . . . sometimes, Mistress.'

'With a dildo?'

'It depends. Sometimes . . .' She blushed.

'Yes?'

'Sometimes I just use my fingers, Mistress.'

'Whilst you are here, you're forbidden to masturbate except when ordered to. Is that clear?'

'Yes, Mistress.'

'Masturbate for me now.'

Once again Carla was completely taken by surprise by the order. It barely seemed credible that such an act could be demanded of her. Then she thought of Bennie, and how the girl had reacted instantaneously to Stone's orders, and she knew that the same would be expected of her. Slowly, her eyes fixed on the instructress, she removed her hands from her head and slipped her right hand down between her legs.

The enforced nudity had already had an oddly perverse effect on the lascivious girl, and her slit was moist as she ran a finger down its length. She sought out her clitoris, teasing it out from between her nether lips and rubbing it gently with her forefinger.

58

At the same time her other hand moved up to her breast and she began to caress her nipple, taking it between finger and thumb and rolling the flesh between them, loving the way it hardened.

She looked up at Laura. She was watching her intently, a slight smile on her face. Behind the woman was one of the mirrors, and Carla could see herself reflected in it, her body hunched forward, her knees bent as she played with herself. The sight sent a sudden thrill through her, and she pushed a finger into her vagina, moaning slightly as her arousal increased.

Carla could never understand the way her body responded to her touches. Any normal woman, she reflected, would be overcome with shame or revulsion at what she was being made to do. But Carla could only think of the heat in her sex and the warm feeling that invaded her body as her ardour increased and her fingers began to move faster.

'You're enjoying that, aren't you?' said Laura.

'Y-yes, Mistress.' Carla's voice was shaky with her exertions as she began to lose herself in her passions.

'Stop now.'

Carla looked up at the woman, almost in despair. Having worked herself so much, she was already close to orgasm, and it took all her willpower to withdraw her finger from her throbbing sex. She whimpered slightly as she straightened up and placed her hands behind her head once more. Laura was staring at her crotch, and in the mirror Carla could see how her sex lips were contracting, almost as if her fingers were still buried inside her.

'Come over here.'

The woman moved across to the other side of the room, and Carla padded silently along behind her, her hands still clasped behind her head. The woman stopped by a bench that stood a little over two feet high. Projecting from the centre of it was a phallus made of black rubber, about nine inches long and very thick.

'Straddle the bench,' ordered Laura.

Carla obeyed, spreading her legs wide and planting them on either side of the device.

'Put your hands behind your back.'

As Carla did as she was told, she felt the cold metal of a pair of handcuffs close above her wrists.

'Now move forward until you're over the dildo.'

She obeyed, standing so that the end of the object was no more

59

than half an inch from her open vagina.

'Would you like it inside you?'

Carla couldn't bring herself to speak, so she simply nodded, dumbly.

'All right then, but you must not come.'

'Mistress?' Carla looked at the woman in surprise.

'Some girls, Carla, take ages to get aroused. They need a lot of care and attention from their man before they can come. That's why we have to train them to respond more quickly to their lovers.'

'Yes but . . .'

'From what I have heard about you, and what I've seen today, you are not one of those girls. Why, your cunt was wet even before you started frigging yourself.'

Carla blushed. 'I don't know why, Mistress.'

'The point is, Carla, that certain men prefer their women not to respond. Some men even like to take a woman against her will. With such men you must learn to respond accordingly, and to restrain your desires.'

'So I mustn't appear too eager?'

'That's right. Some men prefer the woman not to come at all. Others want them at least to wait until their own orgasm.'

'But lots of men really like to see me come.'

'And for that you don't need training. What you have to learn today is how to behave with the other sort.'

Carla looked down at the thick dildo that projected between her legs. How could she possibly not come with that inside her? But she knew that Laura was right. She had come to the Institute to learn, and if restraining her climax was something she needed to be able to do, then she must do as she was told.

'Now, lower yourself onto the dildo,' said Laura.

Slowly Carla began to squat down over the device, tentatively lowering herself until, with a sharp intake of breath, she felt it touch her sex.

'Lower. Let it inside you,' ordered Laura.

Carla began to force herself downward onto the dildo. She gasped as it pressed against her slit, shock waves of excitement pulsing through her at the feel of its bulbous rubbery tip. She manoeuvred herself until it was between her bare sex lips. Then she began slowly to push downwards once more, moaning softly as she felt the walls of her sex forced apart by the object penetrating her wet vagina.

Carla lowered herself all the way down until she was sitting astride the bench, the phallus buried deep within her. As her backside came to rest on the bench, she stared across at her reflection in the mirror. She was scarcely able to credit that it was herself she was seeing, a lovely, petite dark-haired girl sitting naked, her legs spread so that the thick black object buried in her vagina was clearly visible.

'Is that exciting you, Carla?'

'Y-yes, Mistress.'

'Good. Now stand up again. But not too quickly.'

Carla gritted her teeth. Then, slowly, she began to raise her body. Once again the friction of the dildo as it moved inside her brought new waves of pleasure coursing through her, and she whimpered slightly as it finally slipped from within her.

'Now do it again.'

Biting her lip, Carla began to bend her legs once more.

For the next few minutes she was made to repeat the process again and again. She must have gone through the procedure a dozen times whilst the impassive woman looked on. Each time, as she felt her vagina filled by the thick object, she was certain she must come, but each time she managed, somehow, to control herself. Her body was shaking with arousal as she lifted herself yet again from the phallus.

'Good,' said Laura. 'You seem to have got the hang of it. Now, I want you to continue doing that whilst I go out and make a call. And remember, I don't want you to stop, no matter what. Understand?'

'Yes, Mistress.'

'Don't forget, I'll know if you come.'

'Yes, Mistress.'

The woman went out. Left alone, Carla was sorely tempted to stop what she was doing in order to try to bring herself under control, but she had already seen the video cameras in the ceiling of the room, and she knew that, if they were switched on, then she would be found out. Instead, with a groan, she began squatting down on the object of her delicious torture once more.

All at once the door opened again and someone entered. It was Rita, the quiet girl, still wearing the maid's costume that scarcely hid her curvaceous charms. She stopped short when she saw Carla, and the young girl blushed as she thought of how she must look, naked and handcuffed, squatting down over the glistening phallus.

'Oh,' exclaimed Rita. 'Sorry. I didn't know you were here. I was sent to polish the equipment.'

'Mmm.' Carla could hardly speak, such was her arousal.

She continued her strange exercise, emitting muffled moans of pleasure as the thick knob moved in and out of her. Meanwhile Rita got on with her work, bending low over the devices so that Carla was treated to a perfect view of her pert behind and her thick sex lips.

Suddenly the door opened yet again and a man entered that Carla had not encountered before.

'What the fuck are you doing?'

Carla froze, her face crimson, her wet cunt half penetrated by the thick, black device. But it wasn't her the man was addressing. Rita turned to face him.

'I was dusting, Master.'

'You were due to clean my room half an hour ago.'

'I-I got delayed, Master.'

The man strode up to the girl and snatched her duster from her, hurling it to the ground.

'You're supposed to do the staff rooms first, you stupid girl.'

'I'm sorry. I'll go right away.'

Carla watched the scene unfold. For a moment she forgot what she was supposed to be doing, hovering there with the dildo halfway inside her, then the man turned to her.

'What are you staring at. Aren't you on a lesson?'

'Yes, Master.'

'Well, get on with it.'

Slowly, her face still glowing, Carla continued her strange exercise. Meanwhile the man turned back to the girl.

'What you need is fucking,' he said.

'Yes, Master.'

'Suck my cock.'

As Carla watched in fascination, the girl dropped to her knees and began undoing the man's flies, showing the same instant obedience that Bennie had earlier. The man's cock was already stiffening as the girl pulled it from his pants, and she took it into her mouth at once, sucking hard at it. The sight sent new shivers of excitement through Carla's naked body as she fought to suppress her desires, the thick dildo seeming to fill her even more as she drove herself down on it. She wished the couple would go away and leave her alone once more, as the sight of the pretty woman fellating the man's now rampant cock was threatening to release the orgasm she was trying so hard to suppress.

Rita sucked the man with obvious enthusiasm, her head moving back and forth as she caressed his large cock. Then he pulled her off and pushed her back over a bench.

'Pull up your skirt and spread your legs,' he ordered.

Pulling up her skirt was scarcely necessary, since it barely covered her crotch, but Rita obeyed, tucking the hem up to her waist. Carla stared in fascination at the other girl's sex as she opened it to the man, revealing a shiny pinkness. He took hold of the neck of her dress and yanked it down, revealing a pair of small but perfectly shaped breasts, the nipples standing stiff and proud. He grabbed them roughly, squeezing them hard and bringing small cries of excitement from the young woman. Then he took hold of his rampant cock and guided it toward her open sex.

Rita gave a cry as he thrust himself into her, ramming his cock home roughly. The girl cried out again as he began to fuck her, his backside working back and forth. Carla couldn't take her eyes off the couple as they screwed before her eyes, he jabbing hard into her whilst she moaned with arousal, her body spread and open to him. Carla tried desperately to ignore what was happening, as she worked herself up and down. Her body was screaming for an orgasm, and she was barely in control. Yet still she continued to move her body on the thick dildo, which was coated with her juices now, a small shiny pool of them forming on the bench top.

The man gave a grunt, and Carla knew he was coming. At the same moment Rita groaned, her pretty body shaking as she too experienced her orgasm. Carla closed her eyes to blot out the picture of the pair of them writhing together, Rita's legs wrapped around the man's body as he spurted his semen into her, her hips thrusting up against his as they enjoyed their mutual orgasm. Still the sound of their lovemaking filled Carla's ears, and her cunt throbbed with desire as she continued her extraordinary exercise.

At last the pair separated, he tucking his cock back into his pants as she did her best to cover herself with the quite inadequate dress.

'Now get to my room and start cleaning,' he ordered.

'Yes, Master.'

Carla sighed with relief as the pair headed toward the door, going out and closing it behind them. Her mind continued to be obsessed with what she had witnessed, though, her nipples stiff and her sex wet with arousal. She had to summon all her willpower in order to continue to hold back the climax she needed so badly.

The door opened once more and Laura entered. Carla could see the amusement in the woman's eyes at her discomfort. She came across to where the young beauty was continuing to pleasure herself on the dildo.

'That was pretty good, Carla.'

'Mistress?' Carla's voice was strained from her ordeal.

'It's the first time I've seen a girl pass that test.'

'Test, Mistress?'

'Sure. You don't think that was a chance encounter, do you? That little show was put on entirely for your benefit.'

'You mean . . .'

'Those two fucking in front of you. Kind of an ultimate test, and you passed. Most girls don't last more than thirty seconds after he gets his cock into her. You must be gagging for an orgasm.'

Carla lowered her eyes.

'Come on, get off that thing now.'

Carla raised herself from the phallus, which gleamed with her wetness, and climbed from the bench. She was trembling all over, the love juices running down her thigh, her nipples like bullets.

'Lie down on there,' said Laura, indicating a leather-topped table.

Carla did as she was told, and her eyes widened as the woman produced a large bulbous vibrator from her bag. Surely she wasn't going to have to endure even more?

Laura smiled. 'Don't worry. This is your reward. Spread your legs, Carla.'

Carla did as she was told, and she licked her lips as Laura twisted the base of the toy and it began to buzz loudly.

The instructress ran it over the naked woman's nipples, clearly amused at the way Carla gasped aloud at the sensation. She began moving it down over her ribcage, across her belly and down to the centre of her desires.

Carla came even as the buzzing vibrator was slipped into her vagina, crying aloud and thrusting her hips up at it as she finally found relief. Laura went on moving it back and forth as she watched the sheer joy of release on Carla's face. The girl writhed uncontrollably as wave after wave of lustful pleasure shook her small body, her bottom raised clear of the table, her cunt lips devouring the vibrator. No sooner had she come than she was coming again, more cries rending the air as she made up for the sheer frustration of the last hour.

Carla came twice more before her body finally began to relax and she slumped back on the table, her breasts rising and falling as she gasped for breath.

Laura gently withdrew the buzzing object and placed it aside. 'Feel better now?'

Chapter 11

There was complete silence in the courtroom as Carla completed her tale. All eyes were turned in her direction, and she knew they could detect how aroused the narration had made her, her pretty young nipples hard as nuts, her sex glistening with her juices.

'So the Institute taught you how to bring men pleasure?' asked Phaedra.

'Absolutely. From then on every day was filled with instruction on how to use my body for the enjoyment of men.'

'What other lessons did you have?'

'We learnt different sexual techniques. They had a gym in which we worked out every day in order to make our limbs more supple so that we could try all kinds of positions. They showed us how to use our cunt muscles to bring our partner extra sensation, and different ways to accommodate the men.'

'What kind of ways?'

'Our mouths, obviously. How to suck and lick at the same time. Which part of the glans is the most sensitive to the tongue. What to do with your hands whilst you fellated a man. And, of course, they made sure we swallowed his spunk.'

'And other ways?'

'Between our breasts. They taught us how to hold them so the man got the best feeling. And in our backside of course. A lot of men prefer it up there.'

'What about discipline?'

'We were all caned and whipped regularly, usually by Mr Stone here. I think he enjoyed giving us pain. They would strap us to a frame with a dildo inside us, so that every stroke gave us pleasure as well as pain. Then they would check to see how wet we were afterwards.'

'And were you wet?'

Carla blushed. 'I usually am,' she confessed.

'That's because you're a slut,' interrupted Stone. 'All the women in that place were sluts, including that bitch Laura. They were just learning to be unfaithful.'

Phaedra spun round suddenly and faced him. 'Are you saying you never used any of them for sex?'

Stone looked uncomfortable. 'Well, sure. If they made themselves so available, what the hell was a man to do?'

'So you had sex with the defendant?'

'Occasionally, yes. But only because she wanted to.'

'You never took her without her permission?'

'It wasn't like that. She was at the Institute, wasn't she? That meant she wanted it.'

'You admit then, that you screwed my client without her consent?'

'I didn't have to get her consent. Not there.'

'How many times did you have sex with her?'

'I don't know. There were so many other sluts there. It was my job to teach them to accept discipline from a man.'

'So you're not averse to fucking a slut, just so long as you can thrash her afterwards?'

Stone frowned at her. 'It was just a job, that's all.'

'Are you saying you're not a rapist?'

'Of course not.'

'Yet Carla is a slut?'

'Look. All I know is that she was an easy lay.'

'And she gave you pleasure?'

'Sure.'

'Which is precisely what she was training for. To give men pleasure. No further questions.'

Phaedra turned away, and threw Carla a wink as she returned to her seat. Stone was left standing, his mouth open as the clerk moved forward to escort him from the court.

They broke for lunch and Carla was escorted to a cell below ground, where she was served a meal under the watchful eyes of the guard who had frigged her earlier. As she ate he played with her breasts, rolling her nipples between her fingers and grinning at her discomfort. Then she was led back to the court and chained in place once more.

As before, it took a few minutes for the courtroom to fill up. Eventually, though, the judge took his seat and nodded to Wajir. The prosecuting counsel rose to his feet.

'With Your Honour's permission, I should like to call Nick Elliot to give testimony.'

'Go ahead, Mr Wajir,' replied the judge.

'Call Nick Elliot.'

The man who entered the courtroom wore a pinstripe suit that had seen better days. He had a tanned face, his eyes hidden by dark sunglasses. He seemed rather uneasy in the presence of the court officials, shifting nervously from foot to foot as he was sworn in. Then Wajir approached him.

'Your name is Nick Elliot?'

'That's right.' Elliot spoke with a thick Brooklyn accent.

'What is your job, Mr Elliot?'

'I work in security. Personal security.'

'Do you recognise the defendant?'

'Sure. That's Carla all right, I'd know those tits anywhere.'

'Can you tell the court under what circumstances you first met?'

'Yeah. I was working for Lou Bartolsky at the time. She was fucking him.'

'She was his girl?'

'His and everybody else's.'

'What do you mean by that?'

'I mean she was screwing around. Taking Lou for a ride. Then, when the heat was on, she ran out on him.'

'You're saying she wasn't faithful to him?'

'Faithful? That bitch doesn't know the meaning of the word.'

'How do you know this?'

'Hell, I'd see her at night sneaking out of men's rooms. Lou's guests. She'd wait till he was asleep, then sneak up and climb into bed with them. I guess she was some kind of nympho.'

'But in the end, she left him?'

'That's right. Lou was in some kind of trouble. He'd have to give up his business. He was kind of sick, I guess. That's when she ran out on him.'

'She definitely ran out on him?'

'That's right. As soon as she realised he was splitting from his partners. Mind you, they got their share.'

'What do you mean?'

'I mean the whore gangbanged all three of them. Whilst poor Lou was in his sick bed no less.'

'She actually had sex with all three of the partners, knowing that Mr Bartolsky was ill in bed upstairs?'

'Sure she did. She didn't care. As soon as she found out that he was on the way out she went straight to his partners and shagged all three.'

'And did they take her on after Lou had quit?'

'Like hell they did. I guess they saw her for the slut she was. They fucked her, but then they threw her out.'

'So she left?'

'She ran like a startled rabbit. Bitch took all the presents and money Lou'd given her and did a runner.'

'Tell us, then, Mr Elliot, what is your opinion of Mrs Wilde?'

'She's a gold-digger. Screws around with whoever she likes, then takes the money and runs.'

'And did you know Mrs Wilde was a married woman?'

'No. But if she was my wife I'd thrash the bitch. Hell, no man should take that kind of treatment from a woman.'

'Thank you, Mr Elliot.'

Wajir was grinning as he made his way back to his seat, clearly pleased with Elliot's testimony. Phaedra rose to her feet and crossed to the witness box.

'Mr Elliot, were you present when my client met Lou Bartolsky?'

'No. She was already screwing with him when I came on the payroll.'

'So you have no idea of the circumstances under which she was employed?'

'She wasn't employed. I told you, she was fucking him.'

'I put it to you, Mr Elliot, that you weren't very well informed about her relationship with him.'

'What's to be informed about? I've seen her type before.'

Phaedra turned to the judge. 'Your Honour, I think Mrs Wilde should tell you precisely what was going on in her own words.'

The judge inclined his head. 'I'm sure we'd all like to hear her explanation,' he said.

Phaedra approached the dais on which the naked Carla stood.

'Mrs Wilde,' she began, 'you were with Lou Bartolsky for some time, I believe?'

Carla nodded. 'Yes. He was my first client after I graduated from the Institute.'

'I notice you used the word client. It wasn't a casual relationship, then?'

'Certainly not. I signed a contract. I was employed by Lou.'

'A contract?'

'That's right. My position was a professional one.'

'So what about the allegations that you were unfaithful to him?'

'That was all part of the contract. Lou knew exactly what was going on.'

'Tell the court, please, Mrs Wilde, how did you come to meet Mr Bartolsky?'

'Through the agency. After I left the Institute, my name went on their books. Lou was after a woman, and they sent me across to meet him.'

'And he chose you straight away?'

'Not exactly. In fact he very nearly didn't choose me at all.'

'Tell us what happened that day, please.'

'It was in his office, in New York. I guess it was a kind of audition. What I didn't know was that there was going to be competition there . . .'

Chapter 12

As the lift carried her up to the forty-fifth floor of the skyscraper that was Lou Bartolsky's headquarters, Carla found herself more nervous than she had been for some time. Ever since Phaedra had called her the week before to tell her that there was an assignment, and that the organisation for which she now worked was putting her forward for it, she had found it difficult to sleep.

Of course she had always known that this day would come. After all, it was what she had trained for. What she hadn't expected was how underconfident she would feel. Despite her previous experience and the rigorous training she had undergone at the Institute, the anticipation of the interview procedure she was about to face made her feel very young and inexperienced.

Carla had graduated only two weeks earlier. She had passed out with honours, being declared by Laura one of the best students she had ever encountered. At the time she had felt flushed with success. Now, however, her confidence seemed to desert her with every floor they passed on the way up the building.

She had flown back to England to be met by Phaedra at the airport. The woman had taken her straight out to the country mansion that was the headquarters for the organisation she ran. There Phaedra had sat her down and taken her step by step through the rules of the organisation, after which Carla had been formally enlisted onto their books. She had signed a contract for two years.

The object of the group was simple. They supplied beautiful young women at a very high price to those able to afford them. The women were accepted by the clients on a contract, normally of six months duration, and were expected, within reason, to do exactly what was asked of them by their masters. For this the men paid large sums and ensured that the girls were well looked after. Fifteen per cent of all earnings went to the organisation, the rest belonged to the girl. It sounded, Carla reflected, not much more than an extension to the escort agency for whom she had worked previously, although the earnings were much higher, as was the level of commitment required of the girls. There were no one-night stands here. For the duration of the contract, the girl was entirely in the power of her employer.

The lift came to a halt, and the doors slid silently open. Carla stepped out into an expensively furnished lobby with a thick carpet, the walls adorned with colourful abstract paintings. To her right was a desk, behind which sat a neatly dressed woman of about thirty. She eyed Carla without expression.

'Yes?'

'Good morning. I'm Carla. I have an appointment to see Mr Bartolsky.'

'Go through there. The other one's already here.'

Carla was slightly confused by the remark. The other one? What other one? What could the woman be talking about? It was her that Bartolsky was interviewing, wasn't it?

She stepped through the door into a large office with similar plush furnishings to the one she had just left. Standing by the window was a woman, who turned as Carla entered. She was about the same age as the petite English girl, but much taller, about five foot ten, Carla estimated. She had long dyed blonde hair and her face was expertly made up. Her breasts were big. Too big, Carla reflected, clearly the work of a plastic surgeon. She wore a tight red dress, the skirt split up the side to reveal shapely thighs and a tight behind. Altogether she reminded Carla of something out of Baywatch, and she found herself slightly intimidated by the girl's appearance.

There was a mirror on the wall, and Carla stole a glance at herself. She had to admit that she too looked stunning, her hair brushed back, her face almost free of make-up, her lovely eyes peering out from below long lashes. She had on a small red dress that hugged her curves beautifully and, although her breasts couldn't compete in size with the other woman's, they were firm and natural and in perfect proportion to the rest of her young body.

The two girls eyed each other up for a few moments, but before either had time to speak a door opened and a man entered.

Lou Bartolsky was in his mid-forties, and everything about him spoke of his obvious wealth. He wore a beautifully cut dark grey suit, with a yellow shirt and a wide silk tie. His watch was encrusted with diamonds, as was his tie pin. His hair was immaculately groomed, still retaining much of its natural colour, though flecked with grey at the temples in a way Carla found rather distinguished. There was something else about him that she found attractive too, an aura that was difficult to qualify. His confident manner spoke of immense power, so that she found herself strangely attracted to him.

Barely had she taken him in, though, than the taller woman stepped forward, her arm outstretched.

'Hi! You must be Lou. I'm Barbie.'

Carla reflected on the appropriateness of the name as she watched the woman take Bartolsky's hand in hers, closing her other hand over the top and squeezing warmly.

'My, what a firm handshake,' she went on. 'I was expecting to meet a much older man. I'll bet you're good in the sack too. Those muscles. You work out a lot?'

Carla watched silently as the woman pressed herself on Bartolsky, her breasts brushing seductively against his jacket, her eyes fixed on his. Clearly this job was no foregone conclusion. Barbie was competition and, judging by first impressions, a pretty formidable one. Carla felt suddenly rather overwhelmed by the woman's forwardness. Perhaps Bartolsky would prefer Barbie's typically American style to her own. Whatever happened, it was clear that she had something of a competition on her hands to gain Bartolsky's confidence.

The man disentangled himself from the blonde and turned to the English girl.

'I guess you must be Carla, then?'

'Hello,' said Carla, rather shyly taking his hand.

'So, Lou, what is it you're looking for in a girl?' went on Barbie, striking a pose that thrust her breasts forward. 'Li'l Barbie here likes to please her men, any way they like.'

Bartolsky smiled. 'I guess that's the kind of thing I'm looking for.'

'What say you and I go somewhere private to get acquainted then?'

'Hang on,' he said, 'there's two people getting interviewed here. Tell me, Carla, what do you offer?'

'I've had the best training there is, Mr Bartolsky,' replied Carla. 'I know I wouldn't disappoint.'

He looked Carla up and down, then shook his head.

'I'm not sure. I was looking for something a bit more spunky.'

'That's me to a T,' interrupted Barbie. 'Hell, these little English roses are fine enough for serving the tea and cooking scones, but you need a full-blooded American girl for this kind of work.'

Carla looked at Bartolsky. It was clear she was already losing the argument. The American girl's personality was certainly strong, and her body was beautiful, if a little artificial. Carla would need to work pretty hard to make herself noticed. The trouble was, brashness was not in her nature. It was certainly in Barbie's, though, as the girl moved close to Bartolsky again, wrapping an arm about his waist.

'C'mon now, Louie,' she said. 'Tell Barbie just what it is that you like best.'

All at once the door opened and the secretary entered.

'I thought I said no disturbances,' said Bartolsky. Carla couldn't be certain, but she thought she detected a note of embarrassment in his voice at being found in this somewhat compromising position with the voluptuous Barbie.

'I'm sorry, Mr Bartolsky,' said the secretary. 'But you'd better come. It's rather urgent.'

'What is it?'

'Lambeth's here, and he's making a bit of a nuisance of himself.'

'That idiot? Can't you get rid of him?'

'He's very insistent, Mr Bartolsky.'

Bartolsky gave a grunt of annoyance. 'All right then. I'll see him for two minutes. You two stay here.'

'Don't be long, honey,' said Barbie as he went out.

Carla felt slightly awkward at being left alone with Barbie. Not particularly wanting to talk to the American, she sat down in an easy chair on the far side of the room and began flicking through a magazine. Meanwhile Barbie produced a pack of cigarettes and started pacing the room, puffing at one.

Ten minutes passed. Then suddenly the secretary was back with them.

'Listen, ladies, you'd better get out of here. We've got trouble.'

'What kind of trouble?' asked Barbie.

'It's Lambeth. The damned idiot's got a gun in there, and I'm afraid he's going to use it.'

'A gun?' said Barbie, her eyes widening. 'What the hell's happening?'

'He says he's going to shoot Mr Bartolsky,' said the secretary, clearly distressed.

'Who is Lambeth?' asked Carla.

'He used to be Mr Bartolsky's partner way back, but the boss lost confidence in him and bought him out. After that the business really took off and Mr Bartolsky got rich.'

'So he thinks he was cut out on purpose by Bartolsky?'

'That's right. Ever since, Lambeth's blamed him. He's really jealous of Mr Bartolsky. He's never gone this far before though. If I'd known he had a gun I'd never have let him in.'

'You think he'll actually shoot your boss?'

'I just don't know. He's been drinking, you see. He's ranting and raving in there.'

'Shit, I'm getting out of here,' said Barbie.

Carla looked at her, then at the secretary. She knew the sensible thing was to get out of the building. But she knew too that if she did so, she wouldn't be asked back, and the thought of losing out to the brash American girl made her suddenly angry.

'Where is he?' she asked.

'In Mr Bartolsky's office, just down the corridor. I really think we should get out of here.'

'Unzip my dress.'

'What?' The women stared at Carla in disbelief.

'Unzip me. I think I can help.'

'But you can't go in there.'

'Look, do you want your boss to end up another murder statistic?'

'No but . . .'

'Then undo this zip.'

For a moment neither woman moved. Then, shaking her head, the secretary stepped forward. She took hold of the zipper at the back of Carla's dress and pulled it down. Carla dragged the tight-fitting garment down her body and tossed it aside. She stood, wearing only her underwear. This consisted of a small half-cup black bra, that revealed the tops of her areolae, and a tiny pair of matching briefs, the transparent front panel of which clearly showed the dark triangle of her pubic bush.

'Show me the office.'

'Crazy British bitch,' said Barbie. 'Get out while you can.'

'Show me.'

The secretary took her into the corridor and pointed to a door halfway down.

'They're in there.'

'Okay. Wish me luck.'

Carla tried to appear confident as she strode down toward the office, though in reality her heart was pounding. When she reached the door she paused for a second, her hand on the doorknob. What on earth was she doing? The secretary was right, she should get the hell out of here. After all it was only a job.

But it was her first job. How could she return to Phaedra and say she had failed? And to lose out to that brainless Barbie doll! That would be the worst thing of all! Gritting her teeth she turned the handle and pushed the door open.

'Come on, Lou, I thought you wanted to fuck me.'

She walked into the room, letting the door close behind her. Then she stopped, staring in mock surprise at the scene that confronted her. Lou Bartolsky was standing with his back to the wall, his hands clasped behind his head. Before him stood a shorter, balding man in an ill-fitting suit. He was holding a large automatic pistol, and he turned in surprise as Carla entered.

'What the hell . . .'

'Oh sorry, Lou. I didn't know you had company. I'll come back later.'

Carla turned toward the door.

'Wait! Come back here.'

'What is it?' she asked rather petulantly.

'Who the hell are you?'

'I'm Carla. I just wanted Lou, but I guess this is the wrong time. Is that gun real?'

'Of course it's fucking real. Get over there by the wall with him.'

'Look, I don't want to play games with you. I thought Lou was going to fuck me so I got my dress off. Then he disappeared.'

'I'm not playing games. Just do as I say.'

Carla put her hands on her hips. 'What's the problem? You going to shoot Lou or something?'

'Damned right I'm going to shoot him. This bastard robbed me. Now he's got all this, and I've got nothing.'

'That true? Lou robbed you?'

'Sure he did. Would I be wearing a suit like this if I was as rich as he is?'

Carla eyed him. 'I guess not.'

'And just look at this place, it's obscene. Now it turns out he's got a gorgeous chick like you.'

'Lou doesn't own me. I go with who I like.'

'As long as they're rich.'

Carla smiled at him in her most disarming way.

'Hell, it's not money that turns me on. I like a man who's in control.'

'Well right now, I'm in control.'

Carla licked her lips and glanced down at his gun.

'So I see.'

The man ran his eyes down Carla's barely clad body.

'You're quite a doll. Why not show me some more?'

'What do you mean?'

'I mean take off your underwear.'

'What, here?'

'Look, leave the girl alone,' said Bartolsky suddenly. 'Your argument's with me. Go on, get out of here, Carla.'

'You heard the lady,' said Lambeth. 'She doesn't belong to you. Now she's going to prove it. Come on, baby. Forget this bastard.' He waved the gun at her.

Carla shrugged. 'Oh well, I was getting bored with him anyhow. He really thinks he owns me.'

'Prove he doesn't. Strip for me.'

'Don't do it, Carla,' warned Bartolsky.

'Screw you,' replied Carla. 'I'll do what I want.'

'That's more like it, baby,' grinned Lambeth. 'You see, Lou, money can't buy everything. Go on, Carla, show me what you've got.'

Carla looked him in the eyes for a moment, then shrugged. 'Okay.'

She reached up behind her back and unhooked her bra. She let it fall away from her body and dropped it onto the couch. She paused, her hands at her sides, while the men took in the ripe firmness of her young breasts.

'Shit, those are gorgeous,' said Lambeth. 'Now take off the pants too. Show it all.'

'Don't do it, Carla,' warned Bartolsky.

Carla threw him a look of disdain, then turned to the man with the gun once more.

'You're a pretty demanding guy,' she said. 'But I like a man who knows what he wants.'

She let her hands drop and take hold of the flimsy panties. Staring into Lambeth's eyes, she slipped them down and dropped them beside the bra. Then she turned to face him, legs apart, hands planted on her hips.

'Like what you see?'

He nodded silently, and she could see he was aroused by the sight of her naked form. Behind him, on the wall, was a mirror, and she studied her naked body. Her nipples stood out firmly from the pale orbs of her breasts. Below, the patch of sparse hair that covered her pubis gave way to her bare sex lips, which she still kept shaved. She smiled at Lambeth and ran a hand over her breast, teasing the nipple so that it hardened still more. Then she dropped her other hand to her crotch, moving her legs apart and rubbing a finger lightly over her love bud.

'You're making me horny, staring at me like that,' she said.

'Go ahead, touch yourself. I'm enjoying it.'

There was a table at the side of the room, and Carla moved across to it. She leaned back against it, so that the hard edge of the wood dug into the flesh of her behind. Then she opened her legs and began to masturbate, pressing her fingers into her vagina and moaning softly as she became aroused. They had taught her at the Institute to play with her body in a way that would excite watching men, and now she made full use of that instruction, delving her fingers deep inside her sex so that they soon became coated with a sheen of wetness.

She had deliberately moved to the opposite side of the room from Bartolsky in the knowledge that Lambeth would not be able to take his eyes from her, and would be distracted from his original target. Now, as she watched, she saw Bartolsky reach slowly down toward his desk drawer.

'Mmm. Oh God, that's good,' she murmured, thrusting her hips forward as she masturbated, her legs spread wide and her knees bent. 'Christ, I think I'm going to come!'

She cried aloud as a genuine orgasm shook her body, her fingers flying back and forth inside her. At the same moment Bartolsky was on his feet, a small black cosh griped in his hand. Lambeth never had a moment to react as Bartolsky brought the weapon down on the back of his neck with a sickening crunch. For a moment, Lambeth stared vacantly at Carla, then his legs gave way and he crumpled to the ground. Bartolsky took the gun from his fingers and turned to face Carla, who was only just coming down from her climax, still gently rubbing her clitoris.

'My God, I take back what I said about having no spunk,' he

murmured. 'You've got a hell of a lot of guts, Carla.'

She blushed. 'And my tits are real,' she said. 'Try them.'

He stepped forward and closed a hand over her breast.

'They sure are. Carla, you're the best. I think you just got yourself a job.'

Carla smiled, suddenly feeling rather shy. Now that the danger was past, her legs felt like rubber, but she didn't want Bartolsky to know how scared she'd been.

'Will every day be like this?' she asked.

'Christ, I hope not. I can only take so many death threats. Listen, Carla, I was serious. Will you take the job?'

'That's what I'm here for, isn't it?'

'Then it's yours.'

Carla gave a sigh of relief. 'Great,' she said. 'I won't disappoint you, Lou.'

'I can see that.'

'When do I start?'

'Right now. Turn round and lean forward.'

Carla looked at him and raised an eyebrow. 'Is this my first duty?'

'I guess you could call it that. Seeing you standing there is making me horny as hell. Come on, bend over, Carla.'

'Don't you ask a lady's permission before you fuck her?'

'I don't think I need to. You just admitted you were horny too.'

Carla met his eye, and saw the twinkle in it. She grinned at him, then turned and bent forward over the table, spreading her legs wide. There was a rustle of clothing, and she reached behind her, her fingers wrapping about his already stiff shaft. She guided it toward her honeypot and gasped as he began to press against her there.

He penetrated her with a sharp thrust, his thick cock sliding deep within her. Carla braced herself against the table as he started to fuck her with smooth, easy strokes, her passions rising once more at the sense of his throbbing cock burying itself deep in her vagina.

As he took her, Carla found herself pondering her new role. In a sense she was no more than a whore now, selling her body for money. But there was nothing cheap or sordid about what she was doing. She had a beautiful, sensuous body, and she had been born to share it as she was sharing it now. And she had been born to fuck too. Why else was she so quick to become aroused, even with a man she had met less than half an hour before?

He was screwing her hard now, gripping her thighs tight and ramming his cock into her in a way that she loved. Carla, for her part, was responding by tightening the muscles in her cunt, massaging his cock as it slid back and forth inside her.

He came suddenly, and Carla moaned with excitement as she felt herself filled by his hot spunk, the sensation sending another orgasm coursing through her lovely young body. He pressed his body hard against hers, his cock spitting his seed deep inside her.

He spent his load, then gently withdrew. Carla turned to face him, still short of breath after her exertions. He took her face in his hand and kissed her lips.

'Sometimes the best things do come in small packages,' he said.

Chapter 13

'So what you're saying is that you were employed by Bartolsky on a formal basis?' asked the judge, leaning forward over the front of his bench.

'Of course,' replied Carla. 'That's what I do. What I was trained to do.'

'Hold on.' All at once Wajir was on his feet again.

'I beg your pardon, Mr Wajir?' said the judge.

'I'm sorry, Your Honour,' said Wajir. 'I meant to ask if I may approach the bench.'

'You may,' replied the judge, beckoning to Phaedra to join them. Wajir stepped up in front of the judge.

'What we seem to be forgetting here, Your Honour, is that Mrs Wilde is a married woman,' he said. 'What kind of way is it to treat her husband, selling her body to strangers? Surely that's why she's on trial here?'

'Well?' asked the judge, turning to Phaedra.

'If Mrs Wilde's husband had been faithful to her, then your argument might make some sense,' she replied. 'As it is, that bastard had been sleeping around long before Carla discovered her talent for pleasing men. She's been trying to divorce him for years now, but he just keeps stalling. To call Carla a married woman is simply to mock the institution of marriage.'

'Even so, she remains legally married to Mr Wilde,' said the judge.

'Only in name,' said Phaedra.

'I think the defence has a point here, Mr Wajir,' said the judge. 'I suggest you find something that might strengthen your case. Please continue.'

Wajir frowned at Phaedra, then turned back to Elliot, who was still standing in the dock.

'Now, Mr Elliot,' he began, 'you were telling us that Mrs Wilde didn't exactly take her duties to her employer seriously?'

'She sure didn't. The bitch would sleep with anything in pants. Christ, she was in and out of every room in his mansion.'

'Of course I was,' interrupted Carla. 'That's what I was employed for.'

'Bloody liar,' said Elliot.

'It's true,' insisted Carla.

The judge banged his gavel. 'This is a court of law, I'd remind you,' he barked.

'Your Honour, I'd like my client to expand on what happened in Mr Bartolsky's employ,' said Phaedra.

'Go on then.'

Phaedra nodded, then faced Carla once more. 'Can you explain your position in more detail?' she asked.

'Certainly,' replied Carla. 'Lou used me to help close business deals. The guys would come to the house and I'd play hostess.'

'Play hostess?'

'That's right. I'd wear something tight and sexy and serve drinks and food all evening. Later on, if they were interested, I'd go to their rooms.'

'Go to their rooms?'

'That's right. I'd go and fuck them. It was part of my job.'

'So Mr Bartolsky knew what was going on?'

'Of course he did. He'd tell me which ones I had to fuck and what their preferences were.'

'What do you mean by preferences?'

'Some wanted straight sex, some liked to be sucked, others wanted to give it to me up my arse. Sometimes they wanted something even more kinky. It was my job to give them what they wanted.'

'And they knew that you were being paid for what you did?'

'I think some of them guessed. Others just thought I was doing it for pleasure.'

'Which you were?'

Carla's face reddened. 'I enjoy what I do, you know that.'

'Wait a minute,' interrupted Wajir. 'Even if we accept that you were just whoring for Bartolsky, there's still the question of why you left.'

'She left because Bartolsky was in trouble,' interrupted Elliot. 'The moment he had problems she was off like a scalded cat. Like I said, she's a gold-digger.'

Phaedra turned to Carla. 'Is that true?'

The girl shook her head. 'It was nothing like that. He'd had enough, that's all. He wanted out, so I helped him.'

'Tell us about it then.'

Chapter 14

Carla had been with Bartolsky for nearly four months when he had confided to her his plan to get out of what he did. Carla had spent that afternoon with one of his clients in his room. He had fucked her with enthusiasm and she had responded in kind, enjoying multiple orgasms at the hands of this experienced lover. Afterwards, once he had dismissed her, she had showered and, wearing only a towel, had set off to talk to Bartolsky. She had found him in his office going through some papers. He smiled when he saw her and invited her in.

'I don't know why I trouble with all this,' he said, indicating the massive pile of paper on his desk. 'It's not as if I need to get any richer.'

'Why do you bother, then?' she asked, perching herself on the edge of his desk. 'Why not sell up and retire somewhere? After all, you can afford it.'

'It isn't as easy as that, Carla. The line of business I'm in needs friends in high places. It's not exactly legitimate, you know.'

'I'd kind of guessed.'

In fact Carla had no real idea what Bartolsky's business was, but she knew from what went on that it was not exactly straight. She had seen too many of his business associates removing shoulder holsters when stripping for bed not to know that there was something rather dodgy about what he did. In fact it wasn't unusual for her to find a bodyguard outside their doors when she slipped out in the night.

'The trouble is,' went on Bartolsky. 'When you're in as deep as I am, it's hard to get out. People expect you to be there.'

'You couldn't do it if you were ill.'

'Yes, but I hardly ever am. I'm strong as an ox.'

'You know that, and I do. But who else?'

'What do you mean?'

'Well, let's face it. A guy with a heart condition would have 'every right to want to sell up and retire.'

'But I haven't got a heart condition.'

'Like I said, you and I know that, but other people don't.'

He looked at her, then shook his head.

'No, we'd never convince them.'

'Convince who? Who would you have to convince?'

'I guess my three partners.'

'Your partners? I didn't know you had partners.'

'We don't get together much. Just every six months. They're due down next week as a matter of fact.'

'That's your chance then.'

'No. They'd never believe me.'

'But they might believe me.'

His eyes narrowed. 'You?'

'Certainly. If they heard it from me, they might well listen.'

'You really think so?'

'If you're serious about getting out.'

'It sounds damned tempting.'

'Let's see what we can think up then. But first of all I think you need some of that tension relieving.'

Carla stood up and undid the towel, letting it fall to the floor. She stood for a moment as he admired her lovely body. She knew he loved to see her naked, and it excited her to have him stare at her bare breasts and crotch. She dropped to her knees and reached for his fly, pulling the zip down. Then she took his already hardening cock into her mouth and began to suck him.

By the end of the following week their plan was taking shape. Carla had called out his doctor late one evening and had made certain the staff knew about it. Bartolsky had simply complained of a headache to the doctor, but Carla had led the other occupants of the house to believe it was more serious. Soon the house was full of rumours that the boss was unwell.

Bartolsky's three partners arrived the following week. All were men of a similar age to him, and all arrived in expensive cars with an entourage of bodyguards. The four men went into conference almost immediately, and Carla barely saw Bartolsky all day. In fact, she had seen nothing of him until she was invited to join the men for dinner.

She wore a tight, short skirt and a thin, almost transparent black top, her breasts bare underneath so that the dark shape of her nipples showed clearly as they pressed against the material. She knew she looked good, as the three men couldn't take their eyes off her during the meal.

Carla studied Bartolsky's three partners as they ate. Like him, they were men of power, and it showed. The oldest of the three, Goldberg, was a large man with a paunch who wore gold jewellery on his wrists and about his neck. Colson was a much smaller man, who said little, but whose penetrating blue eyes sent a shiver down Carla's spine. The third member of the trio, Curtis, was the most forthcoming, and chatted all through dinner, his eyes seldom leaving Carla's petite form.

After dinner they retired to the drawing room, where brandy was served. Bartolsky drank little, however, and soon excused himself, leaving Carla alone with his three partners.

'A bit damned early to be going to bed,' said Goldberg after the door had closed behind him.

'He often goes to bed early these days,' said Carla. 'Frankly I'm a bit worried about him.'

'Why?' asked Colson. 'He's okay, isn't he?'

'I'm not so sure. Look, maybe I shouldn't be saying this, but I think his heart might be bad.'

Curtis turned his steely eyes onto her. 'What makes you say that?'

'He just hasn't been well. He had the doctor out the other night. Then there's . . . well, his performance.'

'Go on.'

'He doesn't seem to want to do it much these days. I don't think we've had sex for more than a month. That's a long time for him. And for me.'

'So you think he's ill?'

'I'm sure of it. I think the work's getting too much for him as well. Frankly, I think he should give it up.'

'He can't do that,' said Colson. 'We're a team.'

'We won't be much of a team if Lou drops dead on us,' observed Goldberg.

'Don't say that,' put in Carla.

'The fact remains that we need him alive and well.'

'Why couldn't you just buy him out?'

'It's not that easy. He has a great deal of knowledge.'

'Still,' put in Curtis, 'as Goldberg says, the knowledge isn't much use to us if he's six feet under.'

86

'It's true,' insisted Goldberg. 'If Lou's about to drop dead, we're in trouble.'

'But if you bought him out, then you'd still be able to consult him,' Carla went on. 'And as time passes his knowledge becomes spread amongst you.'

'I see what you mean,' put in Colson. 'If he's not working, he'll live longer, and we all benefit. I think buying him out sounds a good idea.'

'But who's going to suggest it to him?' asked Curtis. 'After all, he's a proud man. He may not like the idea.'

'Why not let me do it?' said Carla. 'I'm sure I'd do the best job.'

Goldberg scratched his head for a moment, then nodded.

'I think that's a good plan,' he said. 'You suggest it, then come back and tell us what he says.'

'Meanwhile, we should be thinking about helping the lady out with her other needs,' said Curtis, putting down his drink and crossing to where the young beauty was standing.

'What do you mean?' asked Carla, her face a picture of innocence.

'The fact you've been deprived of sex for so long. That's a shame. I'd like to do something about it.' He reached out a hand and ran it gently over her soft breasts.

'You mustn't do that,' she said quietly. 'What would Lou say?'

'We're partners,' he replied. 'We share everything.'

He began undoing the buttons of her blouse one by one.

'Shouldn't we go somewhere more private?'

'Like I said, we share everything.'

He undid the bottom button of the blouse and pushed it apart so that her firm breasts were displayed to all. Carla stood, her arms by her side, her eyes lowered as he felt the soft flesh of her orbs, rubbing the nipples so that they hardened at once to small brown knobs.

'Such pretty tits,' he murmured. 'I'll bet you love having them sucked.'

'You mustn't,' she said again. But she made no move to stop him.

'Take off the blouse,' he said.

It was not a request but an order. Carla knew that these were men accustomed to being in command. She gazed at him for a moment, then she shrugged off the flimsy garment and let it fall to the floor.

'And the skirt.'

This time the command came from Goldberg. Carla looked round at the three men, who were all watching her closely. It was clear that they would tolerate no disobedience on her part. She felt her cheeks redden as her hands dropped to her waist and she began undoing her skirt. Moments later it was on the floor beside the blouse, and Carla was standing clad only in a pair of tiny black briefs.

'Lose the panties too,' said Colson. 'Show us what Lou's been enjoying.'

'What if someone comes in?'

'So they come in. C'mon, baby, strip.'

'I-I shouldn't be doing this. You won't tell Lou, will you?'

'Sure, he won't find out,' said Goldberg. 'Go on, honey, we know you're hot for it. Show us what you got.'

Carla knew she could delay no longer. Nor did she want to. She had made her point, and already she could already feel the moistness seeping into her vagina as she reached for the waistband of her pants. There was something about the power that these men wielded that made her very aroused indeed, and the quietly confident way in which they had ordered her to remove her clothes sent a shiver of excitement down her spine as she slipped her panties down and off.

She kicked them aside and stood, legs apart, her hands on her hips as the men admired her naked body. She was trembling slightly as Curtis reached for her breast once more and caressed it, making the nipple still harder as her sensitive young body reacted to his touch. She was very turned on now, as she always was when she stripped in front of a stranger, and the thought of the men's cocks stiffening in their pants sent a surge of lust through her.

She heard the sound of a zip being pulled down, and she looked across to see that Goldberg's circumcised cock was sticking out from his fly, stiff and rampant. He caught her glance and beckoned to her, eyes dropping to his penis.

Carla understood the gesture perfectly, yet still she played the innocent, staring at him with wide eyes.

'Come on over here, baby,' he said. 'I've got something for you to suck on.'

Carla crossed slowly to where he stood.

'You-you want me to suck you?'

'You've done it before, haven't you?'

'Yes but . . .'

'Then get on with it. Shit, you're making me horny as hell standing there showing off your tits and cunt.'

Carla hesitated for a moment longer before dropping to her knees before him. She reached out a hand and tentatively grasped his stiff member. As she did so she felt it twitch violently and saw a small bead of moisture escape from the tip. He pressed his hips forward and she knew she could delay no longer. She pulled his shaft downward so that it was just in front of her face. Then she opened her mouth and took it inside.

At once her senses were filled with the taste and scent of the man, and she began to suck greedily at him, her own arousal increasing as she fellated his thick member.

She glanced sideways. The other two men had their eyes fixed on her, clearly fascinated by the way her breasts quivered as she worked her head back and forth. She wondered what other girl would do this, alone and completely naked in a room full of much older men, sucking one of them off with enthusiasm whilst his companions looked on. Yet here she was, not only doing it, but positively loving it. Carla was completely aroused by the whole situation, and was anticipating the mouthful of spunk she knew she was about to receive with positive relish.

She sucked harder at him, her small, slim fingers caressing his tight ball sac as she did so. She could feel his arousal now, his stiff cock twitching between her lips heralding the approach of his climax. As she sucked she ran her tongue back and forth over his glans, bringing groans of pleasure from him.

He came suddenly, his cock seeming to take on a life of its own as he spurted his hot semen into her mouth. Carla kept her lips clamped about his organ, not missing a stroke, continuing her back and forth movement as she swallowed down his seed. The youngster was positively savouring his climax, sucking his spunk from him, her fingers working his foreskin back and forth as she did so. Goldberg grunted aloud with satisfaction, his stiff member emitting jet after jet of his sperm into Carla's eager mouth. She kept his erection deep inside her mouth until there was no more to swallow, and the frantic pumping of his hips had slowed to a stop. Only then did she pull back, gazing up at him, a small dribble of his semen escaping from the side of her mouth and trickling down her chin.

There was to be no respite for the young woman, though. No

sooner had a satisfied Goldberg tucked his deflating cock back into his pants than Colson had taken her by the arm and pulled her to her feet.

'Okay, baby,' he said, his cold eyes staring into hers. 'My turn.'

'You as well?' asked the beautiful girl, her eyes widening in mock alarm.

'Sure. Like we said, we're a team. You do it with one of us, you do it with all of us.'

'But I . . .'

'No buts. Lie down on the couch. You like being tit-fucked?'

'Tit-fucked?'

'Sure. I wanna put my cock between those pretty tits of yours. Get over and lie on the couch.'

Carla walked slowly across to the couch. It was long and wide, with more than enough space to allow her to prostrate herself, her legs spread. She gazed down between her firm breasts as Colson dropped his trousers. His cock was short and thick, standing stiffly to attention. He moved close to her and, taking her hand, closed her fingers about it. It felt hot to the touch, and she began working his foreskin gently back and forth.

'That's it, baby,' he said. 'Just do like you're told and you'll be all right.'

He placed one knee on the couch and lifted the other one across her, so that he was straddling her waist. Then he moved up her body and pushed her hand down so that she was holding his erection between the soft swellings of her breasts.

'Play with your tits,' he said. 'Push them together so I can get some friction, then tease those hard little nipples of yours.'

Carla released her grip on his penis, then took hold of her breasts, closing a palm about each. It was something she often did before she masturbated, using the thrill that massaging her firm mammaries gave her to increase the wetness inside her cunt. Now, as she squeezed them together, the sensation of the stiff cock trapped between them sent an extra spasm of lust surging through her, and she gave a low murmur of excitement as she began to toy with her nipples. At the same time, Colson started moving his hips back and forth, so that his cock moved in and out of the tight gap she had created.

Carla watched his cock emerging and retreating so close to her face, the smooth glans shiny with his secretions. To see it and smell it so near made her want to taste it too, and she licked her lips as her fingers circulated her stiff nipples. Her own juices were running free now and she shivered as she felt a drop of moisture leak out and trickle down to her anus. Her body was totally turned on to what was happening to her and she craved an orgasm. She knew, though, that she must play these powerful men's game.

'Press harder.'

Carla gazed up at Colson, as he thrust his stiff penis back and forth between her breasts. A light sweat had broken out on his forehead, and his expression was intense as he drove himself on. She did as was asked, pushing her breasts still tighter together, at the same time moving a finger round so that it rubbed against his glans with every stroke, bringing a fresh groan of arousal from him.

The finger did the trick, and moments later hot sperm was spurting over Carla's upturned face. She opened her mouth, and was rewarded by a gob of thick spunk on her tongue, which she swallowed greedily whilst more splashed onto her cheeks and chin. Still he continued to pump his hips back and forth, and she pressed her breasts still closer together, loving the way his member twitched as he shot his load over her silky soft skin. He went on coming until the flow had stemmed to a trickle, which ran up her cleavage and settled in the hollow of her breastbone. Only when he was drained completely did he withdraw, turning away from the spunk-spattered girl and picking up his trousers.

Carla was fully aware that she would be required to take on Curtis as well, and she turned to see that he too had opened his flies. The sight of him standing there, his cock jutting proudly from his pants sent a new shiver of anticipation through her. She knew that he would have her any way he pleased, but she hoped desperately that he would fuck her, and relieve the delicious tensions that had been building within her young body ever since they had ordered her to strip.

He leaned over her, running his hand down over her breasts, his fingers lingering on her bullet-hard nipples, pinching them gently and bringing renewed moans from the naked beauty. Then he let them stray lower, sliding them over her ribcage, across the smooth skin of her stomach and down towards her crotch. As he slipped a finger inside her, Carla gave a little cry of arousal, thrusting her hips up at him as if urging him to probe deeper. He slid his finger out again and held it up for the rest to see.

'See how excited she is,' he said to his companions, indicating the glistening wetness that coated his finger. He turned to Carla. 'You want it, don't you?'

Carla's reaction was to moan softly and reach out for his stiff cock, shivering slightly as she felt how hard it was.

He held his finger out to her, and she opened her mouth, taking it between her lips. She sucked it in in the same way she had sucked Goldberg's cock earlier. As she did so, she tasted her own arousal in the juices that had wept into her vagina, and the taste sent a new thrill through her body.

Curtis climbed onto the sofa and knelt between her legs. Only then did she know for certain that she would be fucked, and yet another spasm of lust coursed through her at the prospect. Her hand was still grasping his twitching rod, and she drew it closer toward her burning sex, raising her bottom from the couch and opening her legs still wider.

'Ahhh!'

She came with a cry as he slipped his cock into her, the tension within her finally released, her cunt muscles contracting violently about his stiff organ as it invaded her. Even as the waves of pleasure swept through her she cursed herself for her precipitousness. She had been trained to restrain herself and had lost concentration for a moment. Would she have annoyed him by her premature orgasm? But when she looked into his eyes she saw only amusement tinged with excitement as he began to move his cock back and forth inside her.

He fucked her with long, easy strokes, his large cock sliding deliciously in and out of her. Her orgasm went on and on as she revelled in the sensation. Even as it began to ebb away she felt a new passion building within her.

Curtis lay across her body, the material of his suit feeling coarse against her bare skin. His hands went to her breasts, squeezing and caressing them as he gazed down at her face. She could feel Colson's spunk on her lips, cheeks and neck, and she wondered at the sluttish sight she must make, lying there naked whilst this older man rammed his cock into her and his two companions looked on. He screwed her expertly, his hips pressing down against hers as she thrust up at him, loving the way he filled her so completely, whimpering softly at every stroke. His expression had changed now to one of intense concentration, and she could sense the excitement building within him as his own climax approached.

He came with a groan, his cock spitting semen into her. As so often happened with the wanton girl, the sensation engendered yet another shattering orgasm within her so that, once again, her cries rang about the room. Curtis went on thrusting into her as he emptied the contents of his balls into her, the hot spunk that spurted from him sending new spasms of lust through her small frame.

When he was spent, he slipped his cock out of the moaning woman, leaving her still writhing on the couch, his seed trickling from her. Carla slipped her fingers down and caressed her clitoris, masturbating gently as the excitement slowly drained away, until she lay still at last, her breasts rising and falling, her fingers still moving slowly over her swollen love bud.

She raised her head, and her cheeks glowed as she remembered the three men who were watching her. She ceased her caresses and rose slowly to her feet.

She caught a glimpse of herself in the mirror, and the colour in her cheeks deepened as she saw the dishevelled, naked young girl, her face and hair streaked with sperm, her breasts swollen with the handling they had received, her twitching sex lips leaking a shiny trail of spunk onto her thighs.

'I . . . I'd better clean up,' she said.

'All right,' said Goldberg. 'But don't be long. We haven't finished with you yet. After all, we still haven't sampled the delights of that pretty little arse of yours.'

Chapter 15

The court was silent for a moment, and Carla gazed out at the faces of those listening, all of which were staring at her. She studied their expressions. Most of the men were open-mouthed, and she could almost feel the lust in their expressions as they surveyed the naked beauty who was sharing her most intimate experiences with them. Carla glanced down at herself. The story, especially the part about the tit-fuck, had made her nipples harden once again, and she could feel a trickle of moisture on her thigh which she knew must be visible to all in the harsh lights of the courtroom.

She looked across at Phaedra. Her friend too was silent, and Carla could see the desire in her eyes as she gazed up at her young protégée. She remembered the time when, on a Greek island, she had been tied naked and blindfold to a bed whilst guests at a party downstairs took it in turns to come up and use her helpless young body. One of those had been a woman, and she had always felt sure that that woman had been Phaedra. Now, as she looked into the woman's face, she knew that her friend wanted the sensation of Carla's tongue deep inside her once again.

'Have you finished?'

The judge's words broke the spell, and Phaedra shook her head as the onlookers shifted in their seats.

'Just a few more questions, Your Honour.' Phaedra looked at Carla.

'And did Mr Bartolsky get what he required?'

'His partners bought him out exactly a month later, freeing him to retire. Of course they can still contact him, and they often do. They even pay him for the consultancy.'

'So far from abandoning him when he became ill, you actually helped him to make up the story?'

'That's right. It was what he wanted, so I did all I could to make it happen. He was very grateful to me. Though, of course, he couldn't make it public.'

'And that was why you left?'

'That's right. Now that he wasn't entertaining businessmen any more, there was really no need for me.'

'So he let you go?'

'Yes. My contract was coming to an end anyway. Actually he wanted me to go with him. He even offered to marry me.'

'But you said no.'

'Well, I couldn't marry him, could I? Not whilst that creep keeps blocking my divorce. But I wanted to move on, anyhow. After all, he was only my first customer, and I wanted to get a lot more experience.'

Phaedra turned to the judge. 'Your Honour, I think the truth in this matter is clear. My client acted at all times in the interest of her employer, including some things above and beyond the call of duty.'

The judge inclined his head, then turned to Wajir.

'Have you any further questions, Mr Wajir?'

Wajir frowned. 'No, Your Honour.'

'In that case, the witness is dismissed. This court will adjourn, and will reconvene tomorrow morning.'

He banged his gavel down hard, and all the members of the court rose to their feet as he walked out. As soon as he had gone, a hubbub arose from the rest of the people in the room as they rose and began to file out.

Phaedra made her way across to the dais to which Carla was chained.

'Well, that wasn't too bad, was it?' she said.

Carla sighed. 'But that was just the first day. Wajir's bound to have more witnesses.'

'Yes, but you know you've done nothing wrong. Just speak out like you did today and we'll be all right. I think the jury are taking to you.'

'I think the jury probably want to fuck me, judging by the way they look at me. If only I could have something to wear.'

'I'm sorry about that. I did try.'

'I know you did. It's just that it's not easy standing up here, trying to persuade them I'm not a slut, when they can all see my tits and cunt, and how turned on I'm getting.'

'Still, maybe if the jury fancy you, they'll come down on your side.'

'I hope so.'

The court was empty now, and Carla's guard mounted the dais beside her.

'You go now,' he said to Phaedra. 'Time to take back to cells.'

Phaedra nodded. 'All right. Good night, Carla. I'll see you in the morning.'

'Good night, Phaedra. And thanks.'

As her friend walked away, Carla felt the man's hand begin to slide up her inner thigh, and she braced herself for another groping by her guard.

Chapter 16

'Call Leonard Hardcastle.'

Carla watched as the door at the rear of the court opened, and a man walked in. He made his way to the front with rasping breath and hauled himself into the witness box. The usher stepped forward and placed a Bible in his hand.

As the man was sworn in, Carla studied him. He was stocky, aged about fifty, with white hair and deep bags under his eyes. His voice was wheezy, and he had a strong northern accent. He spoke the words of the oath softly, occasionally pausing for breath.

Once the procedure was complete, the judge nodded to Wajir, who rose to his feet.

Carla had barely been listening to the formalities. Her mind was on her own predicament as she stood, naked and chained before the court. She had not been taken back to the prison the night before. Instead she had been led to a shower room, where the guard had watched her perform her ablutions. Afterwards she had been served a meal, then had been taken to a cell below the court, where she was locked in, naked and alone.

This morning she had been woken early, and had gone through the same routine before finding herself chained once more to the dais in the courtroom. Soon afterwards the jury had been seated and the court had filled once more.

When the judge made his appearance, Phaedra had, again, appealed that Carla be allowed to cover her nudity, but had met once more with a flat refusal. Then her clerk had issued the summons to Hardcastle. Now the court sat expectantly whilst Wajir crossed the floor of the court to the witness stand. As he did so, Carla braced herself for a new ordeal.

'Mr Hardcastle, thank you for being with us today.'

'That's okay,' replied the man. 'Thanks for paying my fare, that's a damned good hotel you've put me in. First class. My room's got its own bathroom and everything.'

Wajir cleared his throat. 'Yes, well, I'm glad you're comfortable.'

'I am.'

'Now, Mr Hardcastle, I have to ask you, do you recognise the defendant?'

Hardcastle reached into the pocket of his jacket and produced a pair of glasses, which he carefully unfolded, then placed on his nose. He glanced across in the direction Wajir was indicating, and Carla saw his eyebrows rise as he focused on her. A smile crossed his face.

'That's her all right.'

'That's who?'

'That's the girl I told you about. Carla's her name. She's a real bad 'un.'

'How do you mean, a bad 'un?'

'The girl's disobedient. She was constantly in trouble at the big house. Poor old Galston was always having to punish her.'

'Punish her?'

'That's right. She was regularly whipped, and had to be kept in restraint a lot of the time. Yet still she wouldn't behave herself.'

'Tell us about Mr Galston.'

'Galston's a well-respected man in my part of the world. He has this great big house just outside the town. He's a great philanthropist.'

'In what way?'

'He takes in girls who are homeless and have got themselves into trouble with the police. Instead of going to prison, they can opt to work for him until their sentences are up. Then he tries to find them jobs elsewhere. He feeds them and houses them, and all he asks of them is a bit of obedience.'

'Obedience?'

'That's right. I mean you can't have chaos in a community like that, can you? He's a fair man, but even he couldn't control that one.'

'You mean the defendant?'

'That's right. He should never have taken her in. She was always in trouble. The bane of his life.'

'So you think she deliberately caused trouble to him?'

'Certainly I do. She drove him to extremes of punishment. I think she's some sort of man hater.'

'And this disobedience, what forms did it take?'

'She'd oversleep and be late for work and for her classes. She'd refuse to do certain jobs, or she'd do them badly. She'd answer back to him. She was just a persistent thorn in his side.'

'So she'd be punished?'

'That's right, for all the good it would do. Basically I think she enjoyed being in trouble.'

'And you think she did this deliberately to annoy her benefactor?'

'I do. She really had it in for him and for men in general.'

'Can you give us some specific instances?'

'Sure. There were lots.'

Wajir questioned Hardcastle for a further half-hour, during which he described a number of episodes of disobedience and bad behaviour involving Carla. Once again, as she watched the faces of the jury, Carla could see that things were not going too well for her.

At last Wajir seemed satisfied. He thanked Hardcastle and turned to Phaedra.

'Your witness.'

Phaedra rose to her feet and made her way across to the witness stand.

'Tell me, Mr Hardcastle, did you actually witness this bad behaviour by Mrs Wilde?'

'Not usually.'

'So you don't know what actually happened?'

'I told you, she was a bad 'un.'

'But how can you be certain?'

'Galston told me. Besides, I'd see her being punished.'

'You'd watch the punishments?'

'Sometimes.'

'And what form did these punishments take?'

'Well . . . sometimes she'd be thrashed.'

'Thrashed?'

'Beaten. With a cane.'

'And was she naked when she was thrashed?'

'Yes. Galston always stripped her when he punished her. He said he wanted her to learn humiliation.'

'And you used to watch. That was rather voyeuristic wasn't it?'

'Galston would invite us. Me and some others. Said it made the punishment worse for her, being watched.'

'And afterwards?'

'What do you mean?'

'After she'd been beaten. What then?'

'I don't understand the question.'

'I think you do, Mr Hardcastle. Isn't it true that after a beating she'd be handed over to you and your companions?'

'She'd be left in custody for a while.'

'And then you'd have sex with her?'

Hardcastle shifted uncomfortably. 'It was part of her punishment.'

'So you thought this woman was, as you put it, a bad 'un, yet not so bad that you wouldn't use her body for your own pleasure?'

'I told you, it was part of the punishment.'

'I see.' Phaedra turned to the judge. 'Your Honour, I think it's time we heard from my client, don't you?'

'Mr Wajir?'

Wajir shrugged, but said nothing.

The judge nodded his assent, and Phaedra moved across to where Carla stood.

'Now, Mrs Wilde. Is it true that you deliberately disobeyed Mr Galston, the man who was apparently your saviour?'

Carla cleared her throat. 'No. I always did exactly what he wanted of me.'

'That's a bloody lie,' burst out Hardcastle. 'She was always disobeying him. Everybody knew that!'

'I was always apparently disobeying him,' said Carla. 'That was what he wanted me to do.'

'Tell me about Mr Galston,' said Phaedra.

'He was basically a good man. He genuinely cared for those girls, and he found them jobs. Sure some of them became whores, but he always made sure they knew what they were letting themselves in for. And he placed them with good pimps.'

'But he had other desires?'

'Galston's sexual preferences were somewhat unusual.'

'In what way?'

'He liked to see women whipped and tortured. It got him off.'

'So where did you come in?'

'I was a kind of scapegoat. I told you, he was basically a good man. That's why he couldn't bring himself to act out his fantasies on those vulnerable girls. So he hired me.'

'So you were, in fact, employed by Mr Galston?'

'That's right. Through the agency. It was my second assignment.'

'Tell us about what you did for Mr Galston.'

'Well, I was supposed to pose as one of the ordinary girls. But, in reality, my role was very different . . .'

Chapter 17

Galston's house was a large, rambling Georgian pile that stood on the edge of a Northern English mill town. The building was surrounded by a high wall with large wrought-iron gates. When Carla had been shown a photograph of it by Phaedra, she had been rather doubtful about the assignment.

'The place is a bit grim, isn't it?' she remarked. 'It looks more like a workhouse.'

'Don't judge too much by appearances,' said Phaedra. 'I think it's reasonably comfortable inside.'

'I'm not sure,' said Carla.

'It's for three months only,' said Phaedra. 'Mind you, the requirements are pretty stringent. Basically the guy's an S & M freak. There'd be lots of bondage and whipping.'

At the sound of these words, a shiver ran through Carla's body. A shiver of fear, or excitement? She wasn't sure.

'I wouldn't be, well . . . damaged?'

Phaedra shook her head. 'No. We've had him well checked out. He might hurt you a bit, but then you've been trained for that, haven't you?'

Carla nodded. 'I can take a bit of pain,' she said. 'In fact it can be quite a turn-on.'

Phaedra looked at her. 'Carla Wilde, is there anything in the world you don't find a turn-on?'

Carla blushed. 'That's why you took me on, isn't it?'

Phaedra laughed. 'It certainly is, and frankly I wouldn't have you any other way.' She kissed the young woman on the cheek. 'Now, my pretty, are you going to take this on, or not? After all, he is paying you double the usual rate.'

Carla thought for a moment. It was certainly somewhat different from what she had expected. She had imagined lying on a millionaire's yacht in Monaco, or sunning herself on the French Riviera, not spending three months in a correctional institution.

She looked at Phaedra. The woman was waiting, a slight smile playing about her lips.

'You're going to take it, Carla, aren't you?'

Carla grinned. 'Of course I am. After all, it's a challenge, isn't it?'

And so she had arrived at Galston's house, carrying a small bundle of belongings, and had been shown down to the long dormitory that was the accommodation for the girls. She introduced herself as Carla Wilson, a single girl who had been thrown out by her parents because they couldn't put up with her behaviour, and who had been arrested for petty theft.

There were eight other young women staying in the house, and Carla found them friendly and helpful. All had been found guilty of persistent crimes, such as burglary, drug peddling, or prostitution, and all had volunteered to allow Galston to take them in. They were a fairly world-weary lot, and many viewed Galston's hospitality with some suspicion. Still, they were happy to have a roof over their heads and to be free of the strict regime they might face in prison, so there were few complaints.

Carla soon settled into the routine of the place. The girls were woken up early every morning and were expected to work in the kitchens helping prepare the breakfast. After the meal, they were taken up to a sort of classroom where, on most mornings, Galston would visit them. He would generally give them a short lecture on the values of being hard-working and of obeying the rules of the house. Then they would be left in the hands of Miss Parker, a stern-looking woman of about forty who would conduct their classes. The subjects covered ranged from good housekeeping through spelling and simple mathematics to hygiene. Miss Parker was a strict disciplinarian, and allowed no talking or inattention during her lessons. The girls didn't complain, though, as all the information she imparted was practical and she was a good teacher.

The afternoons were spent doing household chores or working in the garden and, after tea, the girls' time was their own. Some went out walking in the large grounds, others played games or watched television. Lights out was at ten thirty and most were so tired by then that they were soon asleep.

For the first week, Carla simply went along with all the other girls, obediently attending the lessons and doing her chores. During his morning lectures Galston never spoke to her, though she was often aware of his eyes on her as she sat in her seat, and occasionally

103

she would see him staring at her whilst she went about her housework.

Unlike the others, however, Carla made it clear from the start that she was dissatisfied with her lot and cynical of Galston's methods. In the evenings, after the lights had been turned out, she would rail against Galston and Miss Parker alike, saying how bored she was with their preaching and how she wished she had never allowed herself to be brought to the house. The other girls said little, so that it was clear she was isolating herself from them. In reality, of course, she was acting a part. She had received her instructions before coming to the house, and she knew her behaviour had to be convincing. She didn't like this aspect of her subterfuge, but Galston was paying the bill, so she knew she had to do things his way.

It was at the beginning of the second week that she made her move. Miss Parker was halfway through a lecture on household cleanliness when she threw down her pencil.

'This is all such rot!' she exclaimed.

'I beg your pardon, Miss Wilson?'

'All this crap you talk. For Christ's sake, what does it matter whether you clean the damned sink every day?'

'I must remind you, Miss Wilson, that you are here because of Mr Galston's goodwill. But for him you'd be in jail at the moment.'

'At least in jail they don't pump you full of this kind of garbage,' riposted Carla. 'I can't see what the hell use it is to anyone. I'm going outside for a smoke.'

'You'll do no such thing. Sit down at once.'

'Fuck off.'

Carla pushed back her chair and headed for the door, with the other girls watching in disbelief. Her heart was pounding as she reached for the door handle. The use of such coarse language was not in her nature, and she knew her face was red.

As her hand fell on the handle, Miss Parker's closed over it.

'You're not going anywhere, young lady,' she said. 'Now get back to your desk.'

'Get lost.'

Carla pushed her aside and pulled open the door. Miss Parker grabbed her arm.

'This is your last chance. Sit down now or face the consequences.'

'Sod the consequences.'

Carla shook her off, then marched down the corridor.

She had barely reached the door into the garden before two male servants closed in on her from either side. She tried to run, but they were too fast for her, grabbing her arms and snapping a pair of cuffs onto her wrists. She cursed them as she struggled, but to no avail. They gripped her arms and frogmarched her back down the corridor.

By the time they reached the classroom, Galston was already there, standing beside an outraged Miss Parker. Carla was almost carried into the room and deposited before the pair, as her fellow inmates looked on. Carla was shaking slightly as she faced her benefactor, but still she stared him defiantly in the face.

'What on earth do you think you're playing at?' he asked.

'I'm sick of this place,' replied Carla. 'I want to go back to prison.'

'You know that's impossible. Now stop this nonsense at once.'

'Get stuffed.'

'You know too that I have full power over you. I can punish you any way I like.'

'Bullshit.'

He pursed his lips. 'You leave me no choice,' he said. 'Take her to the punishment hall. She'll receive eight strokes.'

'No!' shouted Carla. 'You've got no right, you bastard!'

But she was helpless to prevent the men dragging her from the room.

The punishment room was huge, with various pieces of equipment scattered about it. It reminded Carla of the room at the Institute where she had received that bittersweet lesson in withholding her orgasm. Like the one at the Institute, the room was filled with frames and benches and what resembled vaulting horses. Each piece of equipment was hung with shining chains and manacles. On one side of the room were arranged three tiers of benches, and the sound of her fellow inmates being led down the corridor toward the room told Carla that her punishment would be a public one. The thought sent a shiver through her. Since arriving at the house all her sexual instincts had been suppressed, but now she felt the first stirrings of arousal deep within her.

The girls filed in and took their places facing Carla. Meanwhile another man had entered the room, and began preparing a large wooden frame that stood in the centre. It was about eight feet high and five wide, and from each corner hung a chain with a shackle attached. The man was loosening the chains and opening the shackles with a large metal key.

Galston came in with Miss Parker behind him. He turned to the stern-faced instructor.

'You will officiate please, Miss Parker.'

The woman crossed to where Carla was being held, her high heels clacking noisily on the wooden floor. Once again Carla shivered as she stared into Miss Parker's cold eyes.

'Undo her hands.'

Carla felt her wrists grasped, then a click as the cuffs were undone. Instinctively she folded her arms, suddenly intimidated by the domineering woman.

'Take off your clothes.'

'Get lost.'

'If we are forced to strip you we will. In that case your punishment will be increased to twelve strokes. Now, take off your clothes.'

Carla glared at the woman, then looked around the room. All about her, the other girls were watching expectantly, as were the guards. For the third time she shivered, and this time she knew it was excitement that was making her do so.

'Must I take everything off?' she asked.

'Everything.'

'But you have no right. And these men . . .' Carla's voice was not so sure now, and a genuine anticipation brought a tremor to it.

'Strip.'

Carla hesitated for a moment longer, then her hand went to the buttons at her neck.

The prison dress was a simple one, just a grey frock that buttoned up the front. As Carla undid the buttons one by one, she could sense the tension amongst her fellow inmates, all of whom were watching her with intense expressions on their faces. She reached the bottom, and the dress fell open. Beneath she wore white underwear, the bra cut low to raise her breasts and show off her cleavage. The pants were brief, dipping down in a vee at the centre, the thin material outlining her sex lips.

Carla shrugged off the dress, allowing it to fall to the floor. She glanced at the guards. Their eyes were fixed on her shapely young body, and she felt the sudden thrill that always engulfed her when she was about to expose herself. She reached behind for the catch on her bra, flicking it undone. As it slid down her arms a low murmur went up from those watching, and she glanced down at the firm, pale flesh of her breasts, the nipples already half erect, projecting proudly upwards.

The atmosphere in the room was electric now, as Carla's hands dropped to her waist. She looked about her at those watching, then slid the tiny garment down over her thighs and off. Then she straightened, her cheeks glowing as those in the room took in her naked body.

The man who had been preparing the frame had wheeled a full-length mirror across from the side of the room, and it was now positioned so that Carla could see her own reflection in it. She glanced at it, taking in the slim, petite beauty who stood there, her firm breasts jutting forward, the dark triangle of hair at her crotch barely concealing the thick lips and deep cleft of her sex.

One of the guards grabbed her arm and pulled her across to the frame. Before she had had a chance to react, the arm was pulled above her head and a manacle snapped about her wrist. Moments later her other arm was immobilised in a similar manner. Next shackles were closed about her ankles and her legs pulled wide apart.

As soon as all four limbs had been thus attached, the chains were tightened, and Carla found her body being pulled into an X shape, her arms and legs stretched wide apart as the shackles dug into her young flesh. They continued to increase the tension in the chains until she almost cried out with the pain. Then they stood back to admire their captive.

Carla eyed her reflection in the mirror, which had clearly been moved across for just that purpose. Her pale, naked body was stretched taut, her breasts pulled almost oval, the sinews in her arms and legs bulging. Her eyes dropped to her sex, which was wide open, the pinkness inside on view to all. Then she gazed out at the audience of white-faced girls and grinning men.

All of a sudden she became aware of Miss Parker standing in front of her. The woman was holding a long, thin bamboo cane and she lifted it up for Carla to see. She swished it through the air a couple of times, making the helpless captive wince as she contemplated what was to come.

'Eight strokes,' she said. 'Let's hope they will teach you a lesson.'

Carla turned away, unwilling to let the woman see the apprehension in her eyes. She had been trained for this at the Institute, but there the punishments were well controlled, and it was unusual for more than six strokes to be doled out at a time. The prospect of eight was almost unthinkable. Yet, at the same time, she could barely suppress the excitement that was building within her. There was something about this enforced nudity and bondage before all these people that was turning her on in a completely perverse way, and already she could feel the moisture seeping into her sex as her more wayward nature began to come to the fore.

Miss Parker had moved round behind her now, and Carla felt the woman tap her bare behind with the cane. Then she pulled back her arm, and Carla bit her lip, bracing herself for what was to come.

Swish! Whack!

The cane descended with devastating force, slicing into the soft flesh of Carla's backside and bringing a cry from her lips as it thrust her forward in her bonds. For a moment she was numb, then the pain hit her like the stinging of a thousand wasps.

Swish! Whack!

Moments later the second blow fell, the cane striking her bottom just above where the first had fallen and immediately doubling her agony. Carla clenched her fists as the pain seared through her.

Swish! Whack!
Swish! Whack!

Miss Parker beat her with a relentless determination, each stroke finding a new area of pale flesh and planting an angry red stripe across it. Carla's body was shiny with sweat now, a sheen of moisture covering her from head to foot.

Swish! Whack!
Swish! Whack!

Not a sound came from the other inmates as they witnessed Carla's punishment, the girls sitting ashen-faced, some with their hands over their mouths as they watched the cane fall relentlessly across her bare skin. Each blow was thrusting her body forward in her chains, making her breasts shake and bringing a grunt of pain from her.

Swish! Whack!

Only one more stroke to go now, yet Carla doubted she could take it. Even her training hadn't quite prepared her for this level of pain. It was as if her backside was on fire. But there was to be no mercy, and she braced herself as best she could as Miss Parker pulled back her arm once more.

Swish! Whack!

The last blow was probably the hardest of all, cutting into her already inflamed flesh and eliciting a hoarse scream from the young beauty as her body was hurled forward once again, the hard shackles biting into her wrists and ankles. Then it was over, and Carla hung panting in her chains whilst Miss Parker tossed the cane aside.

The woman moved up close to the girl, taking her by the hair and pulling her face up to her own. Carla's eyes were welling with tears. Tears that mingled with the sweat on her face and trickled down her neck, between her breasts and on, over her belly to her crotch.

'Now, perhaps you'll learn a little obedience, young lady,' she said.

Carla did not reply, simply staring into the woman's eyes. Miss Parker held her gaze for a moment longer, then shook her head.

'Get back to class now, girls, the show's over.'

The others rose, still silent and subdued after what they had witnessed. As they filed out, some turned to gaze at Carla, but she avoided their eyes, simply staring straight ahead.

The door closed behind them, then something unexpected happened. Someone approached Carla from behind and, to her surprise, a black blindfold was wrapped about her head, obscuring her vision completely. The act confused her, and she shook her head to try to loosen the object, but in vain.

She heard the last of the girls depart, down the corridor, with Miss Parker's footsteps following them. Then there was silence.

Carla twisted in her chains. Her backside was still burning and the metal shackles were extremely uncomfortable. Her body ached dreadfully from the tension of her bondage. But there was another ache which she couldn't shake off. The nudity, the bondage and the beating had awoken an inexplicable emotion deep inside her and, not for the first time, she was astonished at her own perversity.

Carla was turned on! Something about the treatment she had received had brought out a latent masochism in her character that she was at a loss to comprehend. She had felt the same emotion sometimes during her training, but never as strongly as this. Her sex was wet with desire and, had her hands been free, she knew she would have masturbated.

All at once she heard the door to the room open, then close again. Footsteps came across the room toward her and stopped in

109

front of her. It was the heavy tread of a man, and now, as she gazed into the blackness of her blindfold, she knew he was staring at her lovely, naked body, stretched open before him. The thought sent a new gush of wetness into her vagina.

When he touched her, it was as if an electric shock had sparked through her, and she gasped aloud as she felt his coarse fingers close over her soft young breast. He squeezed and caressed her, his fingers seeking out her stiff nipples and rolling them back and forth, so that she had to bite her lip to prevent herself moaning aloud.

She knew it must be Galston. After all, it was he who was paying for her to be there, and he alone knew that he could have her if he wanted. Yet he hadn't laid a finger on her up until now.

A mouth closed over her nipple and began to suck at it. Once again, Carla was taken completely by surprise, and she gave a groan of pleasure as he ran his tongue back and forth over the hard knob of flesh. As he sucked, he moved his hand lower, seeking out her crotch. Carla's body lurched forward as his fingers found her love bud, and it was all she could do to stop herself coming then and there, such was the level of her arousal.

Suddenly his mouth and fingers left her, and she moaned softly with frustration as her body ached for his touch. Then she heard the sound of a zip being pulled down.

'Wh-who are you?' she whispered.

There was no reply. Instead she sensed him moving closer to her, and something hot and hard brushed against her stomach.

'You have no right to do this to me,' she said. Still he said nothing, but his fingers sought out her cunt again, and she whimpered with desire as she felt her lips pulled apart.

His cock slipped into her easily, her wide stretched legs and copious lubrication saw to that. She winced as he took hold of the cheeks of her backside, grasping the still-inflamed flesh as he pressed himself home. Then he began to fuck her.

Carla's mind was a turmoil of emotions. On the one hand, she knew she should be outraged at the casual way in which she was being taken. After all, her arms and legs were bound, leaving her helpless to prevent this anonymous man having his way with her. Yet, at the same time, her carnal desires were so great that she knew she wouldn't have refused him even if he had asked. Besides, the bondage and her own powerlessness were an aphrodisiac to her, and her body reacted eagerly to this violation, her cunt muscles

110

massaging the heavy cock that was invading her so deliciously.

He began to fuck her harder, his strong hands ramming her hips forward against his. Carla was lost in desire, her small frame shaken back and forth with the violence of his screwing, small cries emitting from her as her climax approached.

When he came, she came too, her shouts of lust ringing about the room as she felt his spunk pumping into her vagina. It was an extraordinary orgasm, the pain in her backside and the aching in her limbs forgotten as she abandoned herself to the sheer pleasure of her climax.

He continued to pump his hips back and forth until all his sperm was spent. Only then did he withdraw. She wanted him to speak, to say something to her, but all she heard was the sound of his zip, then his footsteps retreating toward the door.

'No, wait,' she called, but there was no answer, and the door opened and closed once more, leaving Carla alone in her darkness, a warm trickle of spunk beginning to run down her inner thigh.

Chapter 18

The beating that Carla had received that day was the first of many. In concurrence with her agreement with Galston, she was consistently misbehaving, thus bringing down upon herself the wrath of Galston, Miss Parker and many other staff. It soon became a regular occurrence to witness Carla being thrashed, and before long her pretty backside was never without a crisscross of stripes.

Afterwards would come the blindfold, followed by the thick, insistent cock that would invade her and fill her with male seed. She never actually saw Galston, but she was certain it was him. She knew that the punishments turned him on tremendously, and she knew too that that was why he paid for her to be there. What she found harder to understand, though, was the way in which the treatment would arouse her. It was as if the pain itself was an aphrodisiac, and after just a few strokes she would feel the familiar wetness invading her crotch, so that before long the pain of the beating would be overshadowed by the lascivious urges that would well up inside her.

The way in which she was beaten would vary from day to day. Sometimes she was chained to the frame, as on the first occasion. But there were other devices too, all equally fiendish and all designed to produce maximum pain and humiliation. One was like a vaulting horse, which she was obliged to straddle, after which thick straps would be wrapped about her body to hold her flat across it. Once she was in place, with her hands and ankles secured to her legs, her punisher would set about her with a thin leather belt, laying agonising stripes across her back. When the beating was over, the man would make her suck him off, pushing his erection into her mouth and pumping back and forth until he filled it with his spunk and forced her to gulp it down.

Another favourite was a wooden bar suspended between two posts at the height of her crotch. Her feet would be shackled wide apart to the floor, and her supple young body bent double over the bar, her wrists locked to rings in the floor in front of her. On this device, the favoured weapon would be a long horsewhip that cut stingingly into the tight flesh of her behind, leaving pencil-thin stripes that stung terribly. When she was in this position, he would normally bugger her, filling her rectum with his come. Needless to say, the bar and the horse were not popular with Carla, since she seldom enjoyed the release of orgasm afterwards.

After a time she was separated from the other girls and kept in a solitary cell, where she was chained to her bunk at night. Being alone meant that her master was free to make occasional nocturnal visits, where he would take advantage of her bondage, fucking her with vigour so that she often came two or three times. Always, though, she was blindfold and unable to see who it was that invaded her. During this time she was still allowed to attend lectures and meals with the other girls, but was not allowed to speak to them. She often disobeyed this order, though, bringing yet another punishment upon her.

Slowly but surely the pressure on her increased. After one incident she was stripped of her prison dress and forced to go about in her underwear. When this failed to tame her, they confiscated her bra. Finally she was made to give up her panties, and from then on was kept permanently nude, much to the amusement of her guards. The loss of her clothes had a mixed effect on the young beauty. On the one hand she was deeply embarrassed at having her breasts and sex on display to all, with no concession to modesty allowed. On the other hand, being naked all the time made her very aroused. To make things worse, the guards were in the habit of feeling her up when she was alone with them, and the sensation of a stranger's fingers invading her vagina often brought her to the edge of orgasm.

It was in her final few weeks in the house that Galston began the evening sessions that were the climax of her semi-slavery. One morning Carla had arrived late for her lecture and had admitted to doing no preparation. She was made to stand at the front of the class, as she always was, her hands clasped behind her head, her bare breasts jutting forward whilst the other girls giggled at her predicament. They had long since given up on her, and considered her as something of a figure of fun. Carla, though lonely in her solitary situation, took this in her stride. After all, she mused, she was being paid to be here, whilst they had no choice.

Galston arrived at the classroom and listened patiently to Miss

Parker's complaints. When she had finished he shook his head. He walked across and stood, facing Carla.

'I think, Miss Wilson, that new measures are called for,' he said. 'We have tried reasoning with you, we have tried physical punishment, solitary confinement and humiliation, but none has worked.'

'It's given those damned guards something to goggle at,' replied Carla. 'You'd think they'd never seen a pair of tits before.'

'Be quiet!' barked Galston. 'Tonight you will be brought up before the governors of this institution, and will face their judgement.'

Miss Parker's eyes widened. 'The governors? But Mr Galston...'

'That's enough. Take this recalcitrant young woman back to her cell and prepare her.'

It was some hours later when they came for Carla. She had been allowed to shower and given a meal, but had been confined to the room, her leg shackled to a ring in the floor. When the two guards arrived, they were carrying a cloak. Carla was ordered to stand up, and her hands were cuffed behind her. A leather collar was then produced which they buckled about her slender neck, cinching it so tightly that for a moment she feared her breathing might be impaired. Then the cloak was placed over her shoulders and fastened at the neck. It was made of light, thin material that was almost transparent. With every move she made it billowed out behind her, uncovering her body. As a final, humiliating touch, one of the men produced a chain, which he attached to a ring at the front of the collar. He tugged at it, making her stagger forward, then nodded to his companion.

'She'll do,' he said.

'What's going on?' asked the girl apprehensively.

'Quiet, you.'

They released the shackle on her leg, then one of them took hold of her lead and dragged her from the cell. For a moment Carla resisted, but another sharp tug told her that she had no choice but to do as they told her.

They took her down one of the grim, barely furnished corridors that were a characteristic of the house in which she had been incarcerated for so long. They passed the lecture room and, to Carla's surprise, the punishment chamber. Instead they took a route that led out into the garden.

114

It was a balmy summer's evening, and Carla felt the warmth of the sun on her bare flesh as the inadequate cloak blew back behind her. She glanced to right and left as she was led along, fearful that someone might see her. Since losing her clothes she had been kept indoors, an indulgence for which she had been grateful. Now, as she walked in the open air, her breasts and sex bare, she felt distinctly nervous.

They came to a gate in the high fence that surrounded the wing of the house in which the girls were incarcerated. There a guard was waiting, and he swung the gate open as they approached. Stepping through it in her barely clad state, Carla suddenly felt very vulnerable indeed. Somehow, within the confines of the institution, her nudity had been an acceptable thing, forced upon her by her keepers. Here, outside the fence, she was back amongst everyday people. People who would be astonished and outraged at the way she was exhibiting her private parts so openly. She wished that her arms were free so that she could, at least, cover herself with her hands.

They crossed a wide courtyard and approached some steps leading up to another door in the side of the building. The guard who was holding her lead pushed it open, and they stepped into the main house.

The contrast with the institution wing was stark. Here the floor was laid with deep carpets that Carla's feet sank into as she was marched along. The walls were lined with rick oak panelling and the drapes were thick and expensive. They crossed a hallway where a glittering chandelier hung. A pair of maids were dusting there and they stopped in amazement at the sight of the barely clad young woman being led past them, covering their mouths as they giggled at the sight. Carla felt the colour rising in her cheeks, and she wished once more for something with which to cover herself.

They came to a halt in front of a pair of large double doors, and one of the guards knocked, then pushed them open. He dragged Carla inside whilst his companion closed them. Carla barely had time to take in her surroundings as he took her to the centre of the room, where a large silver ring was set in the floor.

'Kneel!'

She obeyed at once. There was a loud click as he fastened the end of her lead to the ring, so that she was no longer able to rise from her knees. Then he turned, and he and his companion strode out, closing the doors behind them.

Carla glanced about her, and for the first time became aware of the occupants of the room. Sitting opposite her, in a large chair, was Galston. He was surrounded by four people, three men and a woman. Carla didn't recognise any of them, but she would later come to know one as Hardcastle, the witness at her subsequent trial. Even now, though, she felt as if she was before a legal tribunal as she looked at these grim-faced people, all of whom were eyeing her with expressions of disapproval on their faces.

To her left, Carla noted that, once more, a mirror had been placed to reflect her image back to her. This was clearly a standard tactic to maximise her humiliation, and she stared at the petite, kneeling figure. The cloak had fallen forward, so that her breasts were just covered, her nipples starkly outlined by the thin, silky material, the valley between them bare. Her crotch too was just protected by the garment, though so thin was it that the darkness of her pubic bush showed through. She glanced across at the woman, whose attire was in such contrast to her own. She was in her late twenties, with a slim waist and a large bust, and she wore a small, figure-hugging red dress. At that moment, Carla would have given anything for that dress, but that was not an option for the hapless woman.

'This, then, is Miss Wilson,' said Galston.

'She seems awfully small for one creating so much trouble,' remarked Hardcastle.

'Nevertheless she's been the bane of my life for too long. That's why I've had her brought here, before the four of you. I thought that, with her sentence drawing to a close, we might all attempt to teach her a proper lesson in good behaviour.'

'I'm sure we can do something to control the shameless minx,' said the woman. 'What's you first name, girl?'

'It's Carla.'

Bang!

Galston brought his fist down hard on the wooden arm of his chair.

'Whilst in our presence you will refer to us as sir or madam. Do you understand?'

'Yes . . . sir.'

'Now answer the question again.'

'My name is Carla, madam.'

'Well, Carla,' went on the woman, 'is it true what we hear about your misbehaviour?'

116

'They call it misbehaviour. I was just speaking my mind, that's all.'

'Despite the fact that it was getting you into trouble?'

'I don't care. They think they can make me behave by thrashing my arse and making me go about starkers.'

'And don't the beatings hurt?'

'Yeah, sure they do, madam. But I can take it. The point is that they give that old bugger the horn, so they keep on with them.'

Bang!

Once again Galston's fist crashed down.

'You will show respect,' he thundered.

The woman shook her head. 'I can see why the little slut's trouble,' she said. 'I think we should begin at once.'

Carla looked up at her apprehensively. Begin what? Why was she here?

The woman rose to her feet and strode across to where the young girl was kneeling. She took hold of Carla's chin and pulled her face up so that she was staring into her eyes.

'Is it true that the thrashings turn you on?' she asked.

'I . . . I don't know what you mean,' said Carla, suddenly blushing.

'So it is true. That's something I'm looking forward to seeing.' She turned to her companions. 'Come on, let's get the equipment set up.'

Galston nodded, and reached for a bell pull that hung beside his chair. No sooner had he pulled it than the door opened and two young women entered. They were dressed in the black uniforms of maids, with small white aprons at the front. They were certainly not warders from the institution, since Carla had never set eyes on either of them before. They both stared at Carla as they entered, then turned to Galston.

'Bring out the frame,' he ordered.

The pair crossed the room and pulled aside a curtain. There, concealed in a niche, was a large wooden frame. It was formed by three poles joined together at the top to form an A shape. These were linked together by beams that ran horizontally about two and a half feet from the ground. The whole thing appeared very sturdy, and was clearly quite a weight as the two girls struggled to carry it into the centre of the room. Once it was in place, they turned expectantly back to Galston.

'Strip her, then strap her to it.'

117

The pair crossed to where Carla was kneeling, and one of them bent down to release the chain from her collar. They pulled her to her feet, then undid the catch on her cloak, allowing it to fall to the ground. Carla felt the heat rising in her cheeks as the party surveyed her nude body. Although the cloak had been inadequate, it had at least provided some concession to modesty. Now she was naked once more, with no way of covering herself.

There was a click, and Carla felt her cuffs being undone. Then the girls were dragging her across to the frame. A chain hung down from the apex with a pair of cuffs attached to it. The maids made her wrap her arms about the struts, then cuffed her hands on the far side. They each took hold of one of her ankles and pulled her legs apart. There was a leather strap attached to each of the legs and these were wrapped about Carla's ankles and buckled. Then the chain that held her wrists was tightened, pulling her arms upward until she was forced to stand on tiptoe. She glanced through the frame at the five, all of whom were watching her closely. So far things had been no worse than the beatings she had received in the punishment chamber, but she suspected that Galston had more fiendish plans up his sleeve, and when she saw the fine silver chain in his hand, she knew she was right.

One of the maids crossed to him and took the chain from him. It was much thinner than the ones that had been used to bind her, and each end had a shiny object attached to it. As she brought it closer, Carla realised that they were clamps, and the girl held them up for her to see. They were held closely by strong springs, and, as the maid pressed them open, Carla saw that the jaws were lined with needle-sharp teeth. The girl smiled as she saw the expression on Carla's face, and she reached out for the naked beauty's breast.

Carla gave a sharp intake of breath as the girl sought out her nipple, rubbing it back and forth between her fingers and making it pucker to hardness at once. At the same time the second maid began to toy with her other breast, sending delicious sensations through her body as her other teat came erect.

Carla's mind was filled with mixed emotions as the two girls fondled her tender breasts. It felt wonderful to be touched so intimately, but all the time her mind was on the clamps, and the thought of what they were for. When the pair withdrew their hands she braced herself for what was to follow.

The maid holding the clamp pressed on the lever once more, making the jaws gape open. Then she let them close slowly over the nipple that projected so invitingly. Carla closed her eyes as the teeth bit into the tender flesh, stinging her dreadfully and pressing the nipple out of shape. She watched as the girl clamped the second one over her other teat, doubling the pain. Worse was to come, though, as the maid took hold of the chain and began to pull on it, making the teeth bite still deeper and bringing a whimper of pain from the young captive. There was a hook attached to the leg opposite where Carla was tied, and the maid looped the end of the chain over it, so that it was held in tension, stretching poor Carla's breasts almost to a conical shape and making the tears well up in her eyes.

The maid glanced across at Galston, who nodded his approval.

'Good,' he said. 'Perhaps now she'll begin to appreciate what real pain is like.'

'But there's still the humiliation she needs to learn,' said the woman.

'Of course. Please oblige us, ladies.'

The pair nodded to Galston, and one of them crossed to a bureau that stood by the wall. She opened the drawer and pulled out a long, black object. Carla stared at it, then swallowed hard as she realised what she was looking at. It was a dildo, a perfect representation of a man's erect penis made of black rubber. As Carla watched, the girl held it out to her. Everything was in place, from the thick, bulbous glans to the bulging vein that ran down its length. Carla shuddered as she imagined it inside her, and once again she felt the familiar sensation of wetness seeping into her sex as she contemplated what was to happen next.

The girl brought the phallus closer, holding it up in front of her face.

'Suck it,' ordered Galston. 'Wet it with your saliva. You'll be glad you did when you see where it's going.'

Carla glanced at him for a second, then opened her mouth. The maid pressed the object between her lips, and Carla tasted the rubber as she forced it into her mouth.

'Suck,' said Galston again.

Carla began to suck, her tongue licking at the black shaft as she did so. It seemed odd, sucking at this inanimate object that so resembled a real cock, yet feeling none of the sensations a warm, living erection would give her. Still she slurped at it with enthusiasm, the saliva escaping from between her lips and running down the shaft.

'Enough!' said Galston suddenly. 'Insert it into the slut.'

Carla had guessed that this order was to come, but even so she felt a knotting of her stomach as the girl removed the dildo from her mouth and dropped to her knees beside her. A gasp escaped Carla's lips as she felt smooth young fingers run up the length of her slit and prise her nether lips aside. Then the thick, hard object began to press against her most private place.

The bondage and the stinging pain of the nipple clamps had already made her very wet indeed, so that the maid had little trouble penetrating her with the phallus, twisting the end as she pressed it home. Carla moaned softly as she felt her vagina filled with hard, rough rubber that chafed against the walls of her sex in the most exquisite way, bringing a new flow of love juice from her. She looked across at her tormentors. All, including the woman, were watching intently, and she knew the sight of her naked, helpless body being penetrated so blatantly would be making them nearly as aroused as she was.

The girl continued to twist and press until the dildo was completely inside her, only the black base showing between the pink of her sex lips. At that moment, the second maid appeared holding what appeared to be a long metal bolt. Carla watched in some confusion as the girl knelt down beside her companion and inserted the bolt into a hole in the slat of wood that ran about the frame at crotch height. Then her eyes widened in horror as the other girl grasped her by the hips and manoeuvered her so that the base of the phallus had been pushed through and tightened, leaving the dildo affixed to the wood, angled upwards so that it penetrated Carla's cunt just as a man's erect penis would.

Carla could scarcely believe the position they had placed her in, her arms and legs helpless, her tender nipples stretched by the dreadful clamps and her sex invaded by a huge black dildo that stimulated her deliciously with every slight movement of her hips. It was a position that was at the same time painful, humiliating and extraordinary arousing, so that she had to clench her teeth to prevent herself from moaning aloud.

The maids stood back, their handiwork complete. As they did so, the woman rose to her feet and crossed to where Carla stood. She ran her fingers through Carla's hair, stroking her face gently, then let her hand drop to her breasts, tracing the stretched skin and feeling the clamps, tugging at them as she watched the pain in Carla's eyes. She moved her hand downwards to the dildo, running her fingers about Carla's sex and rubbing her hard little clitoris.

'You love this, don't you, little guttersnipe?' she said softly. 'For the likes of you, pain is pleasure.'

Carla said nothing, closing her eyes tight as she tried to fight down the emotions that were rising within her at the woman's intimate touch. Once again the rough treatment she was receiving was appealing to the basest desires within her, and her sex was hot with arousal at the way her clitoris was being teased.

The woman withdrew her hand and turned to the men.

'The little whore's really hot,' she said. 'I think it's time she was thrashed. Let's gag her first, though.'

She nodded to one of the maids, who went to the drawer again and returned with a rubber ball to which a pair of leather straps was attached. She handed it to the woman who took hold of Carla's face.

'Open your mouth.'

Carla shook her head. 'No!'

But the woman was too strong for her, forcing her jaws apart and stuffing the ball gag inside. She pulled the straps back behind Carla's head and buckled them tight. Carla tried all the while to protest, but was capable only of a muffled moan as even her power of speech was taken from her.

'Who's first?' asked the woman.

'I am.' Hardcastle rose to his feet and turned to the maids, one of whom produced a long horsewhip from her belt. As the man flexed it in his hands, Carla shuddered. It was the thinnest and whippiest weapon of punishment she had ever encountered, and the sound of the swish as he tried a few practice strokes made her stomach churn.

He moved over to stand behind her, and she felt him tap the whip against the flesh of her bare backside. Then he drew back his arm.

Swish! Whack!

Carla's scream was lost in the gag as the dreadful weapon cut into her tender behind, the end snaking round so that the stripe ran all the way from her buttock to her belly. Never, in all the beatings she had received to date, had she experienced such pain, and she winced as he pulled his arm back for a second time.

Swish! Whack!

The second stroke was, if anything, even more painful than the first, the blow falling at the top of her legs just beneath her buttocks and laying down another thin stripe that immediately darkened to an angry red.

Swish! Whack!

Once again Carla's body rocked forward, forcing the dildo deeper into her, then stretching her nipples anew as she bounced backwards again.

Swish! Whack!

Carla had never known such agony as the whip sank into her flesh for the fourth time, bringing another muffled cry. She wasn't sure that she could endure another such blow, and she tried to beg for mercy, but the words were lost in the gag.

Then something unexpected happened. All at once the five suddenly seemed to lose interest in Carla. Hardcastle handed the whip to one of the maids as the other four rose from their seats and crossed to where a sofa and some easy chairs had been arranged. At the same time the other maid opened a drinks cabinet and began pouring. Soon the five were relaxing, glasses in hand, chatting together as if quite oblivious to the naked woman who stood just yards from them, her breasts and buttocks on fire with pain, her sex burning with desire as her juices seeped from her, forming a silvery trail down her inner thighs.

For the next fifteen minutes nothing happened, and Carla was able to regain some sense of composure. Then, suddenly, one of the other men put down his glass and strolled across to the maids, one of whom passed him the whip. He moved close to Carla and, without a word of warning, raised the weapon.

Swish! Whack!

The whip slammed into her already tender behind, bringing the pain back with a vengeance.

Swish! Whack!

Down it came again, slicing into her with a terrible force and thrusting her down onto the dildo once more. Again she screamed, and again it was lost in the ball that filled her mouth.

Swish! Whack!

Carla's body was bathed in sweat as the agony of the whip filled her senses. Tears rolled down her cheeks, mingling with the perspiration as she rocked back and forth in agony, every movement stretching her nipples and driving the dildo deeper within her.

Swish! Whack!

This blow landed across her back, leaving yet another red stripe that burned with pain as the man, like his predecessor, handed the whip back to the girl and, turning his back on the naked, writhing beauty, returned to his companions, who even now were being served with fresh drinks.

The next hour was a nightmare for Carla, as each of the other guests took their turn to thrash her lovely young body. Leaving the intervals between the whippings made them worse than ever. Not only was there the certainty that there was more pain to come, but they left her just long enough for the previous marks to reach their most tender, so that when the new blows fell, the agony was doubled. By the time Galston stood up to deliver his strokes, Carla was already begging for mercy, but her pleas were inaudible and she had no choice but to accept still more stripes across her stinging backside.

After all five had thrashed her, they settled back to their drinks again, and the talking continued for another half-hour. At last, though, Galston and the woman rose to their feet.

'Well, gentlemen,' said Galston, 'it's time for me to turn in. Thank you for your help this evening, I'm sure I can leave the young lady in your capable hands.'

He said his goodnights to the three men and the woman did likewise. Then they left them, closing the door behind them.

Almost as soon as the pair had gone, Carla saw Hardcastle beckon to one of the maids, and say something in her ear. The girl nodded and went to a drawer, from which she pulled a small jar. Carla watched warily. It was clear that they hadn't finished with her yet, and she suspected that they were about to put her lovely young body to further use. Her apprehension deepened when the maid came up behind her and dropped to her knees.

For a moment nothing happened. Then Carla gave a sudden start as she felt something cold touch her anus. Immediately afterwards came the unmistakable sensation of some kind of cream being rubbed onto her rear. For a second she was confused. Was this some kind of painkiller? Were they, at last, showing her some mercy? Then she realised that the girl was concentrating the cream about the tight hole of her anus, her finger actually slipping inside her as she applied it, and she knew at once what was on their minds. The cream was simply for lubrication. They intended to bugger her.

Once again Carla tried to protest, but she knew already that it was pointless, and when she saw Hardcastle rise to his feet and unzip his fly, she braced herself for what was to come.

123

Hardcastle's cock was pale and stiff, standing up proudly from his groin. He ran his fingers up and down its length, staring pointedly at the helpless young woman. Carla looked away, and he moved round behind her. Moments later she felt his fingers forcing the cheeks of her backside apart.

He pressed his stiff member against her rear hole, holding his shaft in his hand and twisting it as he did so. Carla's natural reaction was to tighten the muscles of her sphincter and deny him access to her, but she knew she might fight that instinct. As he penetrated her, she winced, the pain of the beating almost overshadowed by that of the cock that was invading her anus. He was oblivious to the discomfort he was causing her, however, and went on pressing until his cock was buried all the way inside her rectum. Then he began to fuck her hard.

As he began to pump his cock into her, Carla found herself being pushed forward against the dildo that still filled her vagina, and suddenly a quite unexpected wave of arousal swept over her. Despite the discomfort of the erect penis deep in her behind, it was the thick phallus in her cunt that was capturing her attention now. Even the agony of the nipple clamps was forgotten as she felt the object pump in and out of her sex.

Every thrust of Hardcastle's hips against Carla's body drove the dildo deep into her, sending shock waves of pleasure through her naked body. As so often happened during her ordeals, Carla had been so preoccupied with her pain and discomfort she had been barely aware of the arousal that this treatment was instilling within her. Now, though, she remembered, and she gave a muffled groan of excitement as her sex was suddenly stimulated by the hard, black phallus.

He pumped his hips faster, doubling the exquisite sensation inside her. All at once Carla was barely in control, her senses so confused by the cocktail of pleasure and pain to which she had been subjected that evening that she simply gave up trying to comprehend what was happening.

The sensation of hot semen spurting deep into her rectum was the final stimulus, and she was suddenly overwhelmed by her orgasm, her young body shaking with sheer desire as the dildo continued to thrust itself into her. It was an extraordinary orgasm, the pain, the bondage and the lustful pleasure combining to produce a shuddering climax, and she screamed aloud into her gag as it overcame her.

By the time Hardcastle withdrew, she was exhausted, hanging loosely in her chains, oblivious to the excruciating pain in her nipples as her relaxation made the chains tighten.

But, even now, her ordeal was not over. Already the young maid was rubbing more of the ointment into her anus as the second of the men strode toward her, his cock standing erect from his fly.

Chapter 19

Once again the court was spellbound as Carla completed her account. Not a sound could be heard anywhere in the room, and all eyes were fixed on the naked, petite figure who stood, hands trapped behind her, legs forcibly spread, describing every detail of her debauched life to them. Now, as her words died away, there was a kind of collective sigh from the onlookers. Then Phaedra rose to her feet.

'Did this punishment finally bring an end to your misbehaviour?'

Carla shook her head. 'No. I couldn't stop, even if I wanted to.'

'And why was that?'

'I told you. Galston was paying me to act like I did, so he could enjoy the punishments. So to have stopped would have been to disobey his orders.'

'And how much longer were you there?'

'Another three weeks. I'm not sure I could have taken much more.'

'Yet no damage was done to you?'

Carla shook her head. 'No, they kept their word. There was a lot of pain, but within a fortnight afterwards there wasn't a mark on me.'

'So during those last three weeks, did things change?'

'Yes.'

'Tell us how they changed.'

'Well, for a start I never went back to the institute wing.'

'Where did you go?'

'I was kept in a cell in the big house after that. Down in the cellar. They kept me chained and naked all the time.'

'Why do you think they kept you in the big house?'

'So they could visit me at night.'

'They?'

'I was kept blindfolded all the time, but I was sure it was Galston and the woman.'

'The woman as well?'

'That's right. I recognised her perfume.'

'And they would do things to you?'

'Yes. Galston would have me tied in some odd position. You know, bent over, on my back with my legs in the air, something like that. Then they'd use me.'

'Use you?'

'Galston would fuck me. Sometimes I had to suck him, sometimes he'd want to give it to me in the arse.'

'What about the woman?'

'She'd squat over my face and make me lick her. Sometimes we'd do a sixty-niner. Sometimes I'd suck Galston's balls whilst he fucked her doggy-fashion.'

'And the punishments continued?'

'Yes. Every night they'd have me in that room and punish me somehow. Then the men would take me. Sometimes there were six or seven of them, so the sessions would go on quite late. I don't know who they were, but that man was often one of them.'

She indicated the witness stand where Hardcastle was standing.

'And the truth is that you only misbehaved because Galston wanted you to?'

'That's right. He was a good man really, but he had these desires. Surely it was better that he paid me to act them out than to use one of the real inmates?'

'I agree.' Phaedra turned to the jury. 'And I'm sure these gentlemen will agree too. What you did was for the pleasure of a man, just like everything else you do. If only your husband understood how properly to treat a woman, you wouldn't be standing here today. No further questions.'

As Hardcastle left the dock, Carla glanced across at her husband. He sat, staring straight ahead, his eyebrows knitted in a frown of displeasure.

The atmosphere in the courtroom was sultry after lunch, the fans in the ceiling spinning lazily and giving little respite from the heat. Carla gazed out from her vantage point across a sea of florid, sweating faces. At least being naked kept her cool, she reflected, though it was little compensation for the embarrassment she endured daily from being kept in this condition.

She glanced across at Wajir, who was sorting through a pile of papers, his brow shiny with perspiration. She would have expected him to have the demeanour of a man who was fighting with his back to the wall by now, yet still there was an air of confidence about him as he studied a sheet, then turned and spoke into her husband's ear.

Phaedra moved across to stand beside her.

'Feeling okay?'

'Yes. I'm all right, despite being felt up again during lunch.'

'The guard?'

'That's right. The bastard can't keep his hands off me. Had me pinned to the wall in the corridor, fingering my cunt. I nearly came.'

Phaedra grinned. 'Well, it can't have been that bad, then.'

Carla reddened. 'Even so, I'm accustomed to men asking before they grope me.'

'Do you want me to file a complaint?'

She shook her head. 'No. I doubt if they'd do anything about it, and it would only make him mad. As it is, he just wants to touch me. I can live with that.'

'Sure?'

'I'm sure. What do you think Wajir's got up his sleeve next?'

'I'm not certain. The bastard's looking pretty smug, isn't he?'

At that moment the judge entered the court, and the pair had to curtail their conversation as they watched the tall, dominant figure stride in. Once the judge had taken his seat, the buzz of conversation resumed for a short time. Then he banged his gavel down once more.

'Court is in session!' he announced. 'The case of Mrs Carla Wilde. Mr Wajir, your next witness please.'

'I call the Reverend Zachary Penfold.'

Phaedra turned to Carla. 'The Reverend? He's really a reverend?'

'That's what he calls himself,' said the girl. 'Is that bad?'

'I'm afraid so. They take their religion very seriously in this country. If he's a reverend, they'll assume he's a man of God, and that he doesn't lie.'

Carla sniffed. 'He says he's a reverend,' she said. 'But I don't know what kind of church he's a reverend of. There's certainly nothing very reverential about the way he behaves.'

'Do you know where he trained?'

'No. But I don't believe it was anywhere recognised by the established church.'

Phaedra hesitated. 'Then: 'Do you think I could leave you alone for five minutes? I need to make a call.'

'Of course. But don't be long. There's no telling what lies that bastard might tell.'

As she spoke a figure entered the room. He was dressed in a dark suit, with the classic black-fronted shirt and a clerical collar of a man of the cloth. In his lapel was a large silver cross. He was quite a young man, not much more than thirty years old, though his hair was greying and his silver-rimmed spectacles gave him an air of maturity.

The clerk swore him in, then Wajir was on his feet.

'You are the Reverend Zachary Penfold?'

'That is correct, sir.' Penfold spoke with a Midwestern American accent.

'And you are the founder and leader of the Church of Divinity and Redemption?'

'Yes, sir, I am. The Lord called me to my vocation many years ago to save the sinners of this world from themselves.'

'Where is your church based, Reverend?'

'My church is universal, sir, but we have our centre of worship in Walville, Texas.'

'Tell me, Reverend, do you recognise the defendant?'

'Why of course I do. I'd know that Jezebel anywhere. Look at her, the whore, standing there naked and without shame.'

Carla felt the blood rising in her cheeks as he made the remark. She was feeling very uncomfortable without Phaedra by her side, and she glanced at the door her friend had gone through, willing her to return.

'I tell you she's a slut,' Penfold was saying. 'She's no more than a slut and a harlot.'

Wajir cleared his throat. 'Yes, well, the decision as to the defendant's character must be a matter for the court. Meanwhile, can you name this woman?'

'Sure. Her name's Carla, Carla Wilde. And she's in league with the devil. Why I tell you . . .'

'Objection!' Phaedra had suddenly reappeared, an angry expression on her face, much to the relief of Carla. 'Your Honour,' she said. 'I can't allow this man to speak like this of my client. Surely this court is concerned with the facts, not the opinion of the witness?'

The judge turned to her. 'Madam, are you not aware that this is a man of God? To wear that collar he must have a knowledge of good and bad.'

'Your Honour, of course I respect any man who has trained in the priesthood. But you must understand that, unless he can back those words with solid evidence, it can't possibly be acceptable to the court.'

The judge looked across at Carla.

'Mrs Wilde, what is your religion?'

'I'm an atheist, Your Honour.'

A murmur went up from the crowd, and the judge shook his head. 'So you reject the word of God?'

'I respect others' beliefs, Your Honour. I simply have no faith of my own.'

'You see what I mean?' shouted Penfold. 'I tell you she's the spawn of the devil.'

'Your Honour,' said Wajir. 'I think that if you listen to the evidence of the witness, you will understand why he describes my client the way he does.'

The judge inclined his head. 'Very well. I apologise, Reverend, that there should be any doubt as to your integrity. Please go ahead, Mr Wajir.'

Carla glanced at Phaedra, who cast her eyes towards the ceiling. Clearly, whatever Penfold had to say, the mere existence of his dog collar would give a credence to his evidence.

Wajir turned to his witness.

'Reverend, would you kindly tell us how you met Mrs Wilde.'

'She came to me as a damsel in distress. She told me she was a fallen woman, and that she needed my help. I'm a man of God. How could I refuse her?'

'Tell us about that first encounter.'

'I was ministering to my flock. Once a week we used to hold an evangelical service in the town. We'd put up a tent and invite the brethren in.'

'So it was an open service?'

'That's right. We were there trying to save souls for the Lord. We'd sing some hymns and say some prayers. Then we'd welcome anyone who wanted to join us. That woman came forward and said she wanted to serve God. If I'd known then what I know now, I'd have sent her away. That woman is evil.'

'So what exactly happened?'

'She told me she was seeking salvation. I offered to teach her God's ways. She accepted.'

'So she joined your church?'

'First of all she had to undergo instruction. I took care of that personally.'

'And did she learn quickly?'

'Yes. Very quickly. 'I don't remember anyone responding so quickly to my teaching. That's what impressed me. Of course, I know now that she had a hidden agenda.'

'And she became a full member?'

'Yes. She went through the initiation ceremony and baptism just a week later.'

'Did she prove a good disciple?'

'At first she certainly seemed to. I was very pleased with her. It was only later that I discovered her treachery.'

'Tell me about Mrs Wilde's treachery.'

'She conspired to bring down the church. She stole the church's money, and turned the brethren against me and against God. She lied and blasphemed and tried to break up our happy family. I tell you, that woman is the very devil incarnate.'

As he spoke the words a collective gasp rose from those watching, and Carla saw the shock on the faces of the jury. Clearly, in this place, religion was something they took seriously. For the first time she began seriously to doubt whether Phaedra could win this case for her.

Wajir's questioning continued, and Penfold went on to claim that Carla had plotted against him from within the community, turning members of the church against him and finally leading a rebellion in which half the congregation had left after raiding the church's coffers and destroying the buildings. By the time he came to the end of his questioning, there was a definite air of disapproval in the room, and Carla wondered once again whether her cause was lost. When Phaedra rose to her feet, however, her expression was as determined as ever.

'Reverend Penfold,' she said, 'how long has your church been established?'

'About four years.'

'And you set it up yourself?'

'I set it up with the aid of God.'

'But you were the prime mover, terrestrially that is.'

'I was the chosen one, yes.'

'Tell me, Mr Penfold, when Carla joined your brethren, how many of you were there?'

'We had a flock of more than a hundred.'

'But how many actually lived in your commune?'

'About twenty of us.'

'And of that twenty, how many were male?'

'I'm not sure.'

'I think you are. How many, Mr Penfold?'

'I had six brothers assisting me.'

'And all the rest were women?'

'I guess so.'

'The men, were they recruited in the same way as the women?'

'No. They were with me from the start.'

'So you didn't recruit any men?'

'We spoke to men, but none had the calling.'

'I see.' Phaedra turned to Carla. 'Mrs Wilde, you say you're an atheist. What persuaded you to join Mr Penfold's church?'

'I was asked to do it.'

'By whom?'

'By a group of men whose wives and girlfriends were church members.'

'But why did they approach you?'

'One of them, Glenn Patterson, had once been a customer of our organisation.'

'He had engaged a girl like yourself?'

'That's right. In fact, he'd ended up marrying her. Then she'd joined Penfold's little lot.'

'Tell me why these men wanted you to join.'

'They were convinced their partners were being held against their will. They wanted someone to infiltrate the church and find out what was going on.'

'So you were never actually a convert?'

'Of course not.'

'Tell me, Carla, when you approached the Reverend here, did anyone else try to join?'

'Yes. There were two men and another girl.'

'Were any of them accepted?'

'The two men were told they weren't suitable. The woman was told to go away and pray harder.'

'So the men were dismissed at once. Why do you suppose the other woman was also rejected?'

'She wasn't well dressed. Her clothes were shabby and her hair was a mess.'

'Whereas you?'

'I wore brand-new designer clothes. And I drove up in a Porsche.'

'So you think Penfold was only interested in affluent women?'

'Objection!' Wajir rose to his feet. 'Mrs Wilde has no way of knowing why this other woman was rejected.'

'I withdraw the question,' said Phaedra. 'Now, Carla, tell us again why these men recruited you.'

'They believed that the women were being held against their will whilst Penfold systematically raided their bank accounts. All of them were allowed personal accounts by their husbands and lovers, and the men had noticed that the funds were being depleted at a fast rate. They'd tried to close the accounts, but they couldn't.'

'And couldn't they simply go and speak to these women?'

'No. Penfold wouldn't let them anywhere near them whilst they were inside the compound. When they came out they still wouldn't speak about what went on inside.'

'Why not?'

'That's what I was supposed to find out.'

'And only someone like you could have got inside?'

'That's right. Nobody got inside except the women, his helpers and the associate brothers.'

'Associate brothers?'

'That's what they called them. In fact they were just customers.'

'Customers?'

'Yes. Not content with draining their bank accounts, Penfold ran a high-class whorehouse, and used the women as the prostitutes.'

A gasp went round the courthouse, and the judge banged his gavel.

'That's a very serious accusation, Mrs Wilde,' he said. 'I hope you can back it up with some facts.'

'Certainly, Your Honour. You see, I began to suspect what was going on when my instruction first began . . .'

Chapter 20

Carla arrived at the entrance to the Reverend Penfold's mission late in the afternoon. She stood, gazing up at the heavy, barred gate, suddenly disinclined to go any further. Her experience with Galston's institution was still a very recent memory, and she was reluctant to allow herself to be placed behind bars again so soon. She was wearing a simple blouse and short skirt and carrying a travelling bag, into which she had placed a few clothes and possessions. Penfold had ordered her to travel light, so she had packed very little.

Set into the gatepost was an intercom, and Carla pressed the button. There was silence for a moment, then a man's voice sounded.

'Who is it?'

'My name is Carla Wilde. The Reverend Penfold asked me here.'

'Wait a minute.'

The machine went dead for a few moments, then there was a click and the gate opened slowly. As she stepped through, the note of the electric motor changed, and it began to close again, locking shut with a loud clang. She looked around at her surroundings. She was inside the compound of what could have been a prisoner-of-war camp. Indeed, judging by the height of the fence and the barbed wire about the top, it might actually have been one at one time. In front of her was a long, low building with barred windows, and beyond were similar huts all made of wood and painted white. At the centre was a much larger building, also made of wood, with a small spire at the front atop which was a cross. This, she assumed, was the church.

A figure emerged from the building in front of her. At first she thought it was a woman, but as it approached she recognised the Reverend Zachary Penfold, dressed in a long white flowing gown that hung down to his ankles.

'Sister Carla,' he said, holding out his arms. 'So you have come to join us.'

134

She let him embrace her and plant a kiss on both of her cheeks. Then he held her back at arms' length.

'It is always good to welcome another sister into the fold,' he said.

'I thought I was just here for an initial assessment,' she replied.

'Of course, of course. But I'm sure that will be simply a formality. I have a very positive feeling about you, Carla. The Lord has sent you to do his will.'

'I hope so.'

'Certainly he has. Come along, now. Let me show you to your quarters. We must begin your training straight away.'

'Training? You make it sound as if I've joined the army.'

He smiled. 'We're all part of God's army,' he said. 'Come, let me take your case from you. You won't be needing those things here.'

'But that's got all my clothes in it.'

'Trust me, Sister,' he said, placing an arm about her shoulders. 'We must take you away from worldly things and introduce you to yourself anew. With God's help I believe you can be reborn.'

A young woman emerged from one of the huts. She was tall and slim, and wore a tight-fitting short gown held together with just three buttons down the front. The gown had a low neckline, revealing a deep cleavage, and the lowest button was at the level of her crotch so that the full length of her slender legs was on show. Penfold handed Carla's bag to her.

'Take this and store it safely, Sister Collette,' he said.

'Yes, Brother.'

Carla studied the girl. She was about twenty-four, with auburn hair worn shoulder-length. She had no make-up on, and the only sign of jewellery was a leather collar about her neck, in the centre of which was a shining ring. A small cross was attached to this, and it gleamed in the sunlight. As she turned and walked away with the case, Carla stared at her lovely behind, the soft, rounded globes of which were all but visible below the minuscule gown. She wondered if the girl wore any knickers, and surmised that she probably didn't.

Penfold led her across the compound to one of the huts. He opened the door and showed her inside. A long corridor ran the length of the building, the ceiling and walls painted white, the floor bare boards. Along both sides were white doors. Penfold opened the first one and gestured to her to enter.

The room was decorated in the same stark manner as the corridor. In one corner was a small bed with a plain white eiderdown on it, beside which was a stool. There was no wardrobe, just a line of coat hooks to the left of the door.

'This is to be your room,' said Penfold. 'It is simply decorated, so that your thoughts are not distracted by worldly things.'

'What have you done with my belongings?'

'Don't worry, they'll be safe. Now you must come with me to dispose of those last reminders of the outside world and to be introduced to your new life. Follow me.'

He led Carla back into the bright sunshine. As she left the block she glanced back at it. It was identical to all the buildings on either side of it, being distinguished only by the letter 'I' painted by the door. Each of the other blocks had a different letter, though there didn't seem to be any particular order to them.

As they passed one of these buildings, Carla was distracted by the sound of a woman's raised voice. She seemed to be protesting about something, and Carla clearly heard the word 'No' shouted twice. All at once the door opened and a woman emerged. She was in her twenties, with a pretty face surrounded by blonde locks. Like Carla she was petite, no more than five foot three inches tall, with a trim figure. She wore a white dress identical to that worn by Collette. In her case, though, the top two buttons were undone, so that her breasts were barely covered, and Carla could see the pert brown nipples set high in the soft orbs.

The woman came to a sudden halt at the sight of Penfold, and pulled her dress closed as best she could, though it was a tight fit. A man came out behind her, and he too stopped short.

'Sister June,' said Penfold. 'Is something the matter?'

'It's him,' she said, indicating the man. 'He wants . . .'

'He wants to help you,' interrupted Penfold. 'You know that, June. You need his help.'

Carla looked at the man. He was in his forties, dressed in an expensive business suit, though his tie was askew and the top button on his trousers was undone. He seemed out of place amongst the white-clad commune members, and, from his expression, Carla guessed he was uncomfortable with his situation. She turned to the girl, who was staring into Penfold's eyes, as if hypnotised by his gaze.

'I . . . I'm not sure that . . .'

'Of course you have your doubts, June,' said Penfold,

interrupting her once more. 'But you must understand that you are here to serve. It's what God wants.'

The girl gave Penfold a despairing look, and Carla could see at once that she was beaten. It was clear that Penfold had some kind of power over her that Carla could not yet understand. As the blonde turned and made her way back toward the building, Carla saw the man in the suit and Penfold exchange a glance. Then the man followed June through the door and closed it behind them.

'What was all that about?' asked Carla.

At once she saw a clouded expression cross Penfold's face. It was there for just an instant, then his smile returned.

'June is still in her early days of training,' he said. 'She'll learn what's required of her soon enough. Now we must get on. There's a lot to be done.'

They were headed toward the church building and, as they came closer, the doors swung open and two figures appeared in the doorway. One Carla recognised as Collette, the girl who had taken her bag earlier. The other was of a similar height to Collette, but with a fuller figure, her large breasts straining against the top of her tunic. She had long blonde hair and full lips, reminding Carla of a young Brigitte Bardot. The two girls stood to one side whilst Carla and Penfold entered.

Once inside, Carla glanced about her. Like the other building it was painted white both inside and out. There were simple wooden benches set in rows facing the end wall. By that wall stood a sort of altar topped with marble, behind which, on a raised dais, stood a tall throne upholstered in red velvet with gold trimmings. It was the only object in the room that was in any way colourful, and Carla felt her eyes drawn automatically toward it.

'Carla is our new recruit,' said Penfold. He turned back to Carla. 'Sister Collette you have already met, of course. This other sister is called Sister Laura. Both are here to help you. Take Sister Carla into the dressing room and help her choose her gown, Sisters.'

The two young women took Carla by the arm and led her toward a door at the side of the main church. As she passed through it, Carla saw that it was a locker room, the walls adorned with clothes racks from which hung identical tunics to the ones worn by the other women.

The two women took her across to one of the racks and began holding the garments against her, checking them for size.

'Does everyone have to wear one of these?' she asked. But the girls didn't reply, simply placing their fingers to their lips and indicating that she should not speak.

They picked out a tunic that seemed far too small to Carla, and she protested, only to be shushed into silence once more. She had expected to be made to put it on then and there, but instead they took her back out into the main church. There Penfold was waiting, seated on the throne like some high priest overlooking his flock. He beckoned the trio forward and addressed Carla.

'The time has come for you to put aside still more of your worldly goods,' he said. 'Are you prepared to do so?'

'Is it really necessary?' she asked.

'Of course. How can you concentrate on the rescue of your soul when still surrounded by such reminders of the world you are leaving behind? Sisters, please proceed.'

The two women approached Carla from either side. Collette began undoing the buttons of her blouse, whilst Laura pulled down the zip on her skirt.

'Don't I get any privacy?' asked Carla.

'We are all brothers and sisters,' replied Penfold. 'We have nothing to hide from one another.'

Collette slipped the blouse from Carla's shoulders whilst Laura pulled her skirt down over her hips and made her step out of it. Now clad only in black bra and briefs, Carla stood, her hands dangling at her side whilst Penfold ran his eyes up and down her young body.

He gave another nod to the women, and Carla felt Collette undo her bra strap whilst Laura reached for her pants. In a few seconds she was completely naked, her nipples hardening as Penfold continued to take in her body. She felt the blood rising to her cheeks as he ran his eyes over her trim pubic mound and up her flat belly to the firm orbs of her breasts. The two girls paused, apparently waiting for an order from the man, who was obviously in no hurry to see Carla's charms hidden once more.

'You seem tense, Sister,' he said quietly.

'I'm a little embarrassed. Couldn't I put the tunic on now?'

'You mustn't be embarrassed in front of your brothers and sisters. Collette, get Sister Carla a drink.'

Carla noticed the two young women exchanging a glance, then Collette turned and went to a cabinet attached to the wall. She opened it and took out a decanter of liquid. It was pinkish coloured and opaque, and she poured a measure into a glass before returning to where Carla was standing. She held it out to her.

'Take it, Sister,' said Penfold. 'It's good.'

Carla took the glass and eyed the liquid. She sipped at it. It tasted slightly fruity, and it seemed to warm her throat as it went down.

'Drink it all, Sister Carla,' urged Penfold.

Carla hesitated for a moment longer, then drank down the fluid, draining the glass. She shivered slightly as it slipped down. She handed the glass back to Collette.

'That's better,' said Penfold. 'Now, lie on the slab and the girls will soothe those tensions.'

Carla eyed him once more. 'I'm not really tense,' she said. 'It's just that I'm not used to people seeing me in the nude.'

'I understand. But we're all friends here. Now, lie on the slab.'

Carla felt her arms taken by the two women, and she allowed herself to be led to the plain altar. The pair lifted her to a sitting position then pushed her gently backwards. The wood felt cool and hard against her naked flesh as she lay back against it, but Carla could already feel her muscles relaxing. It occurred to her that the drink might be having an effect on her, and she wondered what could have been in it. Then she felt Collette begin to gently rub her feet whilst Laura massaged her shoulders, and her body started to relax still more.

Carla closed her eyes, enjoying the sensation of the women's hands on her soft young flesh and forgetting for a moment that a pair of male eyes were eyeing her lovely, naked body. The women worked on, their fingers kneading Carla's muscles and stroking her pale skin. Collette began to work her fingers higher, moving them up her calves and on toward her thighs, at the same time gently spreading Carla's legs so that she knew the man could see the open gash of her sex. At the same time, Laura's fingers crept lower, finding the softness of Carla's breasts, occasionally brushing against her nipples, which the naked girl could already feel hardening even more.

Carla knew now that there had been some kind of drug in the drink they had given her. It seemed to relax her, but at the same time she could feel a warmth rising in her belly that couldn't simply be explained by the ministrations of the two women. It was some kind of aphrodisiac, and it was beginning to make her feel very turned on indeed as the women continued their caresses. Laura was rubbing her breasts in earnest now, her fingers teasing Carla's nipples into hard brown knobs, whilst her companion moved her hands up the creamy smoothness of her inner thighs toward the very centre of her desires.

When Collette's fingers found her clitoris, Carla gave a sudden gasp, the muscles of her sex contracting at the intimacy of the touch. She glanced down at the woman, whose eyes were fixed on the pink slit of her vagina, then across at Penfold, who was watching every movement. It was certainly an odd initiation, she mused, but the drug she had imbibed was beginning to overwhelm her now, and when Collette slipped a finger into her, she moaned aloud, spreading her legs wider and thrusting her pubis up at the probing fingers.

All pretence at a simple massage had been dropped now, and Carla squirmed as she felt Laura's lips close over her nipple and begin to suck at it. Then she felt a new sensation, and she shuddered as Collette began gently to lick at her inner thighs, her tongue moving up her leg toward the centre of her desires.

'You like that, Sister Carla, don't you?' asked Penfold.

Carla could only moan in reply, and she offered no resistance as Collette pressed her legs still wider apart, then knelt up on the slab between them. Carla looked up into the girl's eyes, but could detect no emotion in them as she continued to stroke her. Then Collette leaned forward, and Carla gave a cry of pure desire as she buried her face between her legs and slid her tongue deep into her vagina.

The strangeness of her situation was forgotten as Carla pressed her thighs up against the woman's face, panting with desire at the exquisite sensation of the tongue that was invading her so intimately. At the same time her nipples were tingling with pleasure as Laura continued to suck first one, then the other, drawing the hard teats into her mouth and lapping at them as she sucked. Carla was totally turned on now, her pretty behind slapping down against the slab as she continued to thrust her hips against Collette's face, urging her tongue ever deeper inside her.

She came with a cry, her naked body writhing back and forth as Collette kept her mouth locked against her burning vagina, her tongue darting in and out, lapping at the juices that flowed so freely from her. Carla abandoned herself completely to her orgasm, her screams of pleasure echoing about the wooden building as she was overcome with lust.

Collette continued to lick at her even as the pleasure began to ebb from her and her writhing reduced, keeping her tongue inserted within her until the cries had died away, and she lay panting and prone on the altar. Only then did the two girls raise their heads from her young body. Carla glanced down at her breasts and sex, both of which gleamed with the saliva that covered them. Then she looked across at Penfold, who was smiling at her.

'You see, Sister Carla,' he said. 'I knew you were ready to be liberated.'

Chapter 21

Carla stood at the back of the church surveying the rows of people who sat in the pews in front of her. Apart from the front row, all were women. Young and beautiful women, each clad in a tunic identical to the one that Carla wore. As always, the Reverend Penfold's flock appeared subdued to Carla, chanting along with the words of the service, but showing little sign of the enthusiasm she would have expected of a group of religious converts.

The front row was exclusively occupied by men. There were six of them, all of whom were known to Carla. Their ages ranged from around thirty years to fifty, and all stood straight and silent whilst the women chanted, facing Penfold who sat in the throne, staring out at his brethren.

Carla had been with the community for almost two weeks now, and the scene before her was becoming more and more familiar, the men seemingly dominant whilst the women were cowed and obedient. She wondered for the umpteenth time what it was that kept them in this place. None seemed in any way happy or inspired by their guru, though when she had encountered them the first time at the evangelistic meeting they had shown much more enthusiasm for the cause.

Since her arrival, Carla had barely been allowed to be alone with any of the 'sisters'. Always she had been accompanied by Penfold or one of his six male disciples. She had noticed how subdued the other women were in the presence of these men, and had wondered at the power they seemed to wield.

Since her first encounter with Collette and Laura, Carla's training had followed more conventional lines. There had been no more sexual advances, though Penfold had occasionally asked her to strip off her tunic during their sessions, to reduce her inhibitions as he had put it. He had not touched her, however, being content to eye her breasts and sex as she stood before him. The sessions had still been intimate, though, as he had made her recount previous sexual encounters and had listened with rapt interest to her accounts. Retelling such incidents had, as always, an unwelcome effect on the sensuous Carla, making her extremely aroused, and it was often all she could do to resist the urge to masturbate as she related her most intimate secrets. The aphrodisiac drink hadn't been offered again either, though, even as she watched the ceremony unfold before her, Carla could see a decanter of the liquid and a glass on the altar where she had been ravished by the two women.

Carla had attended a number of these services since her arrival, and usually they had taken the form of ritual incantation followed by an oration from their leader. Today, though, was different. Today was to be her initiation into the sect, her baptism, as Penfold had put it. He had declared her ready to be accepted two days before, and now the group had gathered to witness the ceremony.

Once again, Carla was struck by the lack of enthusiasm with which the women accepted the new recruit into their midst. It was almost as if they were trying to warn her off going through with it and, but for her mission to infiltrate them, Carla would most certainly have had her doubts about the whole thing.

All at once she realised that the congregation had turned in their pews and that all eyes were upon her. She transferred her gaze to the front, and saw that Penfold was beckoning to her. Suddenly apprehensive, she made her way slowly to where he was sitting.

'Brothers and Sisters, today we welcome a new convert to our midst,' said Penfold. He had a strong and authoritative voice, one which demanded obedience, and the congregation listened in silence to his words.

'Sister Carla came to us for help,' he went on. 'She was lost and without direction in the hostile world outside, and she asked to be admitted into this haven of peace. Today we shall grant that wish. Come forward, Sister.'

Carla stepped up to the altar. As she did so, one of the men rose to his feet and poured a glass of the fluid. He passed it to Penfold, who held it out to Carla.

'Drink this,' he said. 'It will give you strength for the ceremony to follow.'

Carla took it from him and eyed its contents. She remembered the last time she had drunk the fluid, and the aphrodisiac effect it had had upon her. Carla liked to be in control, and she abhorred the idea of taking any drug that might dull her senses. However, she knew that all eyes were upon her and, at this stage, she didn't want to give anyone the idea that she was not fully involved in what she was doing. She lifted the glass to her lips and drained it and, as she did so, she sensed the tension amongst the congregation suddenly rise as they realised that she had committed herself to what was to happen.

More chanting followed, whilst Carla stood silently at the front of the church. Already she could feel the drink beginning to take effect as the wetness began to seep into her sex, and she shivered slightly as she wondered what was in store for her.

Penfold made a gesture and the congregation rose to its feet. A door at the side of the church was opened, letting the sunlight stream in. Penfold stood and turned, walking slowly toward the door. Two of the men rose to their feet and took hold of Carla's arms. They followed Penfold out, the four other men falling in line behind, with the congregation behind them.

As they stepped into the sunshine, Carla saw that they were heading toward a small pool sunk into the ground at the back of the building. She had seen it before, and had wondered as to its purpose. It was like a small swimming pool about ten feet long and four feet deep, with steps leading down from the edge into the water. In front of it had been placed a table with a red velvet cloth spread across it. Penfold stopped beside this, then turned to face Carla. The men drew to a halt as the rest gathered about them.

'Are you ready for the initiation, Sister Carla?' he asked.

'Yes, Brother, I'm ready.'

'You will first be washed clean of the trappings of the outside world, then you will consummate your attachment to the congregation. Is that clear?'

'Yes, Brother.'

'Prepare her.'

The man on Carla's right reached across and began undoing the buttons on her tunic. Carla stood motionless as he did so, trying hard to stay in control. Even without the effects of the drug, she knew that the move would spark her arousal. As it was, the effects of the fluid were increasing with every moment, and already her sex was burning with a desire to be touched, so that she trembled slightly as the men slipped her tunic from her shoulders.

Beneath she was naked and she felt her cheeks redden at the

thought of all the eyes upon her as she stood there before them. She remained motionless whilst Penfold gave a short oration, welcoming her to the flock. She scarcely heard the words, the excitement rising within her with every second. At last he finished, and addressed her once more.

'Now, Sister, it is time for the cleansing. Follow me.'

He turned and began slowly walking down into the pool, still wearing his flowing gown. When he reached the floor of the pool he turned, the water lapping about his chest, and gestured to the youngster. Carla felt a hand on her bottom pressing her forward, and she stepped down into the water.

It was cool, but not cold, and she walked slowly, allowing the fluid to envelop her beautiful body until she was standing beside Penfold, her breasts just submerged. The nipples were stiff, partly from contact with the water, but mainly due to the sexual excitement that was increasing within her by the second.

'You will be immersed three times,' announced Penfold. 'This will cleanse you of all you have brought with you, making you ready to be wedded to our congregation. Afterwards you will be ready for the consummation.'

Carla pondered on the words he used, particularly the word consummation. She knew what the word meant following a conventional wedding, but here? A shiver of anticipation ran through her as she gazed into Penfold's eyes.

The man placed a hand on the top of her head and began to press. Carla buckled her knees, allowing her head to be pushed down under the water. As the clear fluid enveloped her, she felt suddenly strangely isolated from the ceremony and the people who surrounded her. It was as if she was no longer a part of the strange ritual, but in a cool, silent world of her own. Then a hand closed over her breast and began to squeeze it, sending a sudden pulse of excitement through her. It was the first time that Penfold had touched her intimately, and she wondered if the others could see what he was doing as he fingered her nipples, sending delicious sensations through her body.

He removed his hand from her head and allowed her to surface once more. She drank in the air gratefully, blinded by her hair which wrapped itself about her head. Then he was pushing her down again, and she was once again immersed in green silence.

This time he reached down between her legs, and she gave a gasp as his forefinger circled about the stiff bud of her clitoris,

145

stroking it gently and exciting her anew with the intimacy of his touch. When, at last, she rose to the surface, her heavy breathing was more due to her arousal than the lack of oxygen.

As he pushed her down for the third time, his fingers penetrated her vagina and, without warning, a sudden orgasm shook her young body, her sex muscles convulsing about his hand as the wetness flowed from her. It was all she could do to keep still as the delicious sensations swept through her, and he held her down until the climax had passed, before allowing her to come gasping to the surface, her face bright red as she realised what had happened.

He pushed the hair from her eyes and gazed at her, smiling slightly.

'Nobody has ever climaxed during their immersion before, Sister,' he murmured. 'You are clearly well suited to your vocation.'

Carla said nothing, but, as she looked up at those watching, she wondered if they realised that she had come so quickly and easily.

Penfold took her shoulders and turned her toward the steps.

'Come, Sister,' he said. 'It is time for you to make the full commitment.'

As he said the words, he took her wrist and guided her hand down to his crotch. Beneath the gown, Carla could feel that his cock was stiff and solid and, as she closed her fingers momentarily about it, a shudder of desire ran through her.

Carla rose slowly from the pool, the water dripping from her slim, naked body. Penfold followed closely behind her, his hands caressing the soft swelling of her behind as she ascended the steps. Once out, she paused by the edge, glancing down at her stiff nipples which glistened with wetness as a rivulet of water ran down between her breasts and on to her bare crotch.

'Sister Carla has been cleansed,' announced Penfold. 'Now we shall complete her initiation.'

As he spoke the words, the two men who had stripped her stepped forward and once more took her by the arms. They led her across to the makeshift altar, then turned her so that her backside was pressed against the edge. Carla knew then that the consummation of which Penfold had spoken was to be a public one, and she felt a tight knot form in her stomach as she contemplated what she was about to do. She looked about at the rest of the congregation. The men were watching with hungry eyes as she was pressed back across the table. Many of the women, too, had their gazes fixed on her, and she knew that she wasn't the only one aroused by her extraordinary situation.

She prostrated herself across the red felt cloth, her backside projecting over the edge. As she did so, the men placed their hands on her knees and pulled them apart, so that her slit lay open, the wetness inside glistening. At the same time, two of the women stepped forward, undoing Penfold's gown at the neck.

They pulled the sodden garment down his body and off, revealing that he was naked beneath it. Carla found her eyes inexorably drawn toward his cock, which projected stiffly from a mat of thick, black pubic hair. It was circumcised, and it curved upwards like a long pink truncheon. As the naked beauty watched, one of the women sank to her knees and took it into her mouth, and she saw the passion in Penfold's eyes as the woman began to suck him.

By now the effect of the drink was almost overwhelming the lascivious young woman. Carla longed to touch herself between her legs, but she daren't whilst the ritual continued, so instead she simply gritted her teeth and waited for Penfold to make the next move.

The woman fellated him for two or three minutes more whilst the rest of the congregation waited in silence and Carla writhed in frustration on the altar. Then Penfold placed a hand on his disciple's head and she drew back, then rose to her feet, fingers still clutching his stiff organ. The man moved forward so that he stood between Carla's open thighs, gazing down at her lovely form, her firm breasts barely sagging to the sides, her naked body open and available to him.

The woman retained her hold on Penfold's cock. But now she was guiding it, not toward her mouth, but to the pink gash of Carla's open sex. The prostrate woman shuddered with arousal as she felt the stiff, bulbous end of his erection pressed against her soft nether lips. Almost at once he started to push, and she gave a groan as his erection slipped into her.

Penfold took hold of Carla's hips as he pressed his rampant cock deep inside her. She moaned aloud at the sheer pleasure his organ gave her and glanced again at those watching. Never before had she been so publicly fucked, and the sensation of the congregation's eyes upon her sent new spasms of lust coursing through her, her sex muscles tightening about Penfold's rod.

He began to fuck her with slow, easy movements, his cock sliding back and forth inside her in the most delicious way. Carla's own, natural libido, enhanced by the effect of the drink they had given her, sent her to new heights of wanton enjoyment as he took her, and almost at once she felt another orgasm approaching.

Penfold's even thrusts shook the table on which she was lying, so that her breasts bounced back and forth in a way that clearly fascinated the men. Carla reached up and caressed her stiff nipples, taking them between finger and thumb and rolling them back and forth, sending thrills of pleasure through her young body. As she did so she stared into Penfold's eyes, which were fixed on her own, his gaze almost hypnotic as he took her.

Such was Carla's arousal that she could barely absorb the bizarreness of her situation. Here she was, outdoors in broad daylight, allowing herself to be screwed by this extraordinary man, whilst his followers stood round and watched. Yet, far from trying to hide her shame, she was making no secret of the lust he was engendering in her, caressing her pliant young breasts and moaning aloud as he rammed his cock deep inside her.

Slowly, almost imperceptibly, Carla felt Penfold's own urgency begin to grow, the force of his thrusts increasing as his arousal took control of him. His grip on her hips tightened, his fingers digging into her flesh, and Carla began to sense that his orgasm was not far off. The thought of having him come inside her increased her own desires still further and she thrust up against him, matching him stroke for stroke, urging him on towards his climax.

When he did come, Carla was ready for him and, as the first spurts of his semen were ejaculated into her, she enjoyed her second shuddering orgasm, her moans turning to cries of pleasure as she writhed about on the hard table. For the moment the watching congregation was forgotten as the wanton girl abandoned herself to her lust, spasms of sensual desire shaking her small frame. Penfold continued to thrust his hips against hers, his eyes closed, his face a picture of ecstasy as he emptied his seed into her vagina, his balls twitching with every jet of spunk he unleashed.

By the time he was spent, Carla too was still, her pretty breasts rising and falling as she regained her breath. Now that her passion was past she felt her cheeks glowing as she looked about at those who had witnessed her ravishment.

Penfold withdrew, making her moan anew as his stiff weapon slipped from inside her. He turned to the women. Someone had

148

produced a fresh, dry cloak for him and, as Carla watched, it was pulled over his head by the pair who had originally stripped him. Already he seemed to have lost interest in his beautiful young partner, turning his back on her and addressing the watching congregation once more. Carla barely listened to the words, lying back on the altar and feeling his seed begin to seep slowly from her.

There was a murmur from the crowd and she raised her head to see them filing slowly away. Once again the women were strangely subdued as they moved off, with Penfold following behind them. Then Carla realised that the men were still there, all six of them standing about her, their eyes fixed on her soft young body.

All at once she felt her arms grasped, and the same two men who had laid her out on the altar were pulling her to her feet. She glanced questioningly at them as they stood her upright, and they smiled confident smiles back.

'Where are you taking me?' she mumbled, suddenly aware that she was still under the influence of the drink.

'Just come along with us,' came the reply. 'Your consummation isn't over yet.'

Carla glanced about at them. She realised that she was being taken toward their quarters. This was a place she had not previously visited. The men lived separately from the women, in a building that stood alone at the edge of the compound. Carla had seen women emerging from the building from time to time, but she herself had never been asked in. Now, though, she was being directed toward it.

'What about my clothes?' she asked.

The man holding her right arm gave a short laugh. 'You won't be needing those, Sister.'

They reached the door and it was opened. Carla was pushed inside, and she found herself in a kind of staff room, with a stove and sink in one corner and a series of chairs arranged about a bare wooden table. They led her to this, then released her arms. Carla stared round at them. All were staring at her pert breasts, and she realised that her nipples were still stiff with arousal.

'Lean over the table.' The man who spoke delivered the words with cold authority.

Carla looked into his eyes. It was clear that they were totally confident that she would submit to them. For a moment she felt a spark of rebellion rising within her. What right did these men have

149

to assume that they could fuck her without so much as a by-your-leave? Yet even as the thought entered her head she was forced to dismiss it. It was clear that they would take her whether she consented or not, so why resist? Besides, she was on a mission, and she didn't want to draw attention to herself by showing dissent.

There was another factor though. As she glanced about at these virile men, Carla felt a new spasm of desire shake her frame. She was naked, and helpless to stop them ravishing her, and the thought of it was turning her on strongly.

Slowly she turned and gazed down at the bare surface of the table. Then she felt a hand between her shoulder-blades pushing her forward. She bent over and pressed herself down against the hard, cool wood, her nipples stimulated still more by the contact with the surface. Someone kicked her ankles, and she spread her legs, pressing her pert young behind backwards as she revealed the centre of her desires to their hungry eyes. She could still feel Penfold's seed seeping from her as a hand stroked the soft, pliant flesh of her backside.

Then something else was pressing against her. Something hard and hot that pushed insistently between her sex lips and began to slide deep into her. She gasped aloud as she felt herself penetrated, the desire flooding back into her as she responded to him. Her pubis was pressed down against the edge of the table, and the wood chafed against her clitoris as he began to fuck her, sending new waves of lust flooding through her naked form.

Suddenly she was aware of a figure standing in front of her, and she looked up to see another stiff penis waving just in front of her face. Before she could speak he had grasped her hair, pulling her face up and thrusting his engorged penis between her lips.

Carla was suddenly overcome by the scent and taste of his maleness as she began to suck hard at him. It was a long time since she had been made to take on two men at once, and, as she sensed the urgency of the pair thrusting their stiff cocks into her, she felt her own desires increase still more and the wetness inside her vagina flowed anew.

Out the corner of her eyes, Carla could see the other four men. Two of them had dropped their trousers already and were gently caressing their erections as they watched her being taken. Carla wondered at the sight she must make, her hair still wet and straggling, her bare body bent forward across the table as she was

150

fucked from front and back, her hips banging down against the surface with every thrust.

As the man inside her came, she came too, her cries muffled by the thick cock between her lips. Moments later they were stifled still more as her mouth filled with thick, hot spunk that dribbled from her as she struggled to gulp it down. The two continued to empty their balls into her until both were quite spent. Then they simultaneously withdrew and stood aside.

Carla raised her pretty face, her chin and cheeks streaked with spunk, only to see the next two men moving forward. Moments later she felt a stiff erection penetrating her burning sex whilst another was forced between her lips.

And yet another orgasm began to build inside her.

Chapter 22

As Carla was being led up onto the dais for yet another day of the trial, she watched the public seats filling up in the base of the courtroom. There, as usual, a large crowd was gathering to hear the latest testimony. Although the case was being heard in camera, word had spread fast about the beautiful, naked young foreigner whose exploits were being revealed in such minute detail to the court. Carla soon discovered that, if she climbed up onto her cell bunk in the mornings, she could see, through the small window, the queues of curious onlookers waiting to enter. Many of them had attended every day since the case had begun, and she suspected that they must have begun queuing very early indeed each morning to keep their places. She wondered what thrills they were getting from hearing the details of her escapades, and she would sometimes fantasise that the men were masturbating over her story as she lay in bed at night, an image always guaranteed to turn the lascivious woman on.

It was the second day of Penfold's testimony. The court had adjourned the night before after hearing about how Carla had been gangbanged by Penfold's disciples. Now he was being asked to attend for a second day, and Phaedra was already consulting her notes as the gathering was being called to order by the usher.

The judge entered, stony-faced as ever, barely casting an eye in Carla's direction as he banged his gavel down hard and began proceedings. Penfold was called into the witness box once more, and he made his way to the front of the court, again wearing his clerical collar.

Phaedra rose to her feet.

'Mr— I'm sorry, Reverend Penfold. Would you tell the court, please, was Mrs Wilde's account of her initiation into your church an accurate one?'

Penfold cleared his throat. 'Certainly admission is by baptism,' he said.

'By immersing the candidate in water?'

'That has always been a traditional means of admitting someone to a Christian church. Some modern congregations simply wet the head of the new arrival but many others favour full immersion like we do.'

'Naked?'

'The body is a temple. There is no shame in nakedness, unless you flaunt it to tempt men, as Mrs Wilde does.'

'Yet it seems that you and your disciples succumbed to such temptation?'

'It is a tradition in our church that a coupling with the leader consummates the new recruit's relationship with the group. It is done publicly so that all can witness it.'

'Isn't that a rather strange idea?'

'Not at all. Years ago, when kings married, courtiers would watch them having sex in order to witness the consummation of the marriage and ensure that any offspring were legitimate.'

'So you consider yourself on a par with royalty?'

'I was merely pointing out that a precedent exists.'

'I see. What about your disciples?'

'What about them?'

'Was it normal for them to have group sex with new arrivals?'

'I'm not responsible for their actions, or for Mrs Wilde's. If she wanted to give herself to them that's a matter for her. She's a woman of very loose morals, as we're discovering here, I think.'

Phaedra turned to Carla. 'Did you submit voluntarily to those men?'

Carla felt the blood rise in her cheeks. 'I did,' she said quietly.

A murmur went up from those watching. Penfold smiled in triumph.

'You see. She's a slut. I told you that.'

'What I meant was that I wasn't raped,' said Carla. 'I needed to penetrate the church, and in order to do so I had to conform to their rituals. Penfold knew damned well that his gang of helpers got to screw the new recruit after him. I asked the others. They all got the same treatment.'

'The other women in the congregation were subjected to group sex with those men?'

'Of course. It was one of the perks of the job. Besides, that's where they first started gathering the stuff they needed to lock those women into the organisation.'

'Ah,' said Phaedra. 'Now we're coming to the nub of the matter. Tell me, was this in any way a conventional church?'

'It wasn't any kind of a church. The whole thing was a front for something much more sordid. What Penfold was running was nothing more than a high-class brothel.'

Once again a hubbub of conversation ran about the court as Carla spoke. The judge banged his gavel down.

'Silence in court!' he shouted. Then he turned to Carla.

'Mrs Wilde, that's a very serious allegation to be making about a man of the cloth. Are you able to substantiate it?'

'Certainly, Your Honour.'

He eyed her for a moment, then put down his gavel.

'Proceed,' he said to Phaedra.

'Thank you, Your Honour. Now, Mrs Wilde, after your, er, initiation. How did things go on from there?'

'They changed a lot. Up until then I'd been treated differently from the other women. I'd had private sessions with Penfold and I'd eaten and slept separately. Now I was a full member, I was put in with the others. It was only then that I discovered exactly what was going on.'

'And how did you discover that?'

'It was the very next day. Penfold summoned me and two other women to help him entertain what he called some important guests.'

'Important guests?'

'That's right. They were local politicians. He needed to keep such people sweet in order to maintain the privacy of the organisation. He couldn't afford any type of investigation, so he occasionally gave freebies to such people.'

'Freebies?'

'He didn't charge them, unlike the majority of his so-called visitors.'

'Tell us about this first experience.'

'As I said, it was the day after my initiation. Two of his disciples singled me and the other girls out during dinner. We were called to the master's accommodation . . .'

154

Chapter 23

When it came, the summons was clearly as much a surprise to the other two women as it had been to Carla. They had been sitting at one of the long tables in the dining hut eating their meals in silence, as they were required to, when the three men had arrived. They had moved about the table and one had stopped immediately behind Carla. Each one had then placed a hand on the shoulder of the girl immediately in front of him.

'Brother Penfold has some important guests,' said the man behind Carla. 'He requires you to go and meet them.'

'Why me?' asked Carla in surprise.

'Come with us, all of you,' he said, ignoring her question.

Carla rose to her feet. As she did so she saw the two others also pushing back their chairs and noted the expressions of dismay on their faces as they did so. Carla eyed them up and down. One, like her, was petite in build, with dark hair cut in a pageboy style. She had big brown eyes and a slim, shapely figure. The other girl was taller with long fair hair and large, jutting breasts. Both, like Carla, wore the same simple tunics.

The trio were led from the hut and across toward Penfold's residence. This was a stone-built house set away from the other accommodation. They were taken round to the back door, where they were shown inside. The men took them into a small drawing room. The room was empty. On a table in the middle stood three glasses of the mysterious drink.

'Wait here,' ordered the men. Then they were gone.

'What's all this about?' asked Carla.

The smaller girl put a finger to her lips.

'Shh. Drink the drink.'

'But you know what that does to you,' Carla replied.

'It makes it easier. Just drink it.'

The other women each took one of the glasses from the table and drank the fluid down. Carla picked hers up and looked at it.

She wanted to keep her mind as clear as possible whilst she observed what was happening. It was apparent from the others' behaviour that something was about to occur that would be made easier by being sexually aroused, but she decided that her own wanton nature would be sufficient to see her through. She crossed to the corner of the room where a plant pot stood, and poured the content of her glass onto the soil. Then she replaced the empty receptacle on the table.

'You'll be sorry,' said the fair-haired girl. 'You don't know what Brother Penfold is going to ask of you.'

'Will it be so bad?'

'It might. I've not done this before. Normally I just serve the ordinary clients.'

'Clients?'

The girl looked at her. 'You'll find out,' she said.

'But if it's so bad, why don't you leave?'

'It's not that easy.'

'Nonsense. Anybody could get through the fence with a simple pair of wire cutters. It's not as if there's many guards.'

'You don't understand. It's not the guards or the fence that keeps us here.'

'Surely you don't really believe Penfold's mumbo-jumbo? Why he's no more a man of God than I am.'

'We have to stay. I told you, you'll find out. Now hush, someone's coming.'

The door opened and Penfold stood framed in it. He ran his eyes up and down them approvingly.

'Ah, Sister Freya and Sister Joy,' he said, addressing the fair girl and the dark one respectively. 'And our new recruit, Sister Carla. We don't usually let the new girls entertain our guests so soon after initiation, but I felt in your case that you were ready for it. I'm sure you'll prove me right. Now, Sisters, let us get on our knees and pray that this evening is successful and our guests are not disappointed.'

The two girls dropped obediently to their knees and Carla did the same. Penfold began to intone a prayer, and Carla bowed her head, though she paid little attention to what was being said.

When Penfold had finished, he motioned for them to rise.

'Follow me,' he said, and led them from the room.

They passed down a short corridor and into another room. This was cosily furnished with large armchairs, a log fire blazing in the fireplace. Seated on one side of the room were two men, both in their early fifties, with grey hair. Each was expensively dressed and smoking a thick cigar. Beside their chairs were empty coffee cups and half-full glasses of brandy, indicating that they had just finished eating. The three young beauties were ushered in and made to stand in the middle of the room, where the men eyed them with undisguised interest.

'These young ladies will be our hostesses for tonight,' said Penfold. 'This is Sister Joy, this is Sister Freya, and this little lovely is our latest recruit to the cause, Sister Carla. Now, ladies, it looks as if Mr Carson's cigar has gone out. Who's going to light it for him?'

Joy stepped forward at once, picking up a lighter from the table beside the man and quickly flicking it into life, applying the flame to the end of his cigar.

'Sister Freya, the brandy bottle for Mr Goodrich,' said Penfold.

The fair girl crossed to the drinks cabinet and took the top off the brandy decanter. Then she filled the two men's glasses. Meanwhile Carla was despatched to the kitchen to get the coffee pot.

For the next half-hour, the trio were kept busy attending to the whims of Carson and Goodrich. Their glasses and cups were kept charged, and slippers were brought out and placed on their feet. All the time none of the girls spoke, though Carla could sense the discomfort of the other two as the drinks they had imbibed began to take effect.

All at once Penfold ordered Carla and Joy to step forward, leaving Freya standing at the edge of the room.

'These two are particularly fine young beauties,' said Penfold. 'Don't you agree?'

The two men nodded enthusiastically.

'Sisters, God gave you those beautiful bodies to worship him with. Don't you want to worship him now?'

Carla glanced at Joy. During the last half-hour she had noted that the wary look on the girl's face had gradually been replaced by one of expectancy. Now Carla noticed how short her breaths were coming. In fact she was practically panting, and Carla knew at once that she was excited. Clearly the aphrodisiac drink was working.

'Well, Sisters?'

'How do you want us to worship?' asked Joy, her voice unsteady.

'Sister Carla, take off Sister Joy's tunic please. Let us see the body that God has endowed her with.'

Carla glanced at Joy, but could detect no reluctance in her face as the words were spoken. She moved close to the girl, placing a hand on her shoulder. Joy simply stood, her breasts still rising and falling quickly, so Carla dropped her hand to the front of the girl's tunic. Slowly, staring into the young beauty's eyes, she unfastened the top button. Still Joy did not move. It was as if she was in a trance, Carla mused. She undid the second button, then the third. Finally, in the absence of any protest, she took hold of the garment and pushed it back over the young woman's shoulders, letting it fall to the floor.

Carla paused, drinking in the girl's beauty. Her breasts were small but firm, with neat, conical nipples that protruded proudly. Her stomach was flat, her mound of venus prominent and covered with a layer of short, dark hair. She stood with her legs slightly apart, so that Carla could discern the deep cleft of her sex. The girl was still panting slightly, and Carla wondered again at the effects of the drink she had imbibed earlier.

'Stand aside and let us see her,' ordered Penfold.

Carla stepped away from the naked beauty, allowing Carson and Goodrich an unrestricted view of her lovely body. Carla could see the colour seep into Joy's cheeks as the men examined her, but she made no move to cover herself, clearly suppressing her natural modesty under the gaze of the sect's leader.

'Sister Carla,' said Penfold, 'do you not find Sister Joy attractive?'

Carla tried to speak, but found her throat unexpectedly dry. She coughed.

'Yes, Brother,' she croaked.

'Kiss her. Kiss her on the lips, as you would a man.'

Carla glanced at him, then at the two watching men. Both were leaning forward in their seats now, clearly excited by what they were seeing. She stepped forward to where Joy was standing impassively staring ahead of her. Carla took hold of the girl's shoulders, running her fingers over the smooth silkiness of her skin. Then she pulled the girl close and gently placed her mouth over hers. She opened her lips and pressed her tongue into the girl's mouth.

At first Joy held back, pulling her tongue to the back of her mouth, her body rigid. In response, Carla pulled her closer and the girl's hard nipples brushed against the front of her tunic, making her shiver with pleasure. Slowly, almost imperceptibly at first, Joy

158

began to reciprocate. Initially she simply relaxed her body against Carla's. Then, as Carla pulled her closer still, she began to move her tongue, timidly at first, then becoming bolder, until it was intertwined with Carla's. All at once, her arms were about Carla and she was pressing her naked body hard against her as the passion in the kiss increased.

For Carla too, what had begun as simple obedience to an order, quickly became an act of passion, her own body responding at once to her young partner's enthusiasm despite the fact that she had foregone the aphrodisiac that was clearly affecting the other girl. For a moment she reflected on her own lasciviousness. It seemed that her body was designed for the purpose of arousing others, and would respond almost anywhere to anyone. Certainly, as she ran her hands over the soft curves of Joy's naked body, her desires were as inflamed as if it had been a man she was holding.

All at once Carla wanted to sample more of this sensuous girl's body. Breaking the kiss, she lowered her head and Joy gave a moan as Carla's lips closed over the hard flesh of her nipple. She began to suck at it, whilst at the same time caressing the other with her fingers. Joy simply put her head back and groaned with delight as her body was expertly manipulated by the young English girl.

'Good.'

Carla had all but forgotten Penfold's presence, so involved was she with her young partner, but now, as he spoke, she realised that the cult leader was taking charge again.

'Take off your tunic, Sister Carla,' he urged. 'Sister Joy, lie on the floor.'

Reluctantly Carla released Joy's nipple from between her lips and straightened. As she did so, her young partner dropped gently to her knees and prostrated herself on her back. Then, slowly, she moved her legs apart, and Carla found herself staring at her slit, the pink lips glistening with her juices.

'Sister Carla.'

Carla realised that she had been motionless for more than a minute, fascinated by the lovely young body stretched out at her feet. She looked across questioningly at Penfold.

'The tunic, Sister Carla.'

Slowly, almost as if in a trance, Carla moved her fingers to the top of her tunic. Her fingers trembling, she flicked the top button undone. She loosened the second, then the third, then stood for a moment holding the garment closed, still staring at Penfold. He nodded his head. Carla hesitated for a moment longer, then she let go and, in a single movement, shrugged the tunic from her shoulders. As she did so, she spotted a figure standing on the side of the room, and she remembered Freya. The fair-haired girl was watching, her face flushed, her lovely breasts heaving. Carla looked down at the girl's hands. They were clenched into fists, and she sensed at once the girl's desire to masturbate as she watched her two companions.

'You see how the sisters desire to do God's will,' said Penfold to Carson and Goodrich. 'Look at how their bodies worship Him, and at the same time bring pleasure to yourselves.'

'They're certainly something special, Penfold,' agreed Carson.

'Didn't I say they would be? Now, Sister Carla, I want you to drink from your sister's passion and allow her to do the same to you.'

The words were metaphorical, but Carla knew what he wanted. She knew too that it was what she wanted, and her lovely body was trembling as she knelt down beside Joy, staring at the girl's firm young breasts which rose and fell with a steady rhythm.

'Go on,' said Penfold.

Carla leant forward onto her hands, so that her own pretty breasts dangled down below her. Then she raised a knee and straddled the girl, positioning herself so that her open crotch was just above Joy's face, whilst she herself stared down into the other girl's glistening honeypot.

She moved her face closer, scenting the girl's desire as she did so. She could see Joy's clitoris, a hard little bud of flesh that shone with her love juices, and she slowly protruded her tongue and licked tentatively at it.

'Oh!'

Joy's body gave a sudden convulsion as Carla licked at her in that most intimate of places. It was as if an electric shock had run through the girl, and the cry she gave echoed about the room. Carla withdrew for a second, then she was back, tasting the shiny juices that coated the girl's love bud. This time Joy was ready for her, and a moan arose from her lips as she pressed her pubis upwards against Carla's mouth.

Carla began licking the girl with enthusiasm, her tongue delving into her vagina, lapping at the fluids that flowed from inside her. Joy responded with enthusiasm, her moans increasing in volume as her passion grew.

160

'Stop!' Once again Penfold intervened, and once again Carla had to lift her mouth from the naked, writhing woman beneath her.

'Sister Joy, you must reciprocate. Do you understand?'

Carla glanced back at Joy, and saw the expression of concern on her face. She realised suddenly that the girl had never had sex with a woman before. Now, faced with the prospect of having to perform such a totally intimate act publicly, she was clearly shocked. Carla could see the concern in her eyes, but mixed with it was an unmistakable desire, and she spread her legs wider and pressed her hips downwards toward the girl's face. Then she lowered her own head and resumed her ministrations to her lovely companion.

For a few seconds, nothing happened. Then Carla gave a sudden start as she felt the unmistakable sensation of a tongue licking slowly up her inner thighs. For a second she paused as she felt Joy's hands run about her hips and grasp her buttocks. Then the girl raised her head and Carla gave a sigh as she felt her tongue begin to trace the length of her slit.

All at once, Joy buried her head between Carla's thighs and her tongue slid in between the lips of her sex, diving deep inside her and sending a pulse of excitement through her. Then Carla was eating hungrily at Joy again, her tongue working anew at the girl's hot sex as she was suddenly overcome by her passion.

For a while both remained where they were, Joy prostrated whilst Carla crouched over her, their faces locked against each other's sex, their tongues working hard. Then, as their passion increased, their control started to slip away and they began to roll about the floor, grasping one another, turning over and over as each tried to get on top of the other. Carla knew that they must make an extraordinarily erotic sight, two naked young beauties rolling about on the floor, each devouring the other's cunt with enthusiasm, each driving her hips down against the other's face as she tried to extract the maximum possible sensation from her.

Joy came first, her sex contracting about Carla's aching tongue as her juices flowed. Carla could taste her orgasm, and seconds later she too succumbed to her desires, so that for a second both were motionless, their bodies rigid apart from a regular jabbing of their hips against one another. Then they were moving again, both gasping with lust, devouring each other's crotches until exhaustion overcame them and they flopped apart, gasping for breath.

Minutes passed during which time the only sound in the room

161

was the panting of the two girls. Eventually Carla raised herself up on one elbow. Joy was still flat out, her mouth smeared with saliva and Carla's secretions, her thighs similarly glistening with wetness. Carla glanced down at her own open crotch and knew that she must look the same. She looked across at the two men. Neither had moved, but she could see beads of sweat trickling down their faces as they stared intently at the two naked beauties on the floor.

Penfold rose to his feet and crossed to where the pair were lying.

'Stand up now, Sisters. You have done well. Your actions have pleased your guests. Now bring Sister Freya to me.'

Carla glanced across at Joy, whose red face, she guessed, was only partially due to her exertions. Now that the passion of the moment had passed, she was clearly embarrassed by her actions. Yet Penfold hadn't finished with them. Indeed Freya had been no more than a witness to what had happened.

As they approached the third girl, Carla could sense her apprehension, her eyes darting from one to the other. She had witnessed their passion and shamelessness, and she must know that Penfold had something similar in mind for her, Carla mused. She took her by the hand and began to pull her to the centre of the room, where Penfold was standing. They stopped just in front of him.

'Ah, Sister Freya,' he murmured, taking her face in his hand and gazing into her eyes. 'Pretty one blessed by God with that lovely fair hair. Are you ready to do His will?'

Freya dropped her eyes. 'Yes, Brother,' she said in a small voice.

Penfold turned to Carla. 'Take her into that room,' he said, indicating a door at the back of the sitting room. 'Remove her tunic and have her ready on the bed on all fours. Do you understand?'

'I understand, Brother,' replied Carla. 'What are we to do?'

'There is a bathroom next door. Clean one another, then go back and assist Freya.'

Carla glanced across at the two guests. She could see that they were in a high state of excitement. She took Freya's hand once again and the trio headed for the door.

The room was quite large, with a thick carpet on the floor. To one side was a cabinet with drinks bottles laid out on it. The only other article of furniture was a wide, low bed with a cream-coloured cover spread across it. Immediately above it, covering almost half the ceiling, was a mirror. They stopped beside the bed and Carla turned to Freya. The girl was trembling, and Carla could see that she was agitated. She stroked her hair, then began undoing the buttons on her tunic. Freya raised a hand and grasped hers for a second, as if to stop her. Then she let the hand drop away again, and stood motionless, her eyes cast down, her arms hanging at her sides, whilst Carla undid the other two buttons and pulled the tunic from her.

For a second Carla paused. Freya, like Joy, had a lovely body. Her full breasts stood out proudly. She had large, pale brown areolae, her nipples set high. Her pubis was covered with downy fair hair beneath which was the slit of her sex, her bulbous clitoris projecting between the lips. Carla badly wanted to touch her, to run her hands over the soft globes of her breasts and to feel the warmth and wetness inside her sex, but she had been given her orders.

'Get on the bed, Freya,' she said quietly. 'Like Brother Penfold said.'

The girl looked at her. 'You'll come back soon, won't you?' she said.

Carla smiled. 'Of course we will. You'll be all right.'

She looked across at Joy and nodded. The bathroom door was on the other side of the room, and she followed the other girl to it. As she went through the door, she glanced back at Freya. The young beauty was staring after them, perched on all fours, her lovely breasts dangling below her, her legs spread wide so that the skin across her backside was tight. Carla gave the girl a little wink, then closed the door.

'We'd better hurry,' she said. 'I think Freya needs us in there. Let's get the shower on.'

She switched on the shower, adjusting the temperature to a warm spray. Then she climbed in.

'Come on, Joy,' she said. 'I'll help you get clean.'

The other girl held back for a second, and Carla sensed her reluctance.

'Come on,' urged Carla again. 'Freya needs us.'

'I . . . That thing we did out there,' stammered Joy. 'I've never done it, you know, with another woman.'

'That's all right,' said Carla. 'Sometimes it can be better that way.'

'But I . . . I'm not. I mean . . .'

'You don't want to shower with me, is that it?'

'It's not personal,' said the girl. 'I'm just afraid that . . .'

'Afraid you might be a lesbian?'

'Yes. No. I don't know.'

'All right, Joy,' said Carla. 'I understand. You can have the shower after I've finished if you feel like that.'

'No,' said Joy suddenly. 'I'm coming in.'

She stepped under the spray beside Carla. The cubicle was small, so that their breasts were almost touching as they stood, facing one another.

'Why the change of mind?' she asked.

'I wanted to,' replied Joy. But as she spoke she made a gesture with her head toward the ceiling. Carla glanced up, then her eyes widened. There, on the far side of the room, was a video camera pointing down at them.

Carla glanced down at Joy, who put a finger to her lips. She reached for the tap and turned it, increasing the flow of water. Carla realised that she was trying to make as much noise as possible so as to drown out anything they might say to one another.

'Start washing me,' she whispered.

Carla picked up the soap from the rack and worked up a lather in her hands. Then she began washing Joy's breasts, sliding her fingers over the soft flesh and caressing her stiff nipples. Joy took the soap and began doing the same to her.

'The cameras are everywhere,' said Joy in a low voice. 'Nowhere's safe from them.'

'Is that why everyone's so obedient?'

'You don't know yet, do you?'

'Know what?'

'Why we do this.'

Carla began soaping the girl's belly, running her hands over it in regular circular movements. 'I thought it was because we've all been saved by the Reverend Brother out there.'

Joy gave a little laugh. 'That's what everyone thinks.'

'And that's not the reason?'

'That's how it all started. But you soon learn that the good Brother out there has a completely different kind of organisation. He . . . Oh!'

Joy gave a little exclamation as Carla's hand dropped to her crotch. The girl looked into Carla's eyes.

164

'You didn't have any of the drink, did you?'

Carla shook her head. She began gently rubbing Joy's clitoris, her eyes fixed on the girl's face. Joy bit her lip.

'Maybe this place would suit you after all.'

'Tell me more about what goes on here.'

Joy shook her head. 'No,' she said. 'I'm out of here in two weeks' time. I've done my bit for the time being. Come on, we've got to get back. They're watching us.'

Carla put an arm round Joy's waist and pulled her close so that their breasts were pressed together and she could feel the hardness of the girl's nipples against her own. She kissed her.

'Why won't you tell me?' she asked.

'Go to Penfold tomorrow and tell him you're leaving,' replied Joy. For a moment she remained, her body moulded against Carla's. Then she twisted away and stepped from the shower, reaching for a towel. Carla watched her for a moment, then turned off the light and followed.

As they emerged into the bedroom once more, both stopped short at the door. Freya was where they had left her, but there were two other figures in the room now. Both the men were naked, their large, hairy bodies an odd contrast to the smooth, pale skin of the young woman between them. The one called Carson was behind her, his long, stiff cock embedded in her vagina. He was fucking her with easy strokes. At her face was Goodrich, kneeling up, his head thrown back as Freya sucked hard at his stiff erection. Between them, the young woman's body was being thrust back and forth, making her soft, round breasts shake to and fro deliciously. She turned as the pair entered, and Carla noted the expression of relief on her face as she saw them.

Carla climbed onto the bed beside Carson and wrapped her arms about his body, pressing her breasts against his back. She reached down and cupped his balls, caressing them as he thrust into the girl in front of him. At the same time her other hand slid round his shaft and found the warm wet bud of Freya's clitoris.

Her touch made the girl stiffen for a second. Then came a muffled cry, and Carla knew she was coming. She rubbed at the girl's love bud, feeling the way her cunt muscles contracted as she came, making Carson gasp with desire. It was clear that the girl had been very aroused indeed, and that it had only taken Carla's touch to push her over the edge.

As she felt Freya's ardour begin to drain from her, Carla pulled

Carson onto his back, his thick erection slipping from Freya's vagina and standing wet and shiny from the hairs at his crotch. He gave an exclamation at this rude interruption of his fucking, then gasped with pleasure as Carla leant down and closed her lips about his rampant member.

The taste and scent of Freya's arousal brought a renewed sense of excitement to the lascivious Carla. The session with Joy seemed ages ago, and the feel of her sexy, wet body in the shower had only served to feed that arousal. Now, the familiar sensation of a man's cock filling her mouth felt wonderful.

All at once she felt the delicious sensation of a tongue licking at her vagina. She gave a little moan and, raising her head for a second, looked back. To her surprise it was Freya who was tasting her honeypot, whilst Joy was spread across the bed, her legs wide, guiding Goodrich's erection into her open pussy. Carla just had time to see her erstwhile partner reach out and begin fingering Freya's bare sex before Carson grabbed her by the hair and thrust her face down over his cock once more.

The rest of the evening was like a blur of constant sexual pleasure to Carla as she had cocks thrust into every available orifice. The men's stamina was such that she came to suspect that they too had been given some kind of stimulant by Penfold. They rolled about on the bed with the three naked beauties, alternatively fucking and being sucked, whilst the girls themselves stimulated one another with hands and mouths. The climax finally came with Carla and Joy kneeling face to face kissing passionately whilst the men buggered them hard. Freya, meantime, lay between, licking at one's balls, then the other. This time the men came almost simultaneously, and Carla gasped aloud as her rectum was filled with spunk. Only when the men had drained their balls into the two girls' backsides did they relax, flopping down onto the bed, the three young women beside them.

Carla must have slept. She was wakened by a hand on her shoulder. She looked up groggily to see Joy and Freya asleep beside her in each other's arms. There was no sign of the men. The hand shook her again, and she turned to see Penfold standing beside her. He was naked, his penis hard.

He stroked her hair. 'Come with me, Sister,' he said quietly.

Carla rose slowly, stretching her lithe young body. He took her hand and guided it to his erection. Then he took her from the room and down the corridor toward his own bedchamber.

Chapter 24

'Your story is an extraordinary one,' said Phaedra, after Carla had completed her account of the night in Penfold's house. 'What you describe sounds like no religious group that I've ever heard of.'

'That's because it wasn't a religious group,' said Carla. 'That was a front.'

'A front for what?'

'For something much more sinister.'

'So the so-called Reverend Penfold was nothing of the kind?'

'He's no more a reverend than I am. He was just exploiting those women.'

'Wait a minute,' interrupted Penfold.

The judge banged his gavel down onto the bench.

'Silence in court!' he thundered.

Wajir rose to his feet. 'If it please, Your Honour?'

'Yes, Mr Wajir?'

'I think my client should be allowed to defend himself. After all, it's Mrs Wilde who's on trial here.'

The judge nodded. 'All right, Mr Penfold. Go ahead.'

'Your Honour,' began Penfold, 'these women came to me of their own accord. I didn't seek them out. Even Mrs Wilde presented herself to me, not vice versa. They were all women looking for help, and that's what I offered them.'

'They were seeking help all right,' said Carla. 'But you were offering something quite different.'

'Can you explain that, Mrs Wilde?' asked Phaedra. 'What happened when you tried to leave the group?'

'I was shown some of the pictures and videos he'd collected.'

'What sort of pictures and videos?'

'Of the things they'd been making me do since I arrived. Of me naked. Of me being gangbanged by his lackeys. Of me and Joy in his parlour.'

'And what did he intend to do with these pictures?'

'He told me that, if I left without his permission, it would be sent to my husband, my relatives and to various other people who knew me or had influence over me.'

'In other words, he was blackmailing you?'

'I don't think that's too strong a word for it.'

'And the others?'

'Certainly. He was blackmailing all of us.'

The judge turned to Carla. 'Now let's get this clear, Mrs Wilde. Are you saying that these women were held against their will? Effectively kidnapped?'

Carla shook her head. 'Even Penfold knew he couldn't get away with that. So he just arranged for them to come back to him for a couple of weeks every few months. They'd tell their families and partners it was a kind of retreat. Then they'd work for him for that time.'

'What sort of work?'

'It was just a classy whorehouse.'

At these words a buzz of conversation went round the room, and the judge banged his gavel down again. When all was quiet once more, he addressed Carla.

'Explain yourself.'

'There's not much to explain. The clients were a classy lot, and they paid a lot of money for the discretion, and for the fact that we weren't professional whores.'

'Yet you all seemed capable of giving yourselves,' remarked the judge.

'We gave them what they wanted because we had no choice. A lot of the girls needed to use the potion to get themselves aroused, remember, but in the end they did as they were told.'

'Wait a minute,' put in Wajir. 'Mrs Wilde is surely not suggesting that all this was going on and the local authorities knew nothing about it. That's inconceivable.'

'Of course they knew,' said Carla. 'But they didn't say anything.'

'Why not?'

'What if I told you that Carson was the local police chief, and Goodrich the mayor?'

Once again a murmur arose from the crowd at Carla's words. Penfold said nothing, simply glaring at her.

Phaedra stepped before the judge.

'Your Honour, I think we've heard enough now to discredit any evidence this man might have to give.'

168

'Wait a minute,' said the judge. 'What happened to the Reverend Penfold's community? He's accused her of destroying it. How did she do that?'

Carla laughed. 'That was easy. We simply played him at his own game.'

'I don't understand.'

'Our original plan was to get hold of the tapes and pictures and destroy them. But we realised that was impractical. There must have been hundreds. So we decided to use them instead.'

'How?'

'Well I told you the place was a high-class whorehouse. We worked out that men who could afford the sort of prices Penfold was charging must be pretty important people. So we decided to let them know what was going on.'

'You and who else?'

'Joy and I did it between us. It wasn't easy. The whole place was bugged, so that getting a chance to talk was pretty difficult. But we managed to meet out in the grounds a couple of times. That was when we made our plans.'

'Go on.'

'Well, the rooms in which we entertained the men were all similarly equipped.'

'Equipped in what way?' asked the judge.

'There was a bed, of course, a chest full of sex aids, a video and television, with pornographic tapes in case they needed more stimulation. But the clients knew about that. What they didn't know about was the cameras.'

'There were cameras in every room?'

'That's right. Hidden ones of course. Penfold was filming exactly what was going on all the time.'

'So how did you use them to your advantage?'

'First of all we needed to get into the communications centre.'

'What communications centre?'

'That was where the cameras were monitored and the tapes changed. It was basically the heart of the whole scheme.'

'And you managed to get inside?'

'That's right. It wasn't that difficult. We just waited until we were on kitchen duties, then we made our move.'

'You had to do kitchen duties as well as . . . what you did?'

'Certainly. They didn't just use us as whores. Somebody had to keep the place going. So there was a roster of cooks and cleaners.

I managed to swap my duties with another girl so I was on the same shift as Joy. Then we put our plan into action.'

'Tell us what you did.'

'Well, we waited until the customers had all taken the girls to their rooms. Then we took the coffees to the control room. They always had coffee and biscuits at about ten, so that's when we made our move . . .'

Chapter 25

Carla's nerves were jangling as she knocked on the door of the control room that fateful evening. In her hands she held a tray with two mugs and a pot of coffee on it, and it was all she could do to keep her hands steady as she listened for the reply. Behind her was Joy with a plate of biscuits and a large, black bin bag into which she was to empty the rubbish bins in the building. Carla glanced back at her young friend and gave a nervous smile. Joy returned the smile, but Carla could see that she too was feeling the strain.

'Who is it?'

'Coffee.'

There was a silence for a moment, then a click as the electronic lock on the door was released. Carla pushed the door open and stepped inside.

The control room was, as always, in semi-darkness, and it was a few moments before Carla's eyes became accustomed to the gloom. Before her, two men sat at a large console, consisting of a bank of ten television screens. Eight of these were switched on, and Carla paused for a second to take in the images. Each showed the interior of one of the bedrooms, and on each screen was a scene of debauchery. In one room, a statuesque blonde lay back on the bed, her legs spread whilst a portly man screwed her with vigour. In another a young redhead was on all fours, her lips wrapped about one man's cock whilst another man took her from behind. In yet another, a dark-skinned girl was kneeling between two men, alternately sucking one, then the other.

The two men in the control room scarcely looked round as Carla and Joy entered, both clearly intent on the scenes before them. Behind them a rack of video machines hummed quietly, the tapes slowly turning as they recorded the scenes on the screens.

Joy began laying out the coffee whilst Carla moved between the two men, placing a hand on each of their shoulders as she leaned close to them.

171

'Much action tonight, boys?' she said quietly.

The man on her right nodded. 'Yeah, it's a busy night. That guy in number seven is really going at it hammer and tongs.'

Carla glanced up at the screen. There, in the middle of the screen, lay a naked man, his chest matted with hair. Astride him, his cock buried in her vagina, was a tall, leggy young woman. As Carla watched, she worked her body up and down on his stiff member, her head thrown back, her full breasts shaking with every stroke.

'God yes,' said Carla. 'She looks like she's enjoying it too.'

The man on her right turned to her.

'You're the new girl, aren't you? Carla, isn't it?'

'Sister Carla to you,' said Carla with a mischievous smile.

He grinned. 'You weren't exactly behaving like a nun the other night. I saw you with that other little chick in Penfold's parlour, then with those two old guys.'

Carla tossed back her hair. 'I thought that was what we were supposed to do. Show God how grateful we are for our bodies.'

'I'd certainly be grateful for yours right now,' said the man. 'Watching this lot is making me bloody horny.'

Carla slid a hand up his leg and squeezed his crotch.

'You certainly feel pretty hard,' she said.

He dropped his hand onto hers. 'Does my hard cock make you feel horny too?' he asked.

She wriggled away. 'Maybe,' she said.

He grabbed at her hand once again. 'Why don't we all get some relief then?'

'You want to do some of that?' she asked, indicating the screen.

'Yeah.' He pulled her closer to him and ran his finger over her front, squeezing her breasts through the thin material of her tunic. 'I reckon you do too.'

She glanced about her. 'Anyone likely to come in?' she asked.

'Nah. We're not due to come off duty for a couple of hours yet. Why not take this off?'

Carla hesitated for a moment. Both men were watching her now, their eyes fixed on her curvaceous body. Then, slowly, she reached up and began undoing the buttons. She let the garment fall open, then she shrugged it from her shoulders and let it drop to the floor.

'Carla, what are you doing?' She turned to see Joy staring at her open-mouthed.

'Just having a bit of fun with these two lads.'

'But we're supposed to be emptying the bins and getting back. They'll be looking for us.'

'They can wait a few more minutes.'

'You're not going to do it with those two, are you?'

'Oh don't be such a prude, Joy. It's just a bit of fun. At least these two make a change from the old buggers Penfold's always giving us.' She took one of the men's heads in her hand and pressed it against her bare breast. At once he began to suck her nipple. 'You can join in if you want to,' she said.

Joy shook her head, backing away.

'No.'

'Oh well.' Carla grabbed the other man's hand and placed it on her thigh. 'Looks like I've got you both to myself. Joy's never any good without one of Penfold's little cocktails anyhow. Forget her, I can handle both of you.'

As she spoke, the man touched her between the legs, and she gave a little gasp. The sensation of the other man's lips locked over her swollen nipple was already turning her on, and the sudden feel of his companion's fingers gently stroking her clitoris brought a surge of wetness deep within her.

All at once, Carla had the urge to see the men's cocks. She reached down and unzipped the fly of the man on her right. His rod was straining hard against his nylon briefs and she squeezed it, feeling it twitch as she did so.

'You are excited,' she murmured. 'Let's get you out of there.'

She pulled down the waistband of the briefs, freeing his erection, which sprang from his fly, standing rampant from his groin. Then, licking her lips, she pushed his mouth from her breast and bent over him, taking him into her mouth.

Carla began to lick at his cock, working her tongue under his foreskin and coating the smooth, hard bulb of his glans with her saliva. As she did so he groaned with pleasure and she began to suck him, as always absorbed by the taste and scent of male arousal. Meanwhile the other man slipped a finger into her vagina and a shudder of excitement ran through her as she pressed her nether lips closed about his digit, loving the sensation of his touch. She reached behind her and, still fellating the first man, felt for the other one's crotch. In no time she had his rampant erection in her hand and was masturbating him gently.

She went on like this for some minutes, occasionally switching

173

so that the cock in her hand was transferred to her mouth and vice versa. So absorbed was she in bringing pleasure to the men that for a moment the plan went out of her head. Then she looked across and saw Joy watching her, and she knew she must move.

She raised her head from the penis she had been sucking and looked up into the man's face.

'It's no good,' she said. 'This isn't enough for a hungry girl like me. I need fucking really bad.'

He grinned. 'Come on up,' he said.

Carla rose to her feet, one hand still caressing the other man's knob.

'Climb aboard,' said the man facing her, indicating his rampant organ.

Carla was genuinely aroused now. She straddled his knees eagerly, moving forward so that she was poised above his stiff member. Reaching down between her legs, she took hold of it. Then she began lowering herself slowly down onto it. As it touched her sex she realised with a shock how wet she was. Even here, using her lovely young body to manipulate these men, she couldn't suppress her natural lasciviousness when faced with a hard cock.

She manoeuvred him into position with her hand, then pushed down harder. For a second her flesh resisted, then she gave a groan as she felt him slip inside her. She forced her body lower, closing her eyes as the pleasure of being penetrated flowed through her. His cock was a thick one, and it pressed her vagina apart in a way that made her gasp with delight, her body tingling with excitement as she gave herself to him.

She settled all the way down, so that she was sitting astride his lap, her firm breasts jutting forward in front of him. Then she began to move, working her body up and down his stiff shaft, her head thrown back as she absorbed the pleasure of being fucked. At the same time she resumed her grip on the other man, masturbating him hard as he watched the couplings on the screen in front of him.

Carla glanced momentarily over the man's head at her friend. Joy didn't see the glance, though. She was busy, working her way down the bank of video machines. At each one she would pause and press the Eject button. As the tape slid from the machine she would mark it with a pencil, then pull a blank tape from the black bin bag she was carrying and replace it. Once the machine was running once more she would move on to the next one, stowing the tape she had taken in another bag she had been carrying in her pocket. Carla watched for a moment longer then, satisfied that her friend would soon have replaced all the tapes, concentrated once more on the stiff cock that filled her throbbing vagina.

She was fucking the man hard now, her young breasts quivering with every thrust down against him. His face was a picture of concentration as she screwed him and she knew that her own climax was building swiftly. She looked across at the man beside her. He was watching a pretty brunette, who was kneeling up against the top of the bed, her hands gripping the brass bedhead whilst the man behind her drove his penis into her rectum, each jab of his hips shaking her young frame as she held the metal with whitened knuckles.

Carla's attention was drawn suddenly back to the man she was astride as a hoarse cry escaped his lips. She drove down harder against him, pressing herself right down into his lap before raising herself once more.

Suddenly he was coming, his body writhing as he pumped his seed into her. Carla knew she would never tire of the delicious sensation of a man's spunk as it spurted into her vagina. Even now, during this cold, calculated seduction, she couldn't control her own desires and she cried aloud as an orgasm swept through her. For the next minute or so she was oblivious to all but her own pleasure, her sex muscles contracting rhythmically about the man's cock, as if drawing the spunk from his twitching organ. For his part, he simply sat back, his face a picture of contentment as he shot his load deep inside the lovely, randy young woman.

Carla continued to move up and down, watching the man's face as he descended from his peak, slowing her movements until at last she was at rest, his knob still stretching her sex. She remained like that for a few moments, then slowly rose, letting him slip from her. Immediately she dropped to her knees beside his companion and took his rampant cock into her mouth, beginning to suck once more.

It didn't take long. She had known it wouldn't. The sight of the action on the screens, as well as the noisy copulation so close beside him had worked the man up to a high state of arousal so that the sensation of a pair of soft lips closing about his organ was all it took to bring him to his climax. He came with a gasp, and Carla sucked greedily at him as he released a steady flow of spunk into her mouth, swallowing it down with relish. She kept her hand clamped about his shaft, working her head back and forth and drawing every drop of semen from him until there was no more. Only then did she release him from her mouth and begin licking him clean, her tongue sliding up the length of his erection and delving into the small hole at the tip from which his spunk had flowed.

At last she rose to her feet.

'Feel better, guys?'

'Mmm. Shit, baby, you're good. When are you on kitchen duty again?'

Carla giggled as she climbed back into her tunic.

'I'll let you know.'

Joy was waiting by the door, clutching the bin bag.

'Come on, Carla,' she remonstrated. 'We've got to get back.'

'All right, I'm coming,' she replied. Then, winking at the two men, she followed Joy through the door.

'Did you get all the tapes?' she asked as soon as they were alone.

'All of them. Wow, Carla, you weren't kidding when you said you'd get their full attention. It was like taking candy from a baby.'

'And all the tapes are marked?'

'Yes. I know exactly which tape was from which room.'

'Good. come on, we're going to use one of the spare rooms.'

'Why?'

'To rewind these tapes. Only about ten minutes or so each.'

'Won't they be waiting for us back at the kitchens?'

'Sod the kitchens. They'll forget all about kitchen duty once we've finished.'

Fifteen minutes later, the two girls were ready to emerge from the empty room. They had rewound the tapes and each had a small stack in front of them.

'How are we going to do this, Carla?' whispered Joy.

'I suggest we strip off. The men will be so distracted by the sight of a nude woman walking in, we'll have the tape in and running before they realise what's happening.'

Carla began undoing her tunic. Joy hesitated for a moment and Carla winked at her.

'Come on, Joy, you're not embarrassed, are you?'

The girl looked at her, then shook her head. Moments later her tunic was on the floor beside Carla's. Carla looked Joy up and down, remembering the evening in Penfold's study, and the feel of her soft flesh against her own. She put an arm about the girl and pulled her close, loving the sensation as Joy's hard nipples rubbed against her own. She kissed her on the mouth, then drew away.

'Come on, baby,' she said. 'We've got work to do. You take upstairs, I'll do down here.'

'Make sure you put the right tapes in the right rooms,' said Joy.

'Don't worry. I'll see you here in five minutes.'

'Okay.'

Carla watched as her friend set off down the passage, her pale backside swaying as she walked. Right at that moment she would have given anything to have her on the bed and to taste once more her delectable sex. But there was no time for that now. She looked down at the first tape. It was marked with a number ten. She glanced at the door beside her. Number ten. She drew a deep breath, then pushed open the door.

Inside the room the lights were low, but she could easily discern the man stretched out on his back whilst a naked girl bent forward over him, sucking his penis. He sat up in surprise as she walked in. Then he saw her naked body, and he grinned.

'You the reinforcements or something?' he asked.

'Not quite. Just brought you something to watch.'

She ejected the tape from the machine at the end of the bed and slipped in the one she was holding. Then she pressed the Play button, clicked on the television and was on her way. The man made a grab at her as she was leaving, but she smartly sidestepped him and slipped through the door, closing it behind her.

In the next room a blonde girl was being vigorously screwed on the bed. Carla went through the same procedure, inserting the tape and switching it on before heading out again.

By the time she reached the third room the noise had started. Behind her she could hear a man shouting, whilst upstairs a furious row had broken out. She slipped in and out of the other rooms easily, and in no time was back in the room they had started from. Minutes later Joy joined her.

'Success?' she asked.

'Went like clockwork. Just listen to them.'

The pair fell silent. From all around the building roars of rage were echoing and already they could hear the sound of running feet outside. Carla twisted the key in the door, then turned to Joy.

'I think it'll be a while before it's safe to go out,' she said.

Joy moved closer to her. 'What are we going to do in the meantime?'

Carla took her hand and pulled her toward her, wrapping her arms about her and holding her naked body close to her own.

'I'm sure we'll think of something,' she said with a smile.

Chapter 26

As Carla came to the end of the episode in which the tapes were switched, the room erupted into a hubbub of sound once more. The judge was obliged to bring down his gavel hard a number of times before order was finally restored.

'Silence in court!' he thundered. 'Any more of this and I'll clear the public gallery. Now, please continue your questioning.'

Phaedra nodded. 'What happened next?' she asked.

'Just what we knew would happen,' replied Carla. 'The guests were enraged when they discovered the bastard had been filming them with the girls. There was a hell of a row.'

'They assumed Penfold intended to blackmail them?'

'Naturally. Wouldn't you? He tried to explain that the video equipment was for our benefit, but I don't think that went down very well either.'

'Surely Penfold and his disciples could have taken care of them?'

'No chance. They all had cellular phones. Within fifteen minutes the place was surrounded by the biggest crowd of heavyweights and thugs you've ever seen. These were rich and influential men, remember, and they could afford the best in bodyguards.'

'And I believe a few more of Penfold's customers were soon on the scene too?'

'That's right. The existence of Penfold's little brothel had got around by word of mouth in the first place, so it didn't take long for this bit of news to spread. They were coming in from all over the state.'

'So what did they do?'

'Penfold soon realised that he was in deep trouble. At first he took refuge in his house. When they threatened to burn it down he came out, though.'

'Then what?'

'They ransacked the place. Pulled out every single camera and microphone. Then they made a fire of all the tapes and threw the machines on. For a while it looked as if Penfold would get thrown on too, but by that time the police had arrived.'

'The police?'

'Don't forget the police chief was one of the customers. As soon as he got wind he came out himself. It's a good thing for Penfold that he did. It was only the police taking him into custody that saved him.'

'And the church?'

'That burned to the ground in a mysterious fire two days later. By then we were all well away. Once he'd lost his credibility, Penfold had no power over any of us.'

'So that was that?'

'Yes. I picked up my fee and turned my back on religion for good. Until now, that is. I hadn't realised that that charlatan was still calling himself a reverend.'

'Actually, I think the court would be interested to hear about your latest enterprise, Reverend Penfold,' said Phaedra, turning to him.

Penfold glared at her. 'That's my business,' he said.

'I think it's the business of everyone here,' replied Phaedra. 'You see, Your Honour, I did a little research on our friend here when he first walked into court, and it seems that the Reverend is starting up a new so-called church.'

The judge looked at her curiously, then turned to Penfold.

'Is this true?' he asked.

'It's still in the early stages of planning,' said Penfold, paling slightly.

'Tell him where it is, Penfold,' said Phaedra.

'It's not important,' he replied.

'It's here, in Barovia, isn't it?'

At once there was a babble of conversation from the public gallery. Once again the judge had to bang his gavel two or three times before order was restored.

'Is this woman telling the truth?' he asked.

Penfold looked away. 'This one is going to be different,' he said.

'Don't believe it, Your Honour,' said Phaedra. 'He's already begun recruiting. It's exactly the same set-up as before.'

The judge stared at Penfold for a moment, then beckoned the Clerk of the Court across.

'I think Mr Penfold should be taken into custody for his own protection,' he said.

'Wait a minute,' Penfold protested.

'It's for your own good,' replied the judge. 'The people of this country take their religion very seriously. They don't like cheats, and they especially don't like cheats who prey on their women.'

'But you have no right.'

'I have every right. As soon as I have finished here, I intend to contact the public prosecutor to discuss extradition procedures. I feel, Mr Penfold, that you may well have overstayed your welcome here.'

Two guards stepped forward. Penfold looked for a moment as if he might protest, but the sight of the burly men on either side of him clearly made him think better of it. Instead he allowed himself to be escorted from the court. Moments later the judge adjourned proceedings for lunch.

It was about an hour and a half later that Carla found herself once again standing naked and alone on the dais on which she had stood for the duration of the trial. As before, her feet were shackled and her arms pinned behind her, so that she was allowed no concession whatsoever to modesty. The judge had not yet entered, and Phaedra took the opportunity of having a few words with her.

'That was a real triumph,' she said. 'Penfold's evidence won't count for a thing now. In fact, I reckon you earned yourself a few brownie points with the jury there.'

'I hope so,' sighed Carla. 'How much longer is this going on?'

'I'm told that Wajir has got one more witness. This whole thing will soon be over, Carla.'

'Yeah, but then what? I wonder who the last witness is.'

'We'll soon find out,' said Phaedra. 'Stand up straight, the judge is coming in.'

The judge took his seat and called the court to order in the usual way. Then Wajir came forward once more.

'Your Honour,' he said, 'I call Arianne Gardener.'

All heads turned as the door was opened and the tall, slender woman entered. Arianne Gardener carried herself like a fashion model. Indeed with her long legs and slim frame she might almost have been one. She was dressed immaculately in a mustard-coloured designer suit that clung to her curves. Her elegant high heels rang loudly on the floor of the court as she made her way to the witness stand, and Carla looked on enviously, only too aware of her own lack of clothing.

The swearing-in process was completed, then Wajir rose to his feet and approached the front of the court.

'Miss Gardener, thank you for attending this afternoon.'

The woman flashed a dazzling smile at him. 'Not at all.'

'Could you tell us please what it is that you do?'

'I'm a personal assistant. My last job was working for a merchant banker in the City of London.'

'I see. And do you recognise the defendant?'

The woman glanced up at Carla. 'Of course I do. I see the little slut's got her clothes off as usual.'

'How do you come to know Mrs Wilde?'

'She wasn't calling herself Mrs Wilde when I met her. Just plain Carla, although you didn't have to be on first-name terms with her to get into her knickers. Come to think of it, I'm not sure if she ever wore knickers whilst she was with my employer.'

'Do I take it that you don't particularly approve of Mrs Wilde?'

'You're quite right I don't. She's a whore, a crook and a liar.'

'Objection!' shouted Phaedra, but the judge waved her aside.

'Let us listen to what the witness has to say,' he ordered. 'I presume she has some grounds for making these accusations, Mr Wajir?'

'Certainly, Your Honour. Miss Gardener, your first accusation, that Mrs Wilde is a whore. What evidence do you have for that?'

'It's simple. It was I that handed her her pay packet every month.'

'Go on.'

'As I said, I was working as personal assistant to a London financier. Is it necessary to reveal his name? I'd rather not.'

The judge turned to Phaedra. 'Does the defence have any objection?'

'No, Your Honour.'

The woman gave a little smile. 'I didn't think they would. It's bad for business, after all.'

'Please carry on, Miss Gardener.'

'Well, my employer decided he needed a partner. He was a single man, married to his job you might say. He worked very long hours and scarcely had time for a home life. So he asked me to look into finding him a paid companion.'

'And how did you go about that task?'

'I made some discreet enquiries and found out about the organisation Mrs Wilde works for. They sent some photographs and he picked her out. I believe she was damned expensive, but money meant nothing to Mr . . . my boss. So I called her in for an interview.'

'And it went well?'

'It must have done. I found her bra and pants in the office afterwards. So you see she's a whore. She fucks men for money.'

Carla felt the blood rising in her cheeks as she listened to the woman's words. Of course it was true. She was indeed a member of the oldest profession, though she disliked the use of the word whore.

'You also accused Mrs Wilde of being a crook and a liar. Can you expand on that, please?'

'They both amount to the same thing. She was being paid to be my boss's companion, yet I know for a fact that she went with any man that wanted her. She was constantly cheating on him, whilst at the same time taking his money. If that's not lying and stealing, I don't know what is.'

'Tell us more about what Mrs Wilde would get up to.'

For the next twenty minutes, Wajir questioned the woman closely, as she went on to describe incidences of Carla's so-called infidelity. By the time she had finished, those watching were shaking their heads and tut-tutting loudly, and Carla knew that things weren't going her way. Phaedra, however, seemed unworried at what she was hearing and scarcely spoke a word. When Wajir finally turned the witness over to her, she rose slowly to her feet.

'Miss Gardener, do you recall your employer signing a contract with my escort company?'

'Naturally. He was a businessman. He wouldn't have taken her on without making sure everything was in writing.'

Phaedra took a sheet of paper from her desk and showed it to the woman.

'Does this look like the contract?'

The woman looked at the document. 'That certainly looks like it. And that's definitely his signature and stamp at the bottom.'

'Have you read this contract?'

'No. As it happens I haven't. Sometimes he didn't want me to read them. After all, although I was in a privileged position in the company, I didn't need to know everything.'

'Thank you, Miss Gardener. Now, with Your Honour's

permission, I'd like to question my client about these accusations.'

'Please continue,' said the judge.

Phaedra turned to Carla. 'Is this the contract you signed?'

Carla nodded. 'Yes. He was quite specific about what he wanted from me, and he made sure it was down in writing.'

'And what did he want?'

Carla felt the blood rising in her cheeks. 'A loose woman,' she said quietly.

'Please explain what you mean by that.'

'He had this thing about a girl who wouldn't say no. A nymphomaniac, if you like. You see he was a bit of a voyeur, and he liked the idea of watching me being seduced. So he put down exactly what he wanted in the contract.'

'Tell us about your time with him.'

Chapter 27

Carla sat in her room re-reading the contract she had signed only the day before. This was going to be one of her oddest assignments, she mused, though, as always, it would be well paid. She thought about Terence Murwell. On the surface he seemed a pretty normal sort of man. As normal as any multi-millionaire City financier could be. He had been friendly and polite when they had met, and had made no improper suggestions to her. Yet, as she cast her eyes over the wording of the contract, she saw revealed a side to his nature that no one would easily have guessed at.

Carla's instructions were simple. She was to live with him in his mansion, and to be his partner wherever they went together, helping to host his parties and accompanying him to any social functions to which he was invited. So far so good, she mused. It was the next paragraph, though, that had made her raise her eyebrows. It stated that, at all times, she was to be completely promiscuous. She was to refuse no man what he asked of her, as far as was reasonable, and was to give her body to anyone who propositioned her. Where possible, she was to let Murwell know precisely what she was doing with her lovers, and to allow him every opportunity to watch what went on between them.

The final part was the strangest, though. At no time was she to reveal that Murwell approved of her actions. In fact, she was to openly defy him in public. She was, in short, to appear to be cheating on him, and to have the desires of a rabid nymphomaniac.

It was indeed an odd assignment, and one that both excited and alarmed Carla. With the other men for whom she had worked, she had been generally required simply to be obedient. In this case, however, it would be she that was expected to take the initiative. The prospect of being available to anyone who desired her made her rather apprehensive as well, though she couldn't deny the excitement that the arrangement aroused in her. Above all, though, it was a challenge, and Carla relished a challenge.

She looked about her. The accommodation was certainly up to scratch. She had been assigned a suite of three rooms in Murwell's vast country mansion in the south of France, including a sitting room, a bedroom and a huge bathroom with the biggest tub she had ever seen. Murwell himself had shown her round it, pausing to point out the spy holes and hidden cameras with which he would watch her. If ever anywhere was designed as a love nest, this was it, she thought.

The phone on the bedside table rang, and she picked it up.

'Mr Murwell requests the pleasure of your company by the pool,' said a voice. Then there was a click, followed by silence.

Carla rose to her feet and crossed to the mirror. She was wearing a short summer dress, her breasts outlined perfectly by the tightness of the thin material. She wore no underwear. This was one of Murwell's stipulations, and it felt oddly cool to have her crotch bare beneath the short skirt.

She went down the back staircase that led from her room and out onto the lawn. The swimming pool was on the other side of the house, and she made her way round to it, enjoying the warmth of the French summer sun on her face.

Murwell was sitting at a poolside table with another man. Carla eyed her new employer. He was in his late fifties, but his body was still good. In his swimming shorts and T-shirt she could see that his waist was still slim and his chest broad. His craggy, handsome face was topped with a fine head of silver hair. He looked up as she arrived and smiled at her.

'Ah, Carla,' he said. 'Good of you to join us. This is Mr Gray. He and I have been doing some business.'

'Hello,' said Carla. Gray smiled back. He was younger than Murwell, in his early forties she calculated. His hair was receding, and he lacked Murwell's athletic figure, but he was handsome enough and he ran his eyes over Carla with obvious appreciation.

A servant brought out glasses of fruit juice, and Carla settled down on a sun lounger beside them, half listening as they chatted together. Then she heard her name.

'Carla, my dear, you look hot. Why not take a swim?'

Carla looked across at Murwell, then at the clear green water of the pool. She did indeed fancy a swim. Then she remembered that she had no clothes of her own here. Murwell had provided a whole new wardrobe for her, but it didn't include a swimming suit.

'I haven't got a bikini,' she said to him.

He raised an eyebrow. 'Haven't you? That was careless of you. Oh well, never mind.'

Carla looked hard at Murwell. She knew he had asked her here for a purpose. She thought about the contract. Then she spoke.

'I could always swim nude,' she said.

'But we have a visitor, dear.'

'I'm sure Mr Gray won't object, will you, Mr Gray?'

'Well I . . .' Gray's face reddened as he eyed the young beauty.

'You see, Terence? He doesn't mind at all. Here, help me with my zip please, Mr Gray.'

'Really, Carla, you'll embarrass our guest.'

'Oh, stop being so old-fashioned, Terence,' she scolded. 'Come on, Mr Gray.'

She rose to her feet and, moving close to the man, turned her back on him. She looked back over her shoulder and winked seductively. Gray hesitated, clearly somewhat fazed by the situation. Then he reached out a rather shaky hand and, taking hold of the zip, pulled it all the way down.

Carla wriggled out of the dress and let it fall to the floor. Then she turned to face the two men. Murwell eyed her frankly. It wasn't the first time he had seen her nude. During the interview he had made her strip, and had made a close inspection of her. However, being nude outdoors was something else, and he seemed to be seeing her with new eyes, clearly approving of what he saw. Gray too was obviously enjoying his first sight of her slim, petite body, and she could see beads of perspiration breaking out on his brow as his eyes travelled over her full, firm breasts, then dropped to the neat triangle of thatch below. Carla held her pose for a full thirty seconds, her hands on her hips, her legs slightly spread, genuinely enjoying being the centre of attention. Then she swung round, ran across the terrace and dived into the pool.

The water was cool and inviting, enveloping her in a green silence as she swam gracefully down to the bottom, then stroked across the pool, emerging at the far side. She floated onto her back, her neat brown nipples coming clear of the water as she gently paddled with her hands, staring up at the clear blue sky. Out of the corner of her eye she could see the two men watching her, and she threw them a smile before submerging once more.

She swam for about ten minutes, gliding almost effortlessly up and down the pool, enjoying its coolness and the sensation of the water as it flowed over her naked form. When she finally emerged, the men were still talking, but they looked up as she approached, her body glistening with the water. Once again she stopped in front of the pair, striking a pose, her hands behind her head.

'The water's lovely,' she said. 'Why not join me?'

'I have to go in and make a phone call,' said Murwell. 'But I'm sure Mr Gray would enjoy a swim.'

Once again, Carla was aware of Gray's discomfort as Murwell spoke the words. She glanced down at his crotch and saw the bulge there. Clearly the sight of the naked bathing beauty was exciting him.

'Yes, come on, Mr Gray,' she said, holding out a hand. 'Come and have a swim with me. You'll love it.'

'I . . . er . . . all right,' mumbled Gray. 'Let me just get my things off.'

He pulled his T-shirt over his head and kicked off his shoes. As he rose to his feet he grabbed a towel and held it in front of his swimming shorts. Carla wanted to smile at his embarrassment, but she managed to keep a straight face, taking him by the hand and dragging him to the pool's edge.

Carla dived in, then turned to see Gray discard his towel and quickly follow her. As he glided toward her, she remarked how well he swam, his body looking almost graceful as he stroked through the water. Clearly he had been something of an athlete in his younger days. She looked across at Murwell, who had also risen from his seat and was headed toward the house. As he passed her, he glanced up at the windows that overlooked the pool, giving her a slight smile. At once she guessed that that was where he was heading. The thought brought a knot to her stomach, and she looked at Gray. It seemed that she was about to start earning her keep.

She continued to swim up and down, but made sure that she was never far from Gray. She would come close to him, letting her fingers 'accidentally' brush against him. At one point she deliberately collided with him, pressing her firm breasts momentarily against his skin, allowing him to feel the hardness of her erect nipples.

Eventually he stopped at one end, his hands stretched along the pool's edge as he watched her swim. She moved up and down in front of him for a while, then swam up to him. The water was

187

shallow here, so that it came to just above her waist, leaving her bare breasts clear of the water.

She smiled at him. 'It's lovely, isn't it?'

'You certainly are.'

'I was afraid I would embarrass you, stripping off like that.'

Once again his colour rose. 'It was a little unexpected.'

'But you like what you see?'

He nodded.

Carla moved closer to him, noting the way his eyes seemed fixed on her chest.

'You swim well yourself,' she said, reaching out and running her hand over his arm.

'I used to swim a lot more, but I've let myself get a bit out of shape.'

She moved her hand across to his chest. Her skin seemed pale against his, and she gently stroked the dark hairs that covered his pectorals.

'You're not in such bad shape,' she said. 'I've had men in a worse condition than you. Besides, I like a bit of flesh on my men.'

He looked into her eyes and she returned his gaze, a slight smile playing on her lips. Then she let her hand move lower, closing it about the bulge at the front of his shorts.

'You're rather excited, aren't you?' she asked.

He gulped. 'I'm sorry.'

'Don't apologise. I take it as a compliment when a man finds my body sexy. Besides, it was obvious even before you got in the pool.'

Once again he looked uncomfortable, but his cock twitched noticeably as she squeezed it through the thin material of his swimming shorts.

'I'd like to see your cock,' she said quietly.

'I . . . perhaps we should go inside,' he croaked.

'No need. We're alone here.' She eased a finger into the waistband of his shorts and, taking hold of the drawstring, slowly pulled it undone. Then, watching his face as she did so, she slid them down over his hips.

His cock sprang up immediately. It was long, so long that the uncircumcised tip protruded from the water. She ran her fingers over it, gently pulling back the foreskin to reveal the smooth helmet. As she did so he reached out a shaking hand and closed it tentatively over her breast. He looked her in the eye and, when he saw that she wasn't going to stop him, began massaging the soft flesh.

'Mmm that feels nice,' she said. 'Do you like my breasts?'

'I think you have a beautiful body.'

'And you have a beautiful cock.'

All at once she dropped to her knees in the water, submerging herself to the neck. She was still grasping Gray's shaft, working the foreskin gently up and down. Now she closed her mouth over the end, hearing him gasp as she began to suck him.

She fellated him expertly, moving her head up and down over his long, hard shaft whilst caressing the tight sac of his balls with her fingers. Her face was going right under the water as she sucked at him, so that she had to keep coming up for air. Still she kept at him though, her own excitement increasing as she tasted him.

At last she raised her head and gazed up at him. He was standing, his head thrown back, an expression of intense arousal on his face.

'I need to be fucked,' she said. 'Come with me.'

She took hold of his cock and led him across to the metal steps that led out of the pool, then turned to face him. The position put her immediately opposite the house, and she glanced up at it. There, peering from a first-floor window she could see Murwell's face, and a pulse of excitement ran through her as she realised that she was being watched.

She moved so that her back was pressed against the steps. Then, relinquishing Gray's stiff member, she reached up and took hold of the handrails. Holding onto them she raised her body up until it was flat on the water, the droplets running from her dark pubic mound. Then she spread her legs, revealing the pink crevice that was the centre of her desires.

'Fuck me,' she said.

Gray stared at her for a few moments. Above, a flash of light told her that Murwell had a pair of binoculars trained on her naked body. Then Gray moved round between her legs, and she saw once again the end of his member projecting from the water.

'Come on, Mr Gray, stick it in me,' she groaned. 'I need it so bad.'

He wrapped his fingers about his own shaft as he moved closer, forcing his erection down so that it was pointed directly at her vagina. Carla gave a little gasp of pleasure as he used his other hand to prise her sex lips apart. He paused for a second, then her gasp turned to a cry as he pressed his stiff cock into her. The water

189

and her own wetness inside provided all the lubrication she needed, and he slid easily into her, burying his cock deep in her vagina. As soon as his meaty erection was all the way inside her, he began to fuck her.

There was something about being screwed in the open air and in water that excited Carla more than she could express, and she surrendered herself to him with genuine enthusiasm as he grabbed hold of her hips, using them as leverage to pump in and out of her with vigour. Carla's breasts bounced back and forth with every stroke, the water splashing over them and running in rivulets between them.

Carla glanced up at Murwell, whose binoculars were fixed on her body as Gray lifted it clear of the water, his hips pounding relentlessly against hers. Was this what he wanted of her? He certainly seemed engrossed by the performance she was putting on for him. She gazed down at her nude, glistening body, and at the man who was busily thrusting his cock into her vagina. Her appetite for sex was extraordinary, she mused. Any whore could have seduced Gray, she knew, but could she have done it with such genuine pleasure and enthusiasm? She groaned as a fresh spasm of passion ran through her.

The excitement she felt was clearly infectious, as Gray had begun to increase the force of his thrusts. Carla tightened the muscles of her sex about his stiff organ, sensing his impending climax and urging him on.

He came suddenly, the prolonged vision of Carla's nude form having already excited him to a high state of arousal. As so often happened, the sensation of his spunk spurting deep inside her cunt sent Carla over the top, and her body was suddenly convulsed by orgasm, her sex muscles tightening once more about the long penis that filled her so wonderfully. He held tight to her, pumping back and forth as he prolonged his climax and hers. For a while she thought she would never stop coming, but at last he began to slow, his spurts dwindling to dribbles as his passion ebbed.

He withdrew slowly, making her sigh with contentment as he did so. Then he let go and drifted onto his back, his cock still standing proud. Carla relaxed too, her body sinking back down into the water. She looked up at the window. Murwell was still there, and there was a smile on his face.

Clearly Carla had got off to a good start.

Chapter 28

During her first month with Murwell, Carla scarcely left the villa. Almost every day a new visitor would arrive, and she would be called upon to entertain him. She grew accustomed to the nude swims in the pool. Sometimes the men would simply watch her, too shy to make an advance, though their hard-ons were obvious. Any suggestion of a come-on, though, would receive a positive response from Carla, and many an astonished visitor would find himself screwing her or being sucked off, either in the pool or on one of the sun loungers.

On one occasion there had been three of them, all young men. These three had been confident of their situation. No sooner had Murwell left Carla alone with them than they were dragging her off naked into the garden. There they laid her out under a tree and took it in turn to fuck her, each one driving hard into her and coming quickly, eliciting a series of shattering orgasms in the gasping girl.

And all the time Murwell had watched, whether from his vantage point over the pool, in a quiet part of the garden or via a closed-circuit television camera hidden somewhere on the premises. Although he never laid a finger on her, Carla knew that the millionaire was satisfied with her performance, and the arrival of the occasional present in her room such as a bottle of expensive scent or a bouquet of flowers, told her of his satisfaction.

It was nearly five weeks after her arrival at the mansion that Carla left it for the first time. One morning at breakfast, Murwell simply announced that they were going into the local seaside town for lunch. The decision took Carla completely by surprise. She had emerged for breakfast after spending the night with an Italian man who had arrived the day before to do business with Murwell. He had been an athletic and demanding lover, and Carla had worked hard to please him. He had left very early that morning, but not before taking her from behind, bent forward over the bed, and she had scarcely emerged from the shower when Murwell's summons to breakfast had arrived.

They had made small talk on the way through the hot, dry French countryside to the town. Carla had gazed from the window of the long, chauffeur-driven limousine, diverted by the unexpected change of scenery.

On arrival they had strolled along the promenade together, and Murwell had taken her into some small, expensive boutiques where he had watched her trying on some dresses, spending what seemed to Carla an extraordinary amount of money on some very sexy little outfits. During the fittings she was careful to keep the cubicle curtains open, allowing Murwell and the other shoppers to feast their eyes on her nude body as she changed. One young man, waiting for his girlfriend, was transfixed by the sight of the naked English girl, and she put on a special show for him, sitting down on the bench in the cubicle and gently masturbating whilst watching his reaction. She knew that her outrageous behaviour pleased her master greatly, and she herself found it an extraordinary turn-on to flash herself so publicly.

At the end of the busy promenade was a large and rather grand hotel, and it was there that Murwell took his young companion for lunch. To Carla's surprise, soon after they had sat down they were joined by another couple. The pair were both French, and were introduced to Carla as Monique and Jules. Monique was tall, with small breasts and short, dark hair. She wore white slacks and a matching jacket with big black buttons down the front. She had a pretty, Gallic face, with large brown eyes and thick, pouting lips. Jules was dark-skinned and handsome and wore his long hair tied back in a ponytail.

At first Carla had assumed that the pair were partners, but it soon became clear that Monique was Jules's employer. Monique, it transpired, was a photographer, who had a studio in a village nearby. She was clearly an old friend of Murwell's, and the two chatted animatedly in French. Jules said little, and Carla suspected that he was sightly awed by his surroundings, though he clearly was interested in her, and his eyes seldom left her breasts which strained against the small top she wore. It was made of cheesecloth and knotted just below her breasts, the shape of her nipples perfectly outlined against the thin fabric. Beneath she had a long white skirt with a slit that ran up almost to her waist.

When Monique turned to speak to Carla, it almost took the

young woman by surprise. She had been gazing out of the bay window in which they were sitting at the sparkling blue sea, her mind miles away, when she suddenly realised that she was being addressed.

'I beg your pardon?' she said.

'I was asking if you were a model,' said Monique.

Carla smiled, slightly embarrassed by the question.

'No,' she said. 'Though I've done a little photographic work.'

'But that's perfect,' said the Frenchwoman. 'Who shot you?'

'Just a guy in London called Mitch.'

Carla thought back to those sessions. It hadn't exactly been modelling, she mused. Mitch had been more into pornography, and most of the shots had been of Carla being fucked by one of the many male models of his acquaintance. They had been for publication in men's magazines, and it still aroused Carla to imagine men wanking over the images of her naked body.

'You must let me shoot you,' said Monique, placing a hand on Carla's knee. 'You are so beautiful and so innocent-looking. Would you let me?'

'I . . . I'm not sure,' said Carla, somewhat taken aback by this sudden interest in her.

'But of course she must,' said Monique turning to Murwell. 'Terence, tell her that she must pose for me.'

'Naturally it's up to Carla,' said Murwell. 'Though I hope any shots you took would be tasteful.'

Carla recognised a note in his voice. It was one she had heard often over the past few weeks, and it reminded her suddenly of her role. She eyed Murwell. It was he that had brought her here and had introduced her to Monique. She had suspected that there was some kind of ulterior motive to their outing, but had assumed that the flashing in the cubicle had been it. Now, it seemed, she had been mistaken.

'What do you mean by tasteful?' she asked, her eyes wide.

'I think you understand, Carla,' he replied.

'Oh, Terence, you can be so stuffy at times,' she said. 'Of course I'll pose for Monique in any way she wants.'

'I want to see all of you,' replied Monique, looking Carla in the eye.

Carla held the woman's stare. She wondered if Murwell had actually put Monique up to this, or whether he had relied on her to ask. She guessed that the latter was the case. It was likely that news of the promiscuous beauty who was staying with Murwell had got back to his friends, and Monique was clearly interested in her.

'All right,' she said. 'I don't mind.'

'Wonderful!' Monique clapped her hands. 'Jules, go and get my bag from the car.'

'You want to do it now?' asked Carla in surprise.

'Of course. I want to capture you as I find you. I'm sure Terence will spare you for an hour or two.'

Murwell didn't reply, and there was a stern expression on his face. But Carla had seen that expression before, and she knew it meant nothing.

Ten minutes later Jules returned, bearing a bag containing camera equipment. Monique selected a large, expensive-looking camera from the bag and fitted a lens to it. Then she aimed it across the table at Carla and pressed the trigger.

'Perfect,' she exclaimed. 'You are lovely, Carla. I can't wait to get you properly on film. Come on.'

She jumped to her feet and Jules picked up the bag once more. Carla looked questioningly at Murwell, but he said nothing. She rose slowly.

'Where are we going?'

'Outside of course. The light is wonderful. Come on, Carla. Jules, bring the equipment.'

The hotel had wide stone steps leading up to the front door, flanked on either side by statues of rampant lions. Monique immediately made her pose beside these, her arms wrapped about them whilst the attractive French girl snapped her. Next she was taken across the road and made to stand by the iron railings that ran along the promenade whilst Monique captured her image.

'Down to the beach now,' declared the Frenchwoman, waving Carla toward a staircase that ran down to the sands. Carla glanced across at Murwell, who had emerged from the hotel and stood watching them from the steps. Then her hand was grasped by the photographer and she found herself being dragged toward the steps.

Carla slipped off her shoes as they reached the beach. The soft sand was hot between her toes, but not so hot that she couldn't walk on it. There were a number of people on the sands, mostly couples sunning themselves or bathing in the clear blue waters of the sea. Some watched idly as the lovely young Englishwoman began to pose for the French girl's camera.

Monique was demanding, making Carla pose in all kinds of positions whilst she snapped away, pausing only to hand her camera back to Jules to reload. She had Carla undo the top buttons of her blouse, then made her crouch in the sand whilst she shot her from above. Carla knew that this exposed her nipples to the lens, but made no objection.

As so often happened, the exposure and the attention were beginning to excite her. It had been the same when Mitch had photographed her. His confidence and authority in ordering her to pose for him had always aroused her, and the fact that Monique was a woman made the situation no less stimulating.

However, even Carla was not prepared for Monique's next order.

'Take off your skirt.'

Carla looked at her, trying to maintain the cool, unconcerned image that Murwell wanted of her, despite the fact that the order had brought a tight knot to her stomach.

'I'm not wearing any pants, you know,' she said.

'I know.'

'And you want me to take my skirt off here, on this public beach?'

'Yes.'

'Terence will be cross with me.'

'To hell with Terence. Surely you don't mind having your cunt photographed?'

'What about all these people?'

'They won't mind. Come on, Carla, take it off.'

Carla looked across to the promenade. Murwell was there, watching her, as always. She knew only too well how much it would turn him on to see her remove her skirt. She glanced about at the other people on the beach. She had been naked in front of strangers before. Indeed, before she began working for Phaedra she had once been forced to strip off at a party on a Greek island and spend the whole evening nude. But that had been in a private home. This was a completely public place, where anyone could see her.

She paused for moment longer, then her hands dropped to her waistband. She undid the skirt slowly, then unwrapped it. Jules's eyes were fixed on the short, dark hairs that covered her pubic mound as she passed the garment to him. Then Monique took control again.

'That's better. Now, put your hands on your hips. Legs apart, that's right. Good. Now turn away. Bend all the way forward. Show me that pretty arse of yours. Lovely. Look back at me. No, don't smile, look aroused. I'm your lover and I'm about to fuck you from behind. That's it. Great!'

Once again Carla was given no time to consider the exhibition she was making of herself as she cavorted about, baring her sex to the camera. She noticed, though, the attention she was getting from the others on the beach. One couple, not far from her, were sitting up, frankly interested in her, the woman with a faint smile on her face, the man clearly aroused by what he saw. As Carla looked across at them, the girl winked at her and ran a hand down between the man's legs, caressing the bulge that was forming there.

All at once Monique lowered her camera.

'That's enough on the beach. Let's go into town.'

She turned and began marching back towards the promenade with Jules close behind her.

'Hang on, Monique.'

Carla found herself abandoned by the shore, and suddenly her near total nudity came home to her. She hurried after the pair, her face glowing as all eyes turned to follow her. By the time she caught up with them, they had reached the place where Murwell was standing.

'My skirt,' she said.

'Come on, Carla,' said Monique. 'We're going to find another spot.'

'What, I'm supposed to walk into town like this?'

Monique smiled. 'Does that embarrass you?'

Carla pouted. 'Not at all. I just don't want to get arrested.'

Already passers-by were stopping to stare at the young girl clad only in a skimpy top, and, behind her bold façade, Carla was becoming more embarrassed by the second.

Monique paused, eyeing Carla up and down once more. Then she nodded.

'All right. I suppose you should put something on. Jules, give her back her skirt.'

Carla accepted the garment gratefully and immediately wrapped it about herself. Then Monique had grabbed her hand and they were heading up the steps and across the road.

They took a wide street that ran away from the beach, up towards the centre of the small town. Carla was still barefoot, and the pavement felt hot and hard, but she said nothing. Every now and again, Monique would stop and make her pose against a lamppost or outside a shop whilst she took more shots.

They reached a square with a statue in the centre. There was a bench in front of it, and Monique made Carla stretch out on it whilst she captured her image.

'Undo your top,' she ordered.

Carla knew by now that argument with the woman was fruitless, so she undid the buttons on the small blouse and unfastened the knot.

'Let it fall open.'

Once again Carla glanced about her. It was remarkable to her how little interest the people were taking in what was going on. On one side of the square a group of youths was watching, nudging one another and passing comments, and in the distance she could see the ubiquitous figure of Murwell, his eyes fixed on the scene, but otherwise she was receiving little more than casual glances from the passers-by.

Taking a deep breath, Carla let her top fall open, revealing her firm, plump breasts. From the youths came a wolf whistle and she looked down at her hard, protruding nipples. Then Monique was in control again, and she was pressing her chest forward whilst the girl trained the lens on her lovely body.

They stayed in the square for some time, Carla discarding her top and posing draped about the statue, her pale, vital flesh making a striking contrast to the hard, dull metal. The more Monique asked of Carla, the more turned on the young English girl became. Carla knew that the Frenchwoman could sense her arousal and, as she made more and more demands of her, she realised that her purpose was to excite her as much as possible. Jules too was clearly enjoying the show, and Carla guessed that he was as horny as she was as he watched her bare her body to the camera.

At last Monique indicated that she had finished in the square and, beckoning to Carla, she set off up the street. For the second time Carla was caught off-guard and had to run after the pair of them, her arms clasped across her breasts as she became suddenly aware of her near-nudity. This time Monique ignored her pleas to have her top returned and she was forced to follow on bare-breasted as the pair hurried up the road.

They turned a corner and there ahead of them was a park, with wooded copses punctuated by lush grassy areas. Monique led them in, and down a path that ran between the trees. Here, at least, there were much fewer people, though Carla continued to cover herself with her hands as she followed them. It was cooler here too, so that Carla began slowly to relax once more.

All at once Monique stopped and turned to Carla.

'Take your skirt off and pose by that tree,' she ordered.

'Haven't you got enough photos now?' Carla said.

'Do it, Carla. I want to see you completely nude. Come on, you know you want to.'

For a second Carla felt like rebelling. Snatching back her top and telling the woman what she could do with her camera. But then she remembered Murwell, and her contract with him. She was supposed to be the sort of woman who would enjoy this kind of thing. In fact, if the truth were told, she was enjoying it. Her cunt was wet with desire and her nipples harder than ever after the previous sessions, and she found herself wondering when and how the tensions that were building within her were going to be released.

She undid her skirt and pulled it off, handing it to Monique in a gesture that she knew was one of surrender. She glanced about her. There was nobody else around, but they were on a path, and the place was far from private. The thought of this sent a fresh shudder of excitement through her as she leant back against the tree, now totally naked.

This time Monique was even more demanding than before, forcing her to adopt all kinds of poses, spreading her legs wide as the camera homed in on the pink wetness of her bare sex. These were explicit shots, yet even now, Monique was not satisfied.

'Masturbate for me, Carla,' she said suddenly.

'What?'

'Masturbate. Finger that wet little cunt of yours. You're dying to do it, I know.'

Carla looked at her, then at Jules, whose eyes were wide open.

'Who's going to see these shots, Monique?' she asked.

'Anybody I want to show them to. Men mainly. I'll probably post them on the internet, too. Imagine all those strangers wanking over your body, Carla.'

Carla shivered. That was precisely what she was imagining, and the picture it conjured up made her shiver with excitement. When Monique gave her the order she had been leaning back against a tree, her thighs spread. Now she pressed her crotch forward as she slowly lowered a shaking hand between her legs. She bit her lip as her fingers found her clitoris and she began to rub it gently. Monique crouched down and aimed the lens at her sex, filming the sheen of moisture on her fingers as she caressed her swollen love bud. Then she moved the camera back up, capturing the expression of sheer lust on Carla's face as her passion began to overwhelm her.

A couple passed, their eyes fixed on Carla's crotch as she gently caressed herself, leaning back against the tree, her legs planted wide apart whilst Monique captured her wantonness on film. Carla saw the pair, but she was too aroused to worry abut modesty now. In fact the sight of them simply made her masturbate harder as she thought of the sight she must make.

All at once Carla felt a hand on her breast. She had been relaxing against the tree, her eyes closed as she revelled in the pleasure her fingers were giving her. Now, as the fingers closed over the softness of her breast she opened her eyes and gave a gasp. It was Jules, and he had stripped naked, his large circumcised cock standing up stiff and hard from his groin. Carla glanced questioningly across at the smiling Monique.

'I could see that you wanted more than your fingers,' said the Frenchwoman. 'Jules has a good cock, yes?'

Carla gritted her teeth as he squeezed her breast harder, sending shivers of excitement through her naked body.

'I thought you just wanted photographs, Monique,' she said.

'So I do. I want to photograph you doing what you do best. Now kneel down and suck Jules's cock, Carla.'

Carla eyed the woman. It seemed that everyone took her acquiescence for granted these days. But, of course, that was precisely what she was being paid for. Her eyes dropped to the thick, twitching member that rose up from Jules's matt of pubic hair, and she licked her lips.

Monique closed in with the camera as Carla knelt down before the man and took his cock into her mouth. She was aware of the click and whirr of the camera close to her ear, but the focus of her attention suddenly became the taste and scent of the Frenchman, and she began to suck greedily at his long, hard member, coating it with a sheen of saliva as she went to work on him. Jules gave a groan as she started to fellate him, and she felt his cock twitch as she began to suck harder.

Out of the corner of her eye she saw that another couple had just entered the clearing and were staring at her. She was fellating him hard now, her head moving back and forth, her breasts quivering as she worked on Jules's lovely cock. She raised her head for a moment, still wanking him hard with her hand as she stared across at the pair. Then she tossed her hair back and took him into her mouth once more, suddenly careless of who saw her wantonness.

Monique spoke again, this time in French, and Jules pushed Carla's head off his member.

'Lie on your back,' he said.

Carla did as she was told, the grass feeling cool and soft against her bare skin as she prostrated herself. Jules knelt at her feet, his cock still rampant, then took hold of her ankles and pulled her legs apart.

Carla fully expected to be fucked then and there, but Monique clearly still hadn't got the shots she wanted. Jules leaned forward and, with a cry of surprise and pleasure, Carla suddenly felt the exquisite sensation of a tongue licking at her open crotch.

Jules worked with his tongue like an expert, lapping at the hard bud of her clitoris, taking it gently between his teeth and running his tongue back and forth over it, then delving deep into her vagina and licking out the copious fluids that flowed from the totally aroused young woman. And all the time Monique was there, occasionally giving orders to Jules as she closed in to get the best possible view of what he was doing to Carla. Carla herself required no instructions now, raising her backside from the ground, knees bent as she urged Jules's tongue deeper inside her, showing Monique everything she wanted.

By now Carla was very aroused indeed, and hot to feel Jules's cock inside her, so that, when Monique ordered her up onto all fours, she obeyed without hesitation, crouching forward and spreading her legs wide, making no secret of her need to be fucked. Still she had the frustration of waiting a little longer though, whilst Monique photographed her from in front and behind, capturing her breasts and sex in this new posture before finally waving Jules forward.

The Frenchman needed no further encouragement, and Carla gave a little whimper of pleasure as she felt him press his swollen helmet up against her hot sex. She was already very wet indeed, and he had no trouble slipping into her, jabbing his hips forward as he buried his stiff cock deep inside her whilst Monique continued to snap away.

200

He fucked her with an urgency that Carla reciprocated gladly. She was already almost crying aloud with frustration, and the sensation of his stiff member thrusting hard into her was a wonderful one. He gripped her thighs hard as he took her, his belly slapping loudly against her tight behind with every stroke. Carla braced herself as the onslaught continued, her head thrown back, a soft moaning emerging from her lips as she savoured what he was doing to her. And all the time the snapping of the camera was in her ears, reminding her that her naked body was being captured on film for the delectation of others.

Jules came suddenly, his body stiffening as his spunk spurted deep into her. Almost immediately Carla came too, her whole body convulsing with the delicious sensation of his orgasm. Jules continued to pound into her with enthusiasm, his cock seeming to swell as it spat his seed into Carla's vagina. His ardour was infectious and she seemed to remain at her peak forever, wave after wave of total enjoyment flowing through her until she could take no more and she collapsed forward onto the grass, his body falling onto hers, his twitching member still buried inside her.

Carla raised her head, and found herself staring into the face of Murwell. Their eyes met, and she felt the colour rise in her cheeks as she thought of what he had witnessed. He stared at her for a moment longer, his face expressionless. Then he rose and strode away, leaving her naked and panting on the grass.

Chapter 29

'So, Mrs Wilde, what you're telling me is that all your infidelities were ordered by Murwell?' said Phaedra.

'Precisely.'

'And you can prove this?'

'Of course I can. It's all there in the contract. I was doing exactly what he asked of me at all times.'

'And how long did you remain with the gentleman in qu'

'The contract ran for four months. After that I think he g. bored with me and wanted someone else.'

'Didn't that upset you, being cast aside like that?'

'I didn't mind. Four months is long enough for a contract. I know some girls go on for longer, but I like a change of scene.'

'So you left on good terms?'

'That's right. I was on good terms with everyone. Except, of course, Miss Gardener.'

'You thought she didn't like you?'

'I'm sure she didn't. I would have thought that that's been made pretty obvious today.'

'And why do you think that is?' asked Phaedra.

'It's clear as day, isn't it? She fancied him.'

'Fancied who?'

'My boss. She's had the hots for him for years. When I came along she didn't like it at all.'

'That's a lie,' shouted the woman. 'She's just a dirty, lying slut.'

'Are you lying, Carla?' asked Phaedra.

'Of course not.'

'So how did you know she fancied him?'

'He told me so. He used to laugh about it. He deliberately didn't let her see my contract because he knew my behaviour would make her mad. He hoped she'd resign over it, but as you can see it didn't work.'

'You slut!' shouted Gardener suddenly. 'You lying bloody bitch!'

202

Bang! The judge brought his gavel down hard, stunning the woman into silence.

'Quiet!' he roared. 'Or you'll be in contempt of this court.'

'Tell me, Miss Gardener,' said Phaedra, spinning round to face the witness. 'Are you still in the gentleman's employ?'

The woman looked uncomfortable. 'No, as it happens, I'm not,' she said.

'And why is that?'

Wajir sprang to his feet. 'Your Honour, it's not Miss Gardener who's on trial here.'

The judge eyed him, then turned back to Phaedra.

'Is this relevant?' he asked.

'Yes, Your Honour, I think it is.'

'Carry on then.'

Phaedra looked at the witness. 'Well, Miss Gardener, why did you leave that gentleman's employ?'

Miss Gardener glared. 'It was all those damned women.'

'Which women?'

'All of them.'

'You mean Mrs Wilde wasn't the only one?'

'She wasn't the first, or the last. He was always hiring women like her.'

'So you knew that Mrs Wilde was being paid to behave the way she did?'

The woman dropped her eyes. 'He'd never let me read the contracts, but I guessed what was happening.'

'Yet you persisted in testifying in this case, despite the fact that you knew that your employer had instructed Mrs Wilde to act as she did?'

'Yes.'

The judge cleared his throat.

'Miss Gardener, it would appear that you have been wasting the court's time with your vindictiveness.'

The woman said nothing.

'I sentence you to a fine of five hundred US dollars,' he said. 'You will be detained until you pay.'

The woman looked at him open-mouthed.

'What?'

'Say anything else and I'll double the amount. Guard! Take this woman from my court.'

Miss Gardener opened her mouth to protest, but already a

guard had moved forward to escort her from the room.

It was five minutes before the court was quiet again. Then the judge banged down his gavel once more.

'Mrs Wilde,' he said, 'have you anything more to say in your defence?'

'Only that nothing I did was designed to hurt any man,' said Carla.

'In that case, I intend to close these proceedings. Any objection, Mr Wajir?'

Wajir had been looking visibly shaken. Now he simply shook his head.

'The jury will retire,' ordered the judge.

Carla watched the twelve men filing out of the jury box. There was nothing more she could do now, the die was cast. It was up to them.

The next half-hour seemed to crawl by. Phaedra sat silently with her young friend, who remained tied and naked on the dais where she had been for the entire trial. The public benches had been cleared, and the only other person in the room was Carla's guard.

The young woman's limbs ached from their bondage, and she tried her best to shift her position to relieve the cramp.

'How much longer will they leave me here?' she asked.

'They'll give it another ten minutes or so,' replied Phaedra. 'The judge obviously thinks the jury are going to reach a quick decision. That's a good sign, I think. But if they're not out soon, you'll be let down until they do come out.'

Even as she spoke, though, there was a disturbance at the back of the court, and the door opened. The usher was letting the people back into the public seats.

'Here we go,' murmured Phaedra.

By the time the jury was back in its seats, Carla was feeling very nervous indeed. She surveyed the faces of the twelve men, but they were expressionless. Then the judge banged down his gavel and called for order.

'Gentlemen of the jury, have you reached your verdict?'

One of the men rose. 'We have, Your Honour.'

'And how do you find on the charge that this woman deliberately used her charms to mislead and to rob men in the most insulting manner, contrary to the laws of gender that exist in this country?'

'Not guilty, Your Honour.'

There was an immediate hubbub from the crowd as Phaedra turned to Carla, a smile of triumph on her face.

'We did it, Carla,' she said.

'You did it more like. You were wonderful, Phaedra.'

All at once Carla became aware that the judge was hammering on his bench. The noise died away.

'The court will remain silent until the verdict is heard,' he thundered.

Carla glanced at Phaedra. 'But I thought . . .'

'Silence!' roared the judge. Now, members of the jury, on the second charge, that of indecency in a public place.'

'Guilty.'

Carla's heart sank. She had completely forgotten the original charge, so absorbed had she been in proving her innocence on the second. She stared in dismay at Phaedra, who also looked shaken.

'Don't worry,' she said quietly. 'It's a much less serious offence.'

The judge turned to Carla.

'Carla Wilde,' he intoned. 'You have been found guilty of the crime of indecency contrary to the laws of this land. This is no trivial offence, However, in sentencing you, I must take into account the time you have already spent in custody, and the ordeal you have gone through. I therefore sentence you to one week in prison and six strokes of the cane.'

He rose to his feet and banged down his gavel again.

'Court is dismissed!'

Chapter 30

Carla had been sitting alone in her cell beneath the courtroom for nearly half an hour when she heard the sound of approaching footsteps. Since the announcement of the verdict she had been allowed to speak to nobody, not even Phaedra. She had simply been unshackled from the dais and taken downstairs to this small, windowless cell, where her guard had abandoned her, her wrists still fastened behind her.

Now, as the door swung open, she gave a little cry of relief at the sight of Phaedra standing there with the guard.

'Phaedra, where have you been? What's going on?'

The woman smiled. 'Take it easy, Carla.' She turned to the guard. 'I believe I'm permitted time alone with my client.'

He gave a little nod, then retired, closing and locking the door behind him. Carla waited until she heard his footsteps fade away, then turned to Phaedra once more.

'Come on, Phaedra, where have you been?'

'Just checking up on a few things. And having a word with the judge.'

'What's to talk about? The bastards have found me guilty, haven't they?'

'I'm afraid so. Still, it's only a week. If they'd found you guilty on the other charge, it could have been ten years.'

Carla inclined her head. 'Yeah, Phaedra, I guess you're right. It could have been a hell of a lot worse. I've got you to thank for that.'

'It was a commercial decision to defend you, Carla. You're no good to me unless you're earning money.'

Carla shook her head. 'You know it's more than that, Phaedra.'

Phaedra smiled. 'Well, maybe,' she said. 'Anyhow I'm glad I got you off.'

'Still, another week in this damned country. I'm not sure I can stand it.'

'And six strokes as well. Don't forget that.'

'Do you think I could forget it? What do you suppose they use? I mean I've had a few thrashings in my time, as you well know.'

'That's what I've been talking to the judge about. You see, he has some power over what happens next.'

'Go on.'

'Well, as for your week in jail, I can get you sent back to where you were being held before the trial.'

'And that's good?'

'The alternative is a prison camp in the north of the country. They take three days to reach on foot. Then you'd get a week's hard labour living in with male inmates.'

'But they'd . . . Well, even I'm not up to that sort of thing.'

'Precisely. Whereas in the other place you'd just have to carry on whoring, like you were.'

Carla eyed her. 'You make it sound like I was just making the tea or something.'

Phaedra smiled, reaching out a hand and stroking Carla's breast.

'The point is, it's something you do well, Carla,' she said quietly. 'And you enjoy being fucked, let's face it.'

Carla blushed. 'It's a living,' she said quietly.

Phaedra bent down and kissed the petite beauty on the lips.

'That's my girl. Now, about the six strokes.'

'Yes?'

'By rights they should be administered in a public square with a cat o' nine tails. They'd give you some underwear, but your back would be bare.'

'What? That could cut my back awfully. It might even scar!'

'Precisely. But the judge has the power to grant lenience on this.'

'What kind of lenience?'

'You'd be caned on the bare behind with the men of the jury as witnesses.'

'I see. That sounds a bit better. I think I can take it on my arse.'

'The trouble is, the judge would want something in return for his lenience.'

'Something in return? You mean . . .'

'What do you think?' said Phaedra, caressing Carla's breast again.

Carla looked into Phaedra's eyes. 'You've already made the decision for me, haven't you?'

Phaedra nodded. 'I had to bargain with the judge then and there,' she said. 'They're assembling the jury now. That's okay, isn't it?'

Carla sighed and gave a weak grin. 'Yeah,' she said. 'I know that everything you do is in my interest, Phaedra. Even if it's getting me thrashed on my bare arse.'

Phaedra squeezed her friend's breast, taking the nipple between her fingers and rolling it back and forth, bringing a small gasp of pleasure from her naked friend. She slipped her other hand down between Carla's legs and ran a finger over her clitoris.

'We've got ten minutes,' she said. 'You might even enjoy it if you're aroused. Open your legs, Carla.'

Carla did as she was bidden, giving a sigh as she felt her friend's fingers slip into her vagina.

Chapter 31

Carla followed the guard down the long corridor beneath the courtroom. Her stomach felt like a tight knot had been tied in it, and her heart was beating hard. Her hands were still fastened behind her, and, despite her apprehension, she couldn't help contemplating what an erotic sight she made as she walked along, her bare breasts thrust forward and shaking deliciously with every step. Every now and again they would pass an occupied cell, and she would hear the whistles of the other prisoners as they eyed her naked body.

How long had it been since she had worn anything at all, she wondered. Certainly a matter of weeks, yet she still couldn't reconcile herself to the embarrassment of being displayed like this, totally nude.

They reached a bend in the passageway and there, on the wall in front of her, was a mirror. She eyed her reflection as she approached. Her nipples were still hard from Phaedra's caresses, the teats standing out prominently from the firm, pale mounds of her young breasts. Her eyes dropped to her flat stomach and neat belly-button, then lower to the prominence of her pubis and the short-cropped hairs that covered it. Phaedra had trimmed her bush in the cell, cutting the wiry hairs to a few millimetres so that the flesh was visible beneath. Visible too were Carla's sex lips, still wet from Phaedra's fingers. The woman had masturbated her expertly, bringing her to the edge of climax on at least four occasions and then leaving her at the very point of orgasm, so that, by the time she had finished, Carla was gasping with arousal.

It was in this state that Phaedra had handed Carla over to her guard and left them alone. The guard had been amused by her obvious excitement and had taken the opportunity to touch her up himself, fingering her breasts and sex before fastening a thick leather collar about her neck. To this he had attached a metal chain, which he was using to lead her along toward her place of punishment.

They rounded another bend and there before them was a pair of double doors. The guard brought Carla to a halt in front of them, then knocked. The doors were opened and Carla was led forward.

She found herself in a large, well-lit room, with a wooden floor and white-painted walls. It reminded her of the room in Galston's institute where she had been punished, except that the only piece of equipment was a single wooden bar affixed to two posts set at about the height of her crotch. Like the other room, too, a set of seats had been erected and on these sat the jury, with an extra seat beside them to accommodate Phaedra. Carla tried not to look at them as she was taken to stand in front of the bar. She came to a halt there, and at once she felt her wrists being unfastened.

'Bend your body over the bar and place your hands on the floor.'

The guard's orders were terse, and brooked no disobedience. Carla obliged at once, leaning forward and placing her palms on the floor, the bar pressing into her midriff so that she was bent double. The guard in front of her grabbed her hands and, before she had registered what was happening, snapped a cuff round each wrist. She tugged at the chains, but they were attached to rings set in the floor just in front of her, preventing her from moving them more than a few centimetres.

At that moment she felt the now familiar sensation of shackles being closed about her ankles, rendering her quite helpless.

Her guard moved round to the side of her and, for the first time, she noticed that there was a handle set into one of the posts that supported the bar over which she was bent. He began to turn the handle and, to Carla's surprise and horror, she felt the bar begin to rise. It went higher with every turn, pressing into her midriff and beginning to put a strain on her arms and legs. Still he turned it, pulling the chains tight and stretching her body in the most painful way imaginable until she felt sure something must give. Only when she was bent double over the pole, her feet and hands completely clear of the ground, did he stop.

Carla was suspended in the most extraordinarily uncomfortable way, her limbs in agonising tension, her legs spread wide apart, her backside stretched taut, the gash of her sex and the tight star of her anus visible to all. It was the perfect position for a beating, she reflected, and the thought sent a shiver through her lovely young body. She was still aroused by the ministrations of Phaedra, and the thought of the beating to come released an almost Pavlovian reaction in her as the instincts instilled in her by her training began to take over.

There was a sudden hush in the room, and she strained round to see that the door had opened once again. There, framed in it, stood the judge, still dressed in his robes.

The jury rose unbidden as he entered, the habit having clearly been instilled in them during the long hours in the courtroom. The judge looked neither right nor left, striding across the room to where a large chair had been placed close to the bar over which Carla was chained. When he reached the seat he turned to the twelve men.

'Gentlemen of the jury,' he intoned, 'thank you for granting us this extra time before you are released. It is important that the prisoner's punishment is witnessed and, since she had chosen to forego a public flogging in which her decency would have been maintained, she is to be punished naked before you. I think you can infer from that that your verdict was a sound one.'

There was a murmur of assent from the jury.

'The sentence is six strokes on the backside,' went on the judge. 'Bring out the cane.'

One of the guards pulled a long bamboo cane from a rack on the wall and brought it across to where the judge was standing. The man held it out in his upturned palms for the judge to inspect.

'Show it to the prisoner.'

The guard brought it across and, dropping onto one knee, held the cane in front of Carla's face. She eyed it with trepidation. It was thin and flexible, curved in the middle. It looked as though it would hurt a lot.

'Kiss the instrument of your punishment.'

Carla glanced at the judge. He was staring at her, his hands planted on his hips. She leaned forward and planted a kiss on the cold, hard wood of the cane.

'Good.' The judge lowered himself into his seat and the jury followed suit. 'Let the punishment begin,' he said.

A silence descended on the room, broken only by the clump of the guard's boots as he strode round behind Carla. The young woman shivered slightly as she felt the instrument of her punishment tap against her bare flesh. She braced herself as he drew back his arm.

Swish! Whack!

Carla let out a cry of pain as the thin cane sliced into the bare flesh of her behind. It was as if a hundred wasps had stung her simultaneously, and her body rocked forward as she clenched her fists in agony.

Swish! Whack!

The second blow fell with unabated force, cutting into her behind just above the first and doubling the pain as she screamed once more. She could scarcely believe the agony that rocked her body. The canings she had received under Galston's rule were as nothing compared to this, and the tears streamed from her eyes as she awaited the third blow.

Swish! Whack!

The weapon came down again with a crack that rang about the room, sending new daggers of agony coursing through Carla's body. Her backside seemed to be aflame with pain now, yet she knew that the punishment was only half over.

Swish! Whack!

The fourth blow caught her on the underside of her bottom cheeks, leaving a livid red line across the top of her legs.

Swish! Whack!

Carla was barely in control now, her lovely young body bucking up and down, despite the tightness of her bonds. In her heart she knew that there was nothing she could do to escape the terrible weapon, bound as she was, but her instincts were in charge and she fought hard with her shackles as he pulled back his arm for the last time.

Swish! Whack!

He brought the cane down at an angle across the fiery red cheeks of Carla's backside, cutting across the stripes already there and bringing a final scream from her as the pain hit home. Carla's soft flesh was coated with sweat now, the perspiration making rivulets that dripped from her breasts and feet onto the wooden floor beneath.

For the next few minutes Carla was incapable of speech, her body still writhing in a vain attempt to assuage the pain. Gradually, though, she began to regain her senses, shaking the tears and sweat from her face and slowly taking in her surroundings once more.

An odd rumbling sound filled her ears, and it was a few moments before she recognised that the sound was coming from the jury. They were all on their feet now, and were filing past her, taking in the angry mass of red stripes that crisscrossed her pert backside. Some of them reached out to touch her as they passed, making her wince with pain as they traced the lines that the cane had left.

Slowly the jury made their way out the door, leaving Carla and Phaedra alone with the judge and the two guards. The woman moved across to where Carla was bound. She dropped onto one knee and stroked the girl's head.

'You okay, Carla?'

'Yeah, I'll live,' she whispered, trying hard to keep her voice steady.

'That was some thrashing. Your arse is like a ripe tomato.'

'Thanks, Phaedra.'

The woman moved her hand round and squeezed Carla's breast.

'That's my girl,' she said. 'I told you that training would come in handy.'

At that moment, Carla realised that there was someone else standing beside her, and she glanced up to see the judge standing there.

'One more matter to attend to,' he said. 'I've dismissed the guards.' He began undoing his trousers.

'You ready for this?' asked Phaedra.

'Yes,' she replied. 'I'm ready. After all it's what I do, isn't it?'

Carla watched the judge as he eased his cock from his pants. Clearly the sight of her naked form being bound and beaten had had the desired effect on him, as his tool was stiff and hard. He was working his foreskin gently back and forth as he stared at her, and she could see that his glans was wet with lubrication. As she watched him, Carla felt her own arousal begin to increase once more. The beating had been a terrible shock to her system, but the sensation of nude bondage was one that never failed to excite her and now, as she gazed at the judge's stiff member, she knew she was ready to be fucked.

As he moved round behind her she thought about her second trial. Like the first it had culminated in her being found guilty and sentenced to detention and, like the first, she had ended up in bondage waiting for the judge to fuck her. She looked up at Phaedra. The woman had a faint smile on her face, and Carla wondered if she too was reflecting on the similarity of the two incidents. Then all else was forgotten as, with a start, Carla felt a finger tracing the soft wetness of her sex lips.

The finger slipped inside her, and, all at once, she felt the familiar wanton desires fill her as her body responded to this most intimate of touches. He moved it back and forth, and her sex closed about it, the hot, smooth walls of her vagina caressing it, making her moan softly. Another finger was running down the crack of her behind and it paused at her anus, tracing the puckered flesh of her sphincter before easing into her backside. Carla gasped as he worked his fingers back and forth, penetrating her front and back and bringing the most delicious sensations. The pain in her stretched and beaten body was almost forgotten now, as her lust increased with every second.

When he finally withdrew his fingers and began to press his swollen knob against her sex, Carla was ready for it, her juices flowing freely. She gave a cry of pure lust as he penetrated her with his stiff weapon, driving it hard into her. For a moment she wondered, not for the first time, at her extraordinary appetite for carnal pleasures. Surely no other girl would be as excited as she was at being forcefully taken like this? Surely the pain of the bondage and the beating should have dulled, if not eliminated her desires? Yet the opposite was the case. The cruel treatment had simply fed her passions until she was more horny than she could remember, and, as he pressed himself all the way inside her, the pain as his wiry pubic hairs rubbed against the raw flesh of her behind was as nothing compared with the wonderful sensation his cock was bringing her.

It was the first time Carla had been fucked since the trial had begun. In that time she had been bound, displayed and humiliated, as well as forced to tell her most intimate secrets in open court. Now she remembered the exquisite pleasure of being screwed by a man, and her moans turned to cries as he began to thrust into her.

He fucked her violently and dispassionately, his rod thumping into her, shaking her bedraggled, sweat-stained body as he pleasured himself inside her. Carla didn't care though. In fact she welcomed his attitude. This wasn't two lovers, gentle and caring between the sheets of the conjugal bed, this was a horny young slut and a dominant man, using one another's bodies, neither caring about the other, simply intent on their own pleasures.

Carla glanced up at Phaedra. The woman was watching intensely as her young protégée was rogered by this tall, imposing man. Carla wondered how Phaedra got her pleasure. She had never seen the woman so much as masturbate, though she had long suspected that, during a strange incident when she had been blindfold and tied down to a bed, she herself had once brought Phaedra off with her tongue.

The judge's thrusts were becoming more violent now, forcing the air from Carla's body as he pressed her against the bar. She could hear his breathing becoming shorter, and she sensed the tension within him growing as he took himself and her toward the peak.

He came suddenly, his cock pulsing as he spurted his seed deep into her. As so often happened, the sensation of a man coming inside her was all it took to push Carla over the top and she came almost simultaneously, her sex muscles tightening about his rod as she accepted his seed inside her. It was a wonderful orgasm, one of the best she'd ever had, and she cried aloud as wave after wave of passion shook her young, helpless body.

The judge went on thrusting into her for what seemed ages, his spunk continuing to flow until it was leaking from her and running down her inner thighs. Still he continued, grunting with satisfaction, until the last drop had escaped into her. Only then did he slow, clearly savouring the moment as much as Carla, finally coming to a stop with his body pressed hard against hers.

He withdrew, leaving Carla panting, her body slumped down in her bondage, a trickle of white fluid running down her thighs. He placed a hand on her back, stroking her momentarily. Then she heard the sound of a zip being pulled up, footsteps and the slamming of the door.

There was silence for a few moments more, then Carla felt another hand on her. But this time it wasn't the large, rough hand of a man but a smaller, feminine hand, and it was rubbing something cool into the inflamed flesh of her behind.

'I smuggled this ointment in,' said Phaedra. 'Does it help?'

'Mmm. That's nice,' sighed Carla. 'Keep doing that.'

Phaedra continued to rub the soothing fluid into the flesh of Carla's bottom, bringing her welcome relief from the pain. It was five minutes before the door opened again, by which time the fluid had been massaged into the pores of her skin, so that it no longer showed.

The opening of the door was followed by footsteps crossing the room to where Carla was still tethered. She was too exhausted to raise her head, but gave a sigh of relief as one of the guards cranked the handle, easing the strain from her aching arms and legs.

They undid the shackles, freeing her completely. Then they took her arms and hauled her up to a standing position. For a second Carla found herself staggering, unable to regain her balance. She held onto the bar and slowly straightened her back. Phaedra was gazing at her anxiously.

'You sure you're okay?' she asked.

'I'm fine. Just a little stiff.'

The guards stood by, watching as the young beauty stretched her limbs, windmilling her arms as the feeling came back into them. Then they moved forward again, cuffing her wrists behind her. They went to push her toward the door, but she resisted for a moment, turning to Phaedra.

'Thanks, Phaedra,' she said. 'For everything.'

'You've already thanked me. I'll be waiting when you come out.'

'See you in a week then. And don't, whatever you do, talk to any photographers.'

Phaedra laughed, then stepped forward and kissed Carla on the lips.

'You're really something, Carla.'

'So are you, Phaedra.'

This time she let the guards lead her away, casting a final glance over her shoulder at her friend as they closed the door. They led her down a passageway and through a door. There, standing waiting for her, was Patak.

'Ah, Mrs Wilde,' he said. 'I've been expecting you. There are many people at the prison anxious to make your acquaintance once again.'

Carla gazed at him coolly.

'We'd better get going then, sir,' she said. 'I've only got a week.'